DOGS OF WAR

Book Three of Underdogs

Geonn Cannon

Supposed Crimes LLC • Matthews, North Carolina

www.supposedcrimes.com

This book is typeset in Goudy Old Style.

Chapter One

December 31, Idaho

THE SNOW stopped falling just before ten-thirty. Cyrus Jackson had gone outside the hunting lodge with his coffee to watch the flurries tumble down from the evergreens on either side of the road. It was a beautiful New Years' Eve, and he could hear the others inside getting ready for the countdown. He was bundled up enough that he was sweating under his jacket, but the exposed skin of his face had turned beet red. He lifted the mug so that the steam washed up over his nose and cheeks to melt the ice crystals forming on his whiskers. He inhaled deeply, wondering if there was something in the mix that made it smell especially mouth-watering. He figured his senses were just heightened from being out in the woods away from all the exhaust and people.

The door opened behind him and Bennett Williams came outside. He was the one who had arranged the hunting party for the whole company. There were only eight of them, but it was enough to make the little lodge feel awfully cramped. The older man stuck his hands in his pockets, kicked at the piles of snow that had gathered on the porch and rocked on the balls of his feet.

"Cy-Guy. You're about to miss the whole thing. Swiss, it is cold out here!"

Cyrus frowned over at him. "Did you just say Swiss?"

"Used to say cheese-us instead of blaspheming, you know, and then it was ho-lee cheese-us, and then just holey cheese. Then... Swiss. Anyway, we're all getting ready to count down. Only got a few minutes left in the year, we all oughta spend it together."

"Sorry, Ben. You'll just have to find someone else to kiss when the ball drops."

"I'll drop your balls, jackass." He whapped Cyrus on the back of the head, then rubbed his shoulder. "Nah, just saying. Things are going to be different after tonight."

Cyrus looked at him. "Different how?"

Bennett took a deep breath and tilted his head back to blow the vapor toward the sky. "Well, there's a new year starting up as soon as that ball drops. January. You know what January is, right?"

"Got me, man. I thought after Christmas and New Years' we got a break from the holidays for a little while."

"Most people, yeah, yeah. You're right. But you and me, we ain't like most people. You know that right, m'man?" He put his arm around Cyrus' shoulders. "How you feeling? A little alert? Keyed up? I put a little something extra in your coffee when I made your cup. The caffeine and the whole mix kind of put a fuse on it. Usually it works a lot faster than this, so I needed a head start. Saw you get up and come out here for some fresh air so I knew it had to be kicking in."

Cyrus tensed and looked down into his mug. Now that he mentioned it, there was a little fogginess at the edge of his vision. When he spoke, his voice sounded slower. "What do you mean? What did you put in my coffee?"

"Little thing called wolfsbane. Supposed to drive your kind absolutely bonkers. You can feel it, can't ya? Burning a little hole in you. Right down into your wolf."

"Son of a bitch." Cyrus tried to twist away from his supervisor, but the grip on his shoulder suddenly turned to steel. He fought as he was pulled tight against Bennett's side. "Hold on, hold on. Can't have you running in there half-cocked. I've known about you for a good long while. Wanted to keep my eye on you until I could do something about it. You ever heard of wolf manoth? Used to be, a bunch of hunters would get together every January and hunt down all you mangy dogs. Population control, you know. Everything got screwed up a long time before I was born, but my daddy and granddaddy kept the tradition alive. Taught me what I needed to know in case the day finally came."

Cyrus fought the urge to growl, closing his eyes against the swell of rage. "I guess the day finally came, huh?"

Bennett checked his watch. "Here in about a minute, yep. See, here's what's gonna happen. I can't just pop you. That would be cold-blooded murder. So what's the perfect murder? One you commit in front of witnesses and the cops shake your hands. Hell, I might even get one of them morning-show ladies to interview me. Call me a hero and everything."

Bennett seemed to be convinced of the reality of the situation, so Cyrus didn't see a point in denying it. "You're just going to tell people I'm a werewolf? They'll laugh in your face." He grunted and wrapped his arms around his stomach. The cup of coffee, sadly only holding one more swallow of poison, shattered at his feet. Inside, the rest of their group behind the ten-second countdown. Cyrus began trembling.

"No, see, what this wolfsbane does? It makes your kind go ape shit. You don't always change, but you do turn into a wild animal. Can't control yourself once it gets in you, and it's been brewing in your system for about half an hour."

"I won't... hurt anyone."

"You won't have a choice. You're going in there and start tearing up your friends and coworkers. A couple of 'em will get hurt too bad to save, and that's a damn shame. Not a person in there I wouldn't miss. But sometimes you gotta make sacrifices. I'll come in once I hear the screaming, and I'll pop you in the head." He pulled out his gun and held it up for Cyrus to see. "Bennett Williams, the boss who saved his team from a madman."

Cyrus lunged for the gun, but Bennett swung him around. He impacted the railing with his hip and swung his hand up to Bennett's face. "I'll kill you... I-I'll kill you and run into the woods until it's out of my system a-and..."

Bennett shook his head. "No. Nah, you won't." He grabbed the long hair that extended out from underneath Cyrus' cap and dragged him toward the cabin door. He twisted the knob with his free hand, hurled him inside, and slammed the door behind him. Cyrus spun on his heel and slammed his full weight against the door, grappling for the knob as his nostrils flared and his skin erupted with beads of sickly sweat. He gasped frantically as he struggled against Bennett holding the door shut from the other side.

The room had become silent since he was thrown into it. He

turned and saw his coworkers, friends, teammates, standing in a small cluster and staring at him. Jenny. Sweet Jenny in her maple-leaf sweater. They'd been flirting all night. He was supposed to kiss her at midnight, but instead he'd been outside getting poisoned. She was the closest, and he felt the fog descending on his senses. It was the same fog he felt when he let the wolf take over, but he knew he wasn't changing physically.

"Jen. I'm so, so sorry..."

A part of him was aware of the shrieking, and he tasted copper in his mouth as the others in the room piled on trying to pull him off of his first victim. He saw the bright red maple leaf of Jenny's sweater spattered with blood and fought against awareness. He didn't want to know what he was doing, didn't want to know if Jenny was already dead. He bit and snapped his jaws hard enough to hurt his teeth, and he tasted things he didn't want to identify. Then he heard the door crash open and felt relief that it was almost over. He turned his bloody face toward Bennett, who pressed the freezing barrel of his pistol against Cyrus' forehead.

"Happy New Year."

Cyrus closed his eyes, grateful that he wouldn't live to hate himself for what he had done.

CHAPTER ONE

Seattle, January 1

THE CASCADES prevented the bulk of the snowstorm from reaching Seattle, which was still recovering from the blizzard that had shut it down over Thanksgiving. It didn't protect them from the rain that slipped across the peaks and slicked down the streets during the lull between Christmas and New Years' Eve. The town was used to wet weather but the endless rain combined with plummeting temperatures forced even the most hardened Seattleite to stay indoors unless it was an emergency.

Ariadne Willow trudged down the brick-lined street toward the flashing lights of a police barricade, hands buried in the pockets of the jacket Dale had bought her at Goodwill. She had a scarf tangled around her neck as well, the front of it pushed up like a barricade against the freezing wind cutting between the buildings. It might have been early, but she'd been bundled up in a cozy blanket with her cozier girlfriend watching a movie when she got the call to come out into the elements.

The uniformed cop standing at the curb recognized her as she approached and lifted the crime scene tape so she could duck underneath. The tape separated a wide cul-de-sac where the road curved back to the east and within the limits of it was a row of frosted-over trash bins and a group of houses that stood on a rise above their garages. Ordinarily the ice-rimed trees would have been a holiday card in the making, but the trio of police cars blocking traffic ruined the scene by casting harsh blue and crimson lights on every surface. The EMTs moving slowly at the back of their ambulance told her there was no chance she was visiting the site of an attempted murder.

Detective Kyle Lorne was standing in the shared driveway of the houses and looked up when he heard her coming. He wore a heavy jacket that reached down to his thighs and a hat which looked like he'd stolen it from an Iditarod participant. The furry flaps were down to frame his face, complete with a striking new beard that had a patch of gray on the chin.

"Willow. Sorry about interrupting your evening."

"It's fine. I can stay out until midnight even on school nights."

Lorne checked his watch. "Well, I'll try to make this quick, then. Victim's name is Marcus Kurtz. He came down to throw out some garbage, the killer was waiting outside. Jumped him and went to work with his teeth and fingernails. First responders said it was like something out of that zombie show, and they're skittish about being alone with it. But that's fine for us... gives you and me time to be alone with it."

"Not exactly my idea of a romantic night out, Detective."

"Well, you know how it is. All the romance fades after the first few dates. But don't worry, I got all kinds of tricks up my sleeve."

He led her into the open garage door he and the crime-scene tech had been guarding. Ari smelled the blood before she got close enough to see the body, grateful her scarf was already tugged up so she could cover her nose and mouth as she approached. The body was in the middle of the garage, legs splayed out with the hands resting on the ruined chest. She fought the urge to turn away as she approached and looked down at the dead man.

"Welcome to Seattle's first homicide of the year."

"Damn. Almost made it twenty-four hours." She looked over her shoulder to make sure they were alone. "So you mentioned fingernails and teeth. You think it was a wolf?"

He looked at her skeptically. "The man's throat was ripped out, Willow. You think it's just a coincidence that it happened on the first day of wolf manoth?"

"Just making sure," she said. "Thanks for giving me the call."

Lorne nodded. "Yeah, sure. As far as my captain knows, you're a consultant here because it matches a case you worked a few months back. When we get a few more of these we'll bring you on for the investigation of a serial killer."

Ari fought the grimace that threatened to cross her features. "How many more of these do you expect to find? And I'm not asking Detective Lorne, I'm asking about your side work with the hunters."

"Hard to say. I'm just the clean-up crew. A bunch of other hunters are in charge of distributing the wolfsbane, and then we have to wait for it to actually affect a wolf enough that they go bonkers."

"So you can't give me any hints about where the stuff is being seeded?"

He shrugged. "Sorry. Need to know. For now, you and I just have to settle for being the clueless interns."

She had been hoping his misunderstanding about her true nature - mainly the fact he thought she was a hunter, not a *canidae* - meant she could probe him for information. Unfortunately all she knew was that someone in the hunter organization, a loose-knit group of individuals with no official roster or hierarchy, was being used to plant wolfsbane throughout Seattle. Ari didn't know if it was in food, drinks, sprinkled over the fish sold at the Pike Place Market, and she ran the risk of getting dosed every time she had a snack. So far she'd survived by being very selective with her food. She only ate things that came sealed in factory packaging or that she cooked herself or by Dale. She got a personal look at what the stuff could do to someone a few weeks earlier, and the resulting coma wasn't something she was eager to relive. She didn't even want to think about the potential insanity that came with it.

Remembering the coma triggered a thought, and she turned to look out the garage door. The street stretched out in front of the houses, and to the south she could see the water through a wide copse of trees. When she was dosed by the drug, she had a brief spurt of energy followed almost immediately by a complete loss of energy. She pointed. "What's over there?"

Lorne stepped forward and looked. "I think patrol said it's a dog park."

"Do not approach the dog park," Ari intoned. Lorne stared at her without understanding and she shook her head. "Nothing, never mind. How long ago did this guy get torn up?"

"Neighbor heard the screams about forty-five minutes go. First patrol car on the scene blocked off the area. Witness saw a guy running down the eastbound road, so one officer secured the scene while the other gave chase. Did he find anything?"

"A few patches of ice that had been broken, but nothing else worth noting."

Ari walked out of the garage and Lorne followed. The border of the dog park was marked by a chest-high stone wall. There were entrances cut every thirty yards or so, and Ari followed the sidewalk until she found one with a gate that was free of ice. "He jumped over here, knocked off the ice when he tried vaulting it." Beyond the fence was a winding path that led sharply down along the slope of the hill. She climbed up onto the fence and jumped over.

Lorne rested his hand on the butt of his gun. "You think he's still in there?"

Ari nodded. "He just tore someone to pieces with his bare hands. He's going to be tired."

"Let me go get backup."

"If he's... changed... do you really want a beat cop to see you trying to arrest a wolf?"

He nodded. "These guys are in the know. Wait here."

Ari cursed under her breath as he jogged back to the parked cars. *Well done, Ari. Going out into the sleet to hang out at a gruesome crime scene with a bunch of hunters who would mount your head on their walls if they knew what you really were. Just brilliant work. You know Dale is sitting on the couch with your Netflix paused, right? Imbecile.* She could see Lorne rounding up the uniformed officers to make a widespread search of the park. The *canidae* was a killer, but he wasn't acting in his right mind. He needed to be punished, not executed. She started down the path, letting her sense of smell take over for her eyes as she moved into the darkness.

As Lorne had predicted, the promise of wolf manoth had drawn hunters from all over the world to the Pacific Northwest. It allegedly had the highest concentration of *canidae* in the northern hemisphere, according to records they had been keeping on the off chance their ruling council decided to break the peace and start slaughtering them again. Ari had been doing her part to quietly warn the community without drawing attention to herself. Lorne had detected that she was part hunter, but he had yet to discover she was a wolf at heart.

Something heavy lurched through the underbrush to her right. She slowed down and crouched, took her phone from her pants pocket, and used the light to scan the bushes. "Come out of there."

"Hunter."

The voice was weak, but it helped her pinpoint his location.

"Nope. I'm a wolf, like you. I'm going to make sure you get treated right."

"Killed... killed Mark."

"Yeah. Yeah, but I know it wasn't your fault. You ate something or drank something that was laced with a drug called wolfsbane. It made you lose yourself for a little while."

He sniffled and grunted. "Ate a veggie burger at... the Planet Garden."

"Veggie burger? Vegan wolf?"

He laughed, and it sounded as if the effort pained him. "Wife is trying it. Means I'm trying it, too. Lady, it hurts."

"Were you injured? Did Mark fight back?"

"No. I mean, it hurts. Trying to think. I think... I think you should run."

Ari was about to reassure him she wouldn't run when he suddenly erupted from the greenery with his arms extended out in front of him. He hadn't transformed, but the skin around his eyes had darkened. His jaw dropped much wider than should have been possible, and he was stooped over with his knees bent up near his chest as he launched himself at her. He was naked save for a pair of ragged sweatpants that threatened to slip off his hips as he propelled himself forward.

Ari dropped her phone and raised her arm, using it to redirect his momentum to the left. He twisted in mid-air and tumbled to the ground, but Ari knew he would recover quickly. She jumped on top of him and twisted his arms behind his back at an angle that made it painful for him to struggle.

"I want to help you, okay? Give me a chance..."

"You're a hunter!"

Ari grimaced. The truth was too complicated to explain, not that she was willing to spill the secrets of her heritage to this stranger. Instead she put her knee in his back to hold him down as she leaned closer to whisper in his ear. He reeked of blood, dirt, and grass, but she ignored it as best she could.

"I'm a private investigator, okay? That cop up there thinks I'm a hunter, so I'm playing off that to try and save the rest of us from ending up like you."

"Wants to kill me." His voice was more growl than speech, and he continued to squirm between her and the freezing sidewalk.

"That doesn't mean he gets to." From the edge of the dog park she heard Lorne shouting her name. "He's coming down here with a bunch of other hunters wearing badges. I can keep them from hurting you but you have to trust me. You're going to have to pay for what you did to Mark, you know that, but I can make the punishment a little more bearable. There can be justice here. You want that?"

He exhaled sharply, puffing out his lips as he nodded.

"Good." She pushed herself up. "Over here! I've got him over here."

Lorne came down the path thirty seconds later with two other cops. One of the officers was illuminating the path with his flashlight and Ari held up her hands to show she had the situation under control. "I've got him," she said. "He's down. I need handcuffs from one of you."

"Get off of him, Willow," Lorne said. "Let us handle this."

She got to her feet and hauled the killer up with her. She stepped to one side, moving toward the officers and looking back at the trembling, half-naked *canidae* killer. Lorne brought up his gun and fired once, hitting the wolf in the chest. Lorne fired again in the space of a second, another spray of blood rising from his left shoulder as he fell back to the sidewalk.

"What the hell?" Ari shouted, recoiling from the body now leaking onto the frost-slicked pavement.

"You know what he was, Willow. You know what we are." He holstered the weapon and pulled his coat back over it. "You okay?"

"I... I don't..." She pushed her hair away from her face and looked away from the body. "You didn't have to do that."

"It's wolf manoth now, Willow. If you don't have the stomach to do what you were born to do, stand aside so the real hunters can do it for you." His voice was matter-of-fact rather than hurtful, but it still stung. "Are you sure you're okay?"

"Yeah. He didn't touch me." She wiped the back of her hand over her chin and looked down to see it came back bloody. "Shit. Not mine... his."

"Good to know. Look, we'll deal with this. No reason for you to be tangled up with paperwork all night. I'll call you tomorrow, let you know how it all shook out."

Ari nodded. "Yeah. Okay."

"Let me walk you back to your car."

She was shaken enough to agree, walking beside him up the hill to where she had parked. It was considerably more difficult than going downhill had been due to the accumulated ice, and Ari didn't trust herself to avoid the slick spots in her current state of mind. Lorne had his eye on her during the walk and touched her arm to keep her from getting into the car.

"You need me to get one of the officers to drive you home? I know it wasn't the first time you've seen someone die, but it takes some getting used to."

"That's an understatement. But no. I should be fine. The drive will help me, I think. Thanks, though."

He nodded and crossed his arms over his chest. "It's hard to believe wolf manoth has finally started again. This is going to be big for us, Ariadne."

"Us?"

"Hunters. Humanity in general." He reached into his pocket and came back with a folded handkerchief. Ari tensed as he reached for her face, then let him brush the blood off her cheek. He folded it around the red smears and deposited it back into his pocket. "It's an adjustment period. I know you didn't grow up in the fold so you're not entirely ready for this. But some of us have been training for it our entire lives. This is our moment, and we're going to take down as many wolves as we can before manoth is over."

Ari struggled to look inspired by his speech, when all she felt was a numbness from what had just happened and a churning in her gut at how excited he looked.

"Can't wait."

He smiled. "I'll call you tomorrow. Goodnight, Willow."

Ari said, "Night, Lorne."

She watched as he walked back down the hill, then got into her car. She started the engine and rested both hands on the wheel as heat poured from the vents to thaw out her extremities. Once she was warm enough she realized that she had been trembling from more than the cold. She'd been between Lorne's gun and his target, had been too deafened and surprised by the first shot to hear the second. She could still see the ice cascading off the trees, the blinding muzzle flash in the darkness. She saw the spray of blood from the *canidae*'s chest as he fell, already dead by the time he hit the ground.

Lorne was right, she'd seen people die before. She'd held a dead girl as she took her last breath, and she'd killed people who were trying to kill her. But she had never witnessed something so brutal and pointless. She finally realized she would attract attention if she remained where she was for much longer. She found the bag of wet wipes Dale had put behind her sun visor, wiped the blood from her cheeks and chin as best she could, and finally pulled away from the curb.

The city glowed through the rain, not emerald but gray and pale gold. She passed by the Space Needle on her way back to Dale's apartment, elegant and unearthly as it glistened. They'd been preparing for wolf manoth since the moment it was brought to their attention the previous fall by Ari's mother and a British *canidae* named Milo Duncan. The hunters had been planning for years to shatter a peace that had lasted for two centuries, and the Pacific Northwest seemed to be ground zero. This time the hunters were using a drug called wolfsbane that turned *canidae* feral without triggering a transformation. The result was apparently normal people going completely mad, and the hunters stepping in like heroes to eliminate the threat.

Ari's days were spent tracking down as many *canidae* as she could to warn them, and her nights were occupied dealing with Detective Lorne and his cadre of hunters. Through an innocent miscommunication on Ari's part and an erroneous conclusion by Detective Lorne, he was under the impression that she was a hunter as well. She was using the information to her own ends, but the hellish reality of going out every night to help killers track down "wolves" was already starting to gnaw at her. Now that wolf manoth had begun, she had a feeling their nights were going to start getting bloody. She wondered how many she had to save in order to make up for nights like this one.

The demands on her time meant that she'd had very little time for the two most important girls in her life; Dale, and her wolf. She worked out little moments here and there to appreciate Dale, to show her how important she was. They had lunch together every day, they found time to see movies together, they occasionally closed the office to walk home together and take long naps. They had just gotten back to the city following their Christmas-slash-Hanukkah trip, a much needed excursion that had helped de-stress them both.

The wolf was much harder to work into the tight schedule. Ari had been able to run and stretch her four legs during their trip, but finding time in the city was next to impossible. Adding to the stress was the fact that Seattle was lousy with hunters at the moment. Dale had never said as much out loud, but Ari knew she was worried that one night Ari would end up on the wrong street and Lorne would be waiting with a few of his heavily-armed friends. The last few times she had transformed, she'd forced the wolf to stay home and curled up in bed with Dale. She could feel the wolf getting antsy, and she couldn't blame it. She had to go for a real run, reclaim her territory in the wilds of Seattle, and she had to do it soon.

She finally arrived at Dale's building and drove underground, sitting in the warmth of the car for another moment before she ventured out into the icebox of the parking structure. She embraced herself as she made a bee-line for the elevator, shifting her weight from one foot to the other until the car arrived. She stripped off her jacket as she ascended, checking it for bloodstains before draping it over her arm. She felt the tension in her body ebbing as she approached Dale's door, knocking once with her middle knuckle before she entered.

Dale was in the kitchen washing dishes. Her hair was down, and in Ari's absence she had changed into sweatpants and an oversized sweater that Ari remembered had a habit of falling off her shoulder. She turned, brushing the hair away from her face with the back of one soapy hand. Ari swallowed the lump in her throat and felt the stinging in her eyes become unbearable.

"Puppy?" Dale came out of the kitchen and wrapped Ari up in a fierce hug. "Ari, what's wrong? What happened?"

Ari put her face in Dale's hair and breathed deeply. "Bad night."

Dale kissed her cheek, her neck, and then nestled her face against the curve of her shoulder. She knew she would have forced herself to talk about it if Dale had asked for more details, but she didn't. She was content to just hold Ari as long as she needed it. Ari cupped the back of Dale's head, her other hand resting in the small of her back. When she felt like she could speak without crying, she kissed Dale's ear.

"Thanks."

"For what?"

"You know what."

Dale snuggled closer to Ari. "Tell you what. Get out of these clothes, put on something comfy, and we'll finish watching our movie. Then we'll go to bed and we can sleep all day tomorrow."

"All day?"

"Well. We can stay in bed, but no promises we'll sleep the whole time."

Ari smiled and kissed her. "That sounds like a plan." Dale stepped out of the embrace and took Ari's coat. "Oh, uh, wait...

stop..."

"I'll just hang..." Dale unfolded it and frowned at the collar. "Is this blood?"

The tears Dale had just stopped threatened to make a resurgence. "Lorne shot a *canidae*. I was standing right next to him. He was hopped up on wolfsbane, and he'd just killed someone, but~"

"He didn't deserve that," Dale said, taking the words out of her mouth. She put the coat on the floor and examined Ari more closely. "Are you sure you're okay? Any tinnitus?"

"No." She took Dale's hands to stop her. "I'm fine physically. I got into a scuffle with the guy, but I talked to him. I thought I'd gotten through to him and then Lorne..." She took a steadying breath. "It's fine."

"I don't think it is, Ariadne. You're going out at night with Detective Lorne and you're hunting your own people. Even if you're not actively harming them, it can't be good for you mentally."

Ari chuckled. "I was thinking the exact same thing on the drive home. But I'm the only one who can do this. Lorne made the leap, he made the mistake, and I'm just taking advantage of it. We need someone on the inside who knows what the hunters are doing. Maybe the lives I save will make up for nights like this one."

Dale looked uncertain, but she nodded. "Okay." She stroked Ari's knuckles. "You want to get back to the movie?"

Ari nodded. "Let me change into my pajamas."

She went into the bedroom and undressed, checking her blouse for any blood before putting it in the hamper. She wore an oversized Seahawks jersey and shorts, leaving her socks on in case the living room was cold. Dale was waiting for her on the couch with a glass of wine. She had turned off the overhead lights, and she sat up so Ari could join her under the comforter. The laptop was sitting on the coffee table, and Dale reached out to start the movie at the point where Ari's phone had summoned her away. When she lay back, Ari rubbed her arms and let Dale settle against her.

"One day of wolf manoth down," Ari said softly.

"Thirty to go."

Ari nodded and kissed the top of Dale's head, trying to shut down her brain enough to enjoy the movie on the screen and the woman she loved in her arms.

CHAPTER TWO

January 2

DALE WAS absently stroking the top of Ari's head as she woke up, and Ari slowly realized that she had transformed in the night without realizing it. Her underwear and shirt were tangled under the blankets near her feet. It was awkward, but at least she hadn't ripped them as she had in the past. Her head was resting on Dale's chest and she twisted until to brush her long flat tongue against Dale's throat. Dale's hand stilled on Ari's neck and then she began to squirm as Ari moved up to start licking her face.

"Whoa... hey, stop it!" She put up her hands to block the assault. "I'm awake! I'm awake. Cut it out." She put her hands on either side of Ari's head and turned her head to look up at her. "I don't think you changed just to give me something to snuggle with, but I appreciate it nonetheless. Thank you, puppy." She kissed the tip of Ari's snout. "But now you need to get up."

Ari scrambled off of Dale and dropped to the floor. Dale tugged at her pajamas as she went into the bathroom, leaving the door open behind her. Ari braced her four legs against the floor as she changed from wolf to back to human. Her shoulders rolled back first, her head dropping forward as her arms extended and her fingers uncurled. The thick fur that covered her body receded into the pelt, which then softened to become flesh. She bared her teeth as they retracted into her gums to be replaced by blunt human dentation, and her tongue plumped and shortened.

When Dale came out of the bathroom, her pajamas had been exchanged for a robe and her hair was clipped up out of her face. Ari had climbed back into bed to slump against the soft mattress, breathing heavily in the aftermath of her rough transformation. She had one leg drawn up to her chest and her sweat-lank hair hung in her face. Dale crouched next to the bed and squeezed her shoulder to test how tense the muscle was. She brushed the hair back and examined Ari's face before giving her a chance to lie about how bad she hurt.

"You okay?"

Ari nodded. "Sore."

"Come take a shower with me."

She helped Ari up and into the bathroom. The shower stall was just barely large enough for them both, but they managed. Ari sat on the little bench attached to corner of the tub, and Dale detached the showerhead to spray it over her head. Ari closed her eyes and let herself be pelted. She leaned forward and Dale guided the barrage of water onto Ari's back and massaged the sore muscles with the tips of her fingers. In the years they worked together she had found most of Ari's trouble spots and knew just how to massage the pain away.

Ari turned her head and kissed the curve of Dale's stomach, sliding her lips up to the underside of Dale's breast. Dale's chuckle echoed off the tile as Ari ran her tongue over the nipple and teased until it was hard enough to bite. Dale somehow managed to keep up the massage as Ari kissed across her chest, exploring the spread of freckles as Dale stepped between her legs and ran the spray over Ari's head again. The hair fell forward over Ari's face, obscuring her face as she met Dale's eye.

"How do you feel?"

"A little more human." She put her hand on Dale's neck and guided her down for a kiss. Dale sagged forward between Ari's legs. Ari took the showerhead and ran it over Dale's back before lifting it to douse Dale's hair. Dale laughed into the kiss, then moaned as Ari guided the spray lower, lingering in the small of Dale's back where she sometimes ached after a long day of sitting at her desk. Dale massaged Ari's shoulders before sliding her hands down to tweak her nipples as Ari guided the water between Dale's legs.

"Hah..."

"Good?"

Dale pointed her toes and leaned heavily against Ari. She

nodded slowly, biting her bottom lip as Ari leaned in to kiss her neck. She licked higher, bit her earlobe, and held on with her free hand as Dale tensed with her orgasm. She closed her eyes, her senses still heightened from being in the wolf form, and she breathed deeply the scent of her partner's climax. She felt the micro-tremors in her body, smelled the mingling of sweat and juices being sluiced down Dale's inner thigh by the water. After a few seconds Dale exhaled and kissed Ari's face.

"I thought I was supposed to be making you feel better."

"You just did. But if you want to go double or nothing..." She leaned back and found Dale's lips again. Dale angled her hip and Ari lifted up to meet her. Dale moved carefully, well aware of how slippery the surface was under her feet, holding tight to Ari as they moved against each other. Dale closed her eyes and put her head down on Ari's shoulder, and Ari kept her eyes closed as she rocked her hips. She came quickly, the spasms running through her aching muscles and relaxing them better than even Dale's best massage couldn't achieve.

Dale sighed next to Ari's ear. "I'm awful fond of you, puppy."

Ari smiled. "The feeling's mutual." She stood up and repurposed the showerhead for use as an actual bathing tool. She washed Dale's hair, obediently crouched so Dale could return the favor before they abandoned the steam-warmed bathroom for the cold reality of the outer apartment. They shivered as they dressed in wool socks and layers. Ari had just tied her shoes when Dale took her collar off the nightstand and brought it over to her. Smiling, Ari lifted her hair out of the way and allowed Dale to put the collar on her.

"You changed around three o'clock, by the way. I was freezing and all of a sudden you started thrashing a lot. I stripped you down like you said I should, and a few seconds later there was a wolf in my bed. You stayed asleep through the whole thing, and I got to cuddle with something really soft and really warm. So I hope you aren't in too much pain, because I really appreciated it."

Ari smiled and let her hair drop. "It's worth a little soreness if it made you comfortable."

Dale bent down and kissed Ari's neck just above the leather of her collar. "What's your plan for today?"

Ari sighed. "Lorne said he would have the preliminary stuff on the *canidae* he killed sometime today. I'll call him this afternoon, see if he's identified the guy. If he has a family, I want to be the one to break the news to them. They need to be warned. If he was dosed..."

"Then there's a chance they have been, too." Dale tucked her hair behind her ears and put her laptop on the bed. "I haven't gotten very far on tracking how the hunters have been getting wolfsbane into food. I was thinking about that cult poisoned salad bars in Oregon back in the eighties. In that case, it only took about a dozen people to spread salmonella just by contaminating the food at a few salad bars. Over seven hundred people got sick."

Ari said, "So one hunter could conceivably expose a hundred people. If we assume that ten people out of every hundred is a *canidae*~"

"That many?"

Ari shrugged. "In the Pacific Northwest, it seems reasonable. I've been asking around and it seems like Seattle and the areas around us have a pretty high population. That's just *canidae*, specifically the ones who change into wolves. There are *felidae* and other shifters who won't be affected by the wolfsbane."

Dale nodded. "Right. So there are more than a dozen hunters, obviously, but not all of them are involved with distributing the wolfsbane."

"Right. Lorne said he had nothing to do with spreading the drug. But whatever the actual numbers are, they're creating an epidemic. We can't risk having it spread."

"And on that note, AmazonFresh should be delivering some groceries this morning. I'll wait for them before going to the office."

Ari kissed her temple. "Thank you, baby."

"No problem. I once dated a girl with very strict dietary restrictions, so I learned how to deal with the fridge as a potential landmine."

"Don't make me jealous. I'm going to go bug Lorne, see if he can give me some early information. I'll see you at work."

"Be safe."

Ari kissed two fingers and placed them against Dale's lips before she left. She tugged on a knit cap and her gloves as she rode the elevator down, went to her car, and headed out into the crisp morning. The rain had left the city scrubbed clean and brisk but it came at the cost of further sinking the temperature. If Ari had truly intended to spend the morning bugging Detective Lorne she would have turned north out of the garage. Instead she turned south, hating herself for the lie of omission she'd committed with Dale, but she was still unsure how she felt about the current situation.

She was waiting until she had a firmer hold on it before she revealed everything. It was one thing to work with the hunters, but her other partner was just as devious and untrustworthy.

The homes along Lake Washington Boulevard had always seemed more like estates to Ari, grand and proud domiciles safely hidden behind wild walls of brightly-colored foliage. She parked in front of a Dutch colonial painted cedar-red so it would more easily blend in with the trees, set back from the road behind a beautifully manicured lawn so the eye would skip right over it. The front porch was mimicked by a balcony on the second floor, and despite the early hour most of the downstairs windows were lit. She pulled into the driveway and reluctantly got out of the car.

The front door was open. She hesitated before knocking and took a moment to look back at the street. The lawn, the trees across the street, the smell of water from the lake; the combination had all once been so familiar because it once made up her entire world. She smoothed down the front of her sweater and faced forward to see movement through the door's fogged glass. The woman confirmed who it was with a glance through the peephole before she opened the door and took a step back. Despite the fact she was twenty years Ari's senior, most strangers could have confused her for an older sister. She was dressed down in a light blue cardigan and a black skirt, her feet bare on the hardwood. Ari knew she had chosen the outfit for its ease of removal; she was the sort of *canidae* who felt comfortable in human form if she could switch to the wolf with a second of warning.

"You know you don't have to knock, Ariadne. This is your home, too."

"Maybe for a while it was. Not anymore." She wanted to put her hands in her pockets, but she felt that would be too defensive. "Morning, Mom."

"Good morning. I was just making breakfast, if you'd care to join me."

Ari shook her head. "No, thanks. I'm not very hungry." It was a lie, but one she could live with. On the other hand, the warmth washing through the open door was too inviting to ignore. "But I will come inside. It's kind of freezing out here."

"The blessing and curse of living with a lake view. Come in."

She brushed past Gwyneth Willow and entered the house in which she'd grown up. The living room took up the majority of the ground floor, with a kitchen and dining room tucked to one side as an afterthought on the other side of the stairs. The house was cozy and inviting, absolutely nothing like the haunted house she often remembered it as. All of the trauma that occurred within its walls should have darkened the atmosphere and forever tainted its aura, but it was just a home. She felt like a ghost, in the house but unable to touch anything. She finally succumbed to the urge and stuffed her hands into her pockets as her mother shut the door.

They had reunited a few weeks before Christmas. Ari came to her with information gained from Detective Lorne that she thought her mother's cronies needed to know, and she'd delighted in sharing it. He had revealed the truth about the peace ceremony Gwyneth and her British friends had tried using to prevent the wolf manoth from beginning. The wolves wanted to recreate the marriage of a human to a *canidae* to reseal the peace. The human they'd chosen was Dale, but the *canidae* wasn't Ari.

The plan had fallen apart, largely due to Ari and Dale's refusal to play their roles. Gwyneth had tried to lay the blame for the coming war at Ari's feet, but Lorne revealed the hunters had never intended to let the accord to take place. They were only playing along to get a large number of *canidae* in one room so they could take out as many as possible in one fell swoop. Since discovering the truth, she'd used it as a stick to prod her mother whenever she was acting too haughty.

So far they'd only had three awkward conversations, none of which Ari had told Dale about simply because she hated the idea she was relying on her mother for any kind of support. All the rent checks she'd just barely made, the business she had helped build with the help of her mentor Glory, the nights when she carefully only ate half her dinner so she would have lunch the next day, and she had never once asked her mother for help. It was a source of pride for her that she never once came crawling back for a handout. But despite every stride she'd taken to be independent, here she was in her mother's living room relying on her for help. She was ashamed of herself for it.

"I take it something happened last night," Gwyneth said as she pushed up the sleeves of her sweater and crossed her arms. "Last night was the first night of wolf manoth. I was up the entire evening waiting for someone to come knocking." She passed Ari on her way into the kitchen. "I hope you don't mind if I eat in front of you. I'm famished."

Ari followed her mother through the house. "Someone

attacked and killed a guy up in Queen Anne. The wolfsbane made him lethargic, and I tracked him down in a nearby park. I wanted to bring him in, but Detective Lorne..."

"He shot him. You can't be surprised, Ariadne. This is what you get for working with a hunter."

Ari stifled her anger. "I'm doing what is necessary. Lorne made the mistake, and I'm just going along with it for the benefit of everyone."

Gwyneth said, "How did the man who died benefit?"

"He..." She forced herself to rein in her anger. "I'm going to get information from Lorne about his family on the pretense of checking them out to see if they're also wolves. In reality I'm going to warn them. I'm going to find out how he was exposed to the wolfsbane and make sure those close to him are safe. That's how I'm helping, Mom. I figure it's better than arranging some cockamamie ceremony that the hunters use to slaughter all of us."

Her mother glared at her. Ari raised her eyebrows, inviting a defense, but she knew it was pointless to defend herself and continued preparing her breakfast.

"Lorne is a hunter. He's going to kill wolves no matter what I do. If I'm standing next to him, maybe I can save one or two."

"What about the ones you can't save? What about the ones you have to watch die?"

"I guess I'll have to learn to live with that."

Gwyneth calmly took her plate to the dining room table and sat facing the window. Her position forced Ari to move so she wouldn't be talking to the back of her mother's head.

"And what if he discovers the truth about you, Ariadne? What if one night he calls you to some dark alley and shoots you the moment you arrive? Will I just have to learn to live with that? Will Dale?"

Ari swallowed the lump in her throat. "That won't happen."

"Benjamin Moss and I worked with hunters to coordinate the ceremony we hoped would prevent this atrocity from starting. The entire time we were meeting up, arranging candidates, compromising, plotting... we were careful and we took precautions but they still outmaneuvered us. They were lying in wait to massacre us as you seem to delight in reminding me. *Canidae* have a dual nature, but so do hunters. They are serial killers who must put on a good face for society while plotting their next murder in secret. Beware of them, Ariadne. Do not let your guard down, even for a moment."

"I'll keep that in mind. But someone has to do this, Mom. We have to know what they're up to. I happened to be on the right side of a stupid misunderstanding, so I'm elected whether I want to be or not. We can't pass up the opportunity just because it's dangerous. If I wasn't your daughter you would be cheering about this turn of events."

"So I'm supposed to just forget you're my daughter? That's not as easy as you might think."

"Tell me about it. I've been trying to forget since I was a teenager." Gwyneth flinched at that and Ari felt a twinge of regret. She softened her voice. "I should go. I'll call you when I have the name of last night's victim in case he was someone you might know."

Gwyneth nodded but didn't meet her gaze. "Thank you. You said the killing occurred in Queen Anne?"

"Yeah. Close to Kinnear Park. The wolf's victim was named Marcus Kurtz."

"Doesn't ring a bell. Still, it's a rather pricy neighborhood."

Ari scoffed and turned to leave. "Yeah. Looks like you're not the only rich wolf in town."

"Be careful, Ariadne. It's easy enough to fall into the habits of those you chose to work with even without the genetic disposition you have."

"I'm not a hunter."

"You're at least part hunter. The man who sired you, regardless of whether it was my choice or not, was a hunter. He passed the trait to you whether you like it or not. His DNA tried to prevent you from achieving your true destiny as a *canidae*. Perhaps all this time you've spent with Mr. Lorne and his ilk is changing you in ways you don't notice. In ways you can't notice until it's too late."

Ari faced her again. "I may be part hunter, but I'm also part you. And I've overcome that part of my genetics just fine so far. I think I'll be okay."

"I hope so. Give my love to Ms. Frye if you would."

Ari ignored the last comment as she left her mother's house again, once more hoping it was the last time but knowing fate had ways of making people end up right where they didn't want to be.

The grocery delivery arrived a half hour after Ari left, and Dale took the time to examine each item before she put it in the fridge.

They were being extremely careful about what they ate, cautious to the point of obsession so Ari didn't have a second exposure to wolfsbane. Lorne had bragged about the fact they had hunters placed throughout Seattle's food service industry, from chefs to waiters to convenience store clerks, so the idea of eating something that wasn't snugly stored inside a securely sealed wrapper was out of the question. They were eating at home a lot more often, and despite the inconvenience, she had to admit she had lost a few pounds now that fast food was off the menu.

She sent Ari a text so she'd know there was safe food at the apartment and headed to the office. She walked since it was less than a mile to the office, and she spent the walk listening to voice mail from the business line. Two potential clients wanted to set up an appointment, and she saved them for later when she could take down the contact information for Ari. No matter how busy she was with the hunters, she still had to make a living. They'd taken a break for the holidays, but the time had come to start meeting clients again. She just hoped Ari wouldn't stretch herself too thin and make a fatal error.

She stopped at the corner store to get a cup of tea, feeling like she was betraying Ari as she bought a cup that was completely mixed and prepared by someone she didn't know. She didn't have a vulnerability to wolfsbane, as humans were almost completely unaffected by exposure to it. She might get a strange aftertaste, or a few hours later she might have a mildly upset stomach, but it was nothing she could use to taste-test Ari's food for her. She was extremely careful about brushing her teeth and rinsing with mouthwash before kissing Ari so nothing passed between them.

She felt so helpless in the face of the citywide poisoning that threatened Ari's safety. And, to be perfectly honest, it threatened her safety as well. If Ari ate something tainted with wolfsbane, the wolf would come out like never before. It wouldn't be Ari, and it wouldn't be the playful beast that woke her up with kisses. It would be like those stories about the family dog that suddenly and inexplicably turned on its owners with teeth flashing and claws out. Ari told her flat-out that if she was ever exposed to wolfsbane that Dale had to stop her "by any means necessary" before she attacked.

Dale didn't know if she could do that, even in self-defense, but she also didn't know what the alternative was. Either she had to live with the fact she'd killed Ari, or she forced Ari to live with the knowledge she was responsible for the death of her partner. No matter how she looked at it, there was no winning. So to save them from that particular Sophie's choice they paid a staggering fee for AmazonFresh, they examined all the packaging before it was put away since they had no idea of knowing if the delivery driver was associated with the hunters, and they cooked everything right up to the point of burning it just to be certain any contaminants were rendered inert.

But that didn't mean she didn't cheat from time to time. She sipped the illicit tea, her guilt rendering it bland as she unlocked the office and turned on the overhead lights. The air was polar, and she shivered as she turned on the thermostat, held her hand over the vent, and began to reluctantly peel off her winter wear. She turned on the desktop and sat down, placing her phone next to the keyboard to replay the voicemails. First, however, she logged on to see what she could find about other *canidae* murders linked to wolf manoth.

Despite Ari's assurances to the contrary, and the revelation that the hunters had never planned to honor the ceremony in the first place, Dale still felt guilty about the attacks that were killing Ari's people. A small, irrational part of her brain insisted it was all happening because she'd been too stubborn to go along with Gwyneth Willow's plan. There was no way marrying Milo Duncan could have worked but she couldn't fight the feeling she could have done something to prevent the hunters from coming out in force. She found a story about a hunting lodge in Idaho that had turned into a blood bath just minutes after the clock struck midnight, a man in Oregon who had been thrown off a balcony after he tried to attack a woman at a New Years' party, at least six cases in Vancouver, et cetera, and so on.

In every case, they were ordinary people who had simply "gone berserk" and started attacking without provocation. In some cases their victims fought back and the *canidae* was dispatched before anyone else died. Dale found herself calling those the "best worst case scenarios," but no matter how many people were attacked, in every case the assault ended when the *canidae* was killed. Instead of finding the "wolves" in human form and killing them in cold blood, wolfsbane forced the *canidae* to not only reveal themselves, it forced them to become murderers so the killing was justified. The hunters were sacrificing innocent human lives to protect themselves from looking like serial killers. The very idea made her sick to her stomach.

She got up and went into Ari's office to the map of the area she had on the wall. It was large enough to show a portion of Canada and the majority of Idaho and Oregon, and she marked the locations of the new kills. She remembered the death Ari had witnessed and added a mark for it on the smaller city map. There could be dozens more, other deaths that weren't being reported or had just fallen under the radar. She knew by the end of the month the map would have more red than any other color, and she whispered a quiet prayer that Ari wouldn't end up as one of the pins on her own map.

CHAPTER THREE

NO MATTER how many times Ari's work took her there, she still wasn't used to visiting the police station. For a decent part of her life she'd lived on the streets. A uniform and a badge meant getting picked up and taken "downtown." Even now a few of the cops she'd met in the course of her work knew she was a private investigator and gave her a wide berth. She used to know the gatekeeper at this precinct, but he'd retired and been replaced with a guy who had a very strict sense of who belonged and who didn't. The new guy told her he'd call up to see if Detective Lorne was free to talk to her and pointed to a row of uncomfortable plastic chairs where she could wait.

After five minutes she was leaning forward with her elbows on her knees, watching everyone around her to calculate a moment when she could sneak upstairs without being seen. She was about to make a run for it when two detectives entered and Ari forced herself to abort her plan. She settled back into the seat and sighed heavily when the female detective slowed to stare at her.

"Ari? Ari Willow."

It took her a moment to recognize the familiar face without the benefit of a uniform and due to the fact her black hair was cut in a flattering pixie style. Once all the contradictory evidence was excluded she realized the woman was Diana Rios.

"Diana. Wow..."

She knew Diana from the old, old days, before Dale when the

agency was still called Willow Investigative Services. They dated until Ari took advantage of spending the night in Diana's apartment to get her hands on classified police files. The violation of trust ended their romantic relationship, but Diana still worked the late shift and occasionally encountered Ari post-transformation. Due to their past she usually didn't arrest her, but Ari knew she was worried about her eccentric ex-girlfriend who frequently turned up barefoot in the park wearing Goodwill rejects.

It had been nearly two years since they'd seen each other, and Ari was ashamed she hadn't been concerned about her old friend. Apparently the absence was due to a well-deserved promotion, and ascending to detective was a very good look for her. Her shorter hair was now accented by a few strands of gray that looked good enough that she knew most people would assume it was dyed to look fashionable. She wore a dark blue suit over a lilac blouse, her badge hooked on the hip of her trousers opposite her holster.

She motioned for her partner to continue upstairs and changed direction to meet Ari halfway across the lobby. She self-consciously touched her hair and smiled. "Ariadne Willow. God. You look really good."

"You too," Ari said. "Civvies suit you. As does the hair."

"Ah. The length or the color?"

"Both, actually."

Diana chuckled. "Thanks. Still getting used to it."

"How long have you been off third shift?"

"Oh, uh. About two years?" She nodded. "The exam came around and I figured what the hell, you know? Little did I know how often detectives get called out in the middle of the night. Joke's on me, huh?"

Ari smiled. "Well, at least you get paid more the same for more work."

Diana returned her smile. "Yeah... so, um. How are you? Still doing the private eye thing? I heard about the whole thing with the Gavins."

Ari nodded. "Yep, still doing that. Still, uh... Dale is still working for me. We're actually together now."

"Wow! Together as in... wow. That's great, Ari. I'm happy for you. And since we're talking about significant others..." She brought up her left hand to show off a ring. "I got this three days after the ban was lifted."

"Oh! Wow. That is..." She laughed and shook her head. "That's amazing. Congratulations. So are you still Detective Rios?"

"It's Macallan now. I took Lucy's name. We should have you and Dale over for dinner sometime. You would really like her, I think. And it would give us a chance to catch up." She stepped back to look Ari up and down. "Looks like Dale is taking care of you. I'm used to seeing you dressed like some thrift shop reject, discombobulated, strung out. Looks like you've gotten back on the straight and narrow. For the most part, anyway."

Her eyes dropped and Ari knew that she was noticing the collar. "Oh, this. This is something Dale gave me. Kind of an inside joke. We didn't want rings, and all the meaning that comes inherent with that, so we decided this was the next best thing."

"Aha. So, you get the collar. What does she wear?"

Ari's smile wavered. "Uh, nothing."

"Nothing? That doesn't seem fair. Someone might snatch her up when you're not looking."

She could tell Diana was teasing her, but they hadn't even discussed an exchange. The collar had been Ari's idea; Dale proved her loyalty by putting it on her, and Ari proved hers by wearing it. Maybe there should have been something else, something that Dale could touch when they were apart so she could feel closer to her. She was annoyed she hadn't realized it on her own.

Diana said, "Uh-oh. Sorry, I didn't mean to open up a can of worms there..."

"No, you didn't. Sorry. I just spaced a little bit."

"Uh-huh. So hopefully you're not here because you're in trouble."

"No. I'm actually working with another detective. Kyle Lorne."

It was Diana's turn to scowl. "You're working with him? On purpose?"

"He seems pretty stand-up to me. For the most part." At least he had before she discovered he was a hunter, and he'd relaxed about showing his more brutal side. They had worked together on a handful of jobs and before wolf manoth brought out his bloodlust, he was a fine colleague.

Diana shook her head and looked past Ari's shoulder as if viewing a montage of Lorne's Greatest Hits on the wall behind her. She finally shrugged and met Ari's eye again. "He rubs me the wrong way. Just don't put yourself in a position to rely on him, okay? And watch your back."

"Watch yours," Ari said softly. "Speak of the devil..."

Diana turned and saw Lorne stepping off the elevator. He had a file open in one hand, thumbing through it as he walked. Diana began to retreat and held up her hand in farewell. "I should catch up with my partner. It was really good seeing you again, Ari. We have to catch up again soon."

"We really do."

Lorne reached them before she could get away, and he nodded at her. "Detective Macallan."

"Detective Lorne. I was just heading upstairs."

"Don't let me stop you." Once she was gone, he lowered his voice. "Watch yourself, Willow. She might try to flip you."

Ari frowned. "Flip me how?"

"You know. She plays for the other team."

"Other..." She blinked in surprise when she realized what he meant. "Wow. I knew the year had changed, I just didn't realize it had changed to 1955. You can say she's a lesbian, Lorne. And..." She stopped herself. Could it be possible that he didn't know she was dating Dale? That she was even gay? He'd driven them home after a case, he'd heard them call each other sweetheart. Then again, there were people who could explain away any evidence. Still, what kind of detective was he? She decided to just say, "It's not a crime."

"Didn't say it was a crime. Free to be you and me, don't 'h' number-eight and all that. I'm just saying that you might want to watch your step around her. You never know when they might be recruiting."

"She's married. Pretty sure I'll be fine."

"Right. Married." Lorne sighed and held up his file. "Got some info on that wolf we took down last night. Want to take a look?"

"Yeah, absolutely."

"Victim's name was Logan Ahearn. He was a chef at some hoity-toity place in Redmond. Turns my stomach thinking of a wolf making my food." Ari struggled not to scoff at the hypocrisy, considering the fact he and his cronies were poisoning her people. "Not like I could afford to eat there anyway. And get this, he's got a family of little wolflettes living on Yarrow Point. You ever meet anyone who lives on Yarrow Point?"

"I think I'm about to." Lorne raised an eyebrow. "Come on, you think she'd talk to a cop? Even if it was self-defense, you're the guys who killed her husband. Let me go check her out, see what's going on. If she's a wolf~"

Lorne shuddered. "She's a wolf, trust me. Humans don't marry wolves. God, how sick would that be?"

Ari clenched her jaw and forced back her initial response. "Yeah. So I'll go check it out and let you know if the family's been infected as well."

"Sounds good to me. Not like I have time to run off to Yarrow anyway..." He took the page with the address out of the file and handed it to her.

"Is the department going to reimburse me for gas and the toll bridge?"

Lorne smiled. "I'm lucky if they reimburse *me* for that stuff. You're doing one this as an extracurricular activity, not as an officially-hired consultant. But I tell you what, since you're doing this as a favor to me, I'll buy you dinner sometime."

Ari said, "Wow, two dinner invites in ten minutes. I'm really going to save a ton on groceries this month."

"Two? Who else invited you to dinner?"

She cursed herself mentally for the slip. "Uh, Off- Detective Macallan."

"See? What did I tell you? Watch yourself, Willow." He winked at her as if to indicate his homophobia was meant playfully, then started toward the elevators. "Let me know what you find out."

"Will do."

Ari checked the file as she walked, using the map on her phone to figure out where exactly the Ahearn family lived. She sent Dale a text to keep her informed of where she was going and what she was going to do. She was definitely going to meet with Logan Ahearn's widow as she had told Lorne, but she also planned to find out how he was infected and protect his family from suffering the same fate.

She drove across the floating bridge and thought about the distance between Ahearn's home and the place where he'd been killed. The entire city of Seattle was between the two locations, which meant it was unlikely the victim had been chosen at random. Ahearn had called the victim by name so either he sought out a specific victim or they'd been together when Ahearn was dosed with the wolfsbane. Ari found herself hoping for the latter; if he was at a business dinner or hanging out with friends there was a smaller chance his family would be at risk from something in their home.

As Ari arrived on the peninsula, she realized that even though she'd grown up with a wealthy mother, and despite being taken under the wing of another rich woman in Glory, she now understood there was still a whole higher level of money that she'd never gotten close to achieving. Yarrow Point was an enclave of the super-rich, their sprawling homes hidden behind artfully landscaped hedges and bushes that shut out the plebian world. She caught glimpses of private basketball and tennis courts behind towering walls of privacy foliage, and could smell the chlorine from swimming pools tucked away out of sight. These were the people who had private docks in their backyards for when they felt like tooling around Lake Washington.

Ari ignored a No Parking at Any Time sign next to a row of dumpsters. She looked down at her sweater and slacks, which had seemed so nice in Dale's bedroom, and felt self-conscious as she walked down the winding driveway to the Ahearn home. It was tucked away at the bottom of a slope, only a small segment of it visible from the road. As she came around the curve, however, she saw that it hugged the curve of the land like a serpent, large picture windows reflecting the still waters of the lake.

The back door opened as Ari approached, and a pretty woman in a blue dress stepped out to intercept her.

"Hello, may I help you?"

"Mrs. Ahearn?"

"I work for the Ahearns."

Ari said, "My name is Ariadne Willow. I'm a private investigator. I need to speak with Mrs. Ahearn about her husband."

The woman's demeanor changed. "Should I prepare her for bad news?"

"Yeah... I would."

"Stay here for a moment." She turned and went back inside, and Ari was left alone in the driveway. She supposed it was a driveway, at any rate, even though it was long enough to qualify as a side street. It curved along the slope of the lawn to end at a three-car garage with a basketball hoop over the middle door. She tried to remember if she'd seen any luxury cars parked on the street near the crime scene but Queen Anne wasn't exactly a slum. Luxury cars wouldn't have looked at all out of place there.

The door opened again and a surprisingly tall, unexpectedly young woman with pale brown hair came outside. She wore a giant sweater that appeared hand-knit swaddled her torso, leaving only her hands and legs exposed. She pushed her sleeves up to her elbows and crossed her arms as she looked at Ari and seemed to mentally process the reasons for her to be there.

"Something happened to Logan."

Ari couldn't tell if it was intended as a question. She was stunned at the idea Lorne hadn't had someone break the news. "Yes, ma'am."

"You'd better come inside."

She turned and went back into the house, leaving Ari to catch up with her. She paused just over the threshold and saw the first woman sitting in the small office just off the living room. Mrs. Ahearn had gone into the kitchen and Ari followed her. "Would you like something to drink?"

Ari said, "No, thanks. Mrs. Ahearn~"

"Serena."

"I'm sorry I have to tell you this, but your husband was killed last night."

Serena stopped next to the kitchen island and rested her hands on the marble. She bowed her head and took a deep breath. Ari stepped closer and put her hand on the woman's shoulder, shocked at how much taller she was up close. Ari herself was five-seven, but she still only came up to the new widow's shoulder. Serena closed her eyes and curled her fingers on the countertop, her chest rising and falling with each slow intake of breath and measured exhale.

"How did it happen?"

"A police officer shot him."

Serena looked at her, a wave of hair blocking most of her face, but her eyes were clearly visible. "Why? What was he doing?"

Ari looked toward the front of the house where the other woman was working. "Jacqueline isn't listening. She knows better. And I can tell from your scent that you're one of us. So let's not beat around the bush. What happened to my husband?"

"Do you know about wolfsbane?" Serena shook her head. "It's a drug being used by a group of hunters to turn *canidae* into feral monsters. That gives them permission to kill us in cold blood. They've been dosing us through food, drinks, I've even heard a rumor that they're trying to aerosolize it. When one of us inhales or ingests it, we go feral. Then the hunters swoop in to save the day by taking us out. Your husband was under the influence of it last night. He was shot by a detective."

"God, this is so unbelievable. You said this wolfsbane gives hunters a reason to kill us. What did Logan do to make the officer open fire? Do I even want to know?"

Ari hesitated. "Do you happen to know where he was last night? Do you know who he was meeting with?"

"He was visiting one of the men who invested in the restaurant. We had a bit of a downturn last year but things were improving. He wanted to thank Mark for staying with us."

Ari said, "Marcus Kurtz?"

Serena began to nod but stopped mid-motion. "Oh, God. Please don't tell me."

"Sorry."

Serena swallowed hard and pushed away from the counter. She went to a teapot sitting on the stove and took a cup off a hook. "This is unbelievable."

"Ah," Ari said. "I would be careful about drinking that..."

Serena looked at her cup. "This is from a brand-new bag. I opened it myself this morning."

"Where did the tea come from?"

"I don't know." She found the bag in the cupboard and looked at the bag. "Illinois. I've been drinking it all morning."

"I guess it should be fine. Just be careful about what you buy and where you buy it." She eyed the fruit on the counter. "I'm guessing most of what you buy is organic?"

"Yes."

"Make sure you wash it carefully before you eat it. Things like bananas and apples... things that come with natural safety wrappers, those should be fine. But tea or soup can have a pinch of something nasty mixed in. Anything someone else prepares for you should make you wary."

Serena shrugged and took a drink. "These hunters. How are they operating? How can they just go around killing us?"

"They're ordinary people for the most part. Police officers, bus drivers, mailmen. They put themselves in a position to be attacked and then claim self-defense when they pull the trigger. If you're asking how they justify sacrificing innocent bystanders, then you're asking the wrong woman. Do you have any idea how your husband might have been exposed?"

"If it could have been anything he ate or drank..." She looked out the window as she thought. "He was always sampling things at the restaurant. It's amazing he didn't weigh five hundred pounds. It could have been anything that crossed his table. Oh, God, if it was in something he served then he might have helped infect some people. They have to be warned."

Ari said, "I'm doing my best to warn as many *canidae* as I can. If you have any kids..."

"Two kids. They're still away with their grandmother... they went out for Christmas and to celebrate the new year." She anticipated Ari's next question. "Ireland. We thought they should get in touch with their roots."

"They should still be warned. And if you don't mind keeping them out of school for a while, they might be safer staying right where they are. And we should warn Jacqueline about it as well."

Serena said, "Does it affect humans?"

"It gives them a stomachache sometimes, but nothing worth noting."

"Then she'll be fine. Jackie doesn't have to worry about infection."

Ari kicked herself for not noticing earlier when Serena had casually mentioned the assistant wasn't like them. "She's not *canidae?*"

"No. We hired her about six weeks ago as my personal assistant. I'm an artist... the gallery sent her over."

"Do you trust her?"

Serena said, "Yes," but she hesitated and looked as if she was saying it because she didn't have quite enough evidence to say no. She looked toward the other room with a wary expression as Ari slipped off her stool.

"Stay here." She walked slowly through the living room and peered around the corner into the office. Jacqueline was on a laptop with her back to the door. She was small but well-muscled, her black hair cut short. Ari wished there was some telltale sign, a tattoo or a bracelet which indicated someone was a hunter. Lorne said he'd grown the beard in honor of wolf manoth, but what did would a woman do? Cut her hair to avoid having her vision impeded?

She sensed the scrutiny and turned around to find Ari watching her. "Hello. I'm sorry, I didn't catch your name."

"Ariadne Willow. I'm a private investigator. I'm working with Detective Kyle Lorne. Know him?"

Jacqueline's mouth twitched slightly toward a smile. She lowered her voice and leaned closer. "Ah, yes. Lorne... I've heard of him. You can tell him everything's under control here. Serena's a fighter but I know I can overpower her when the time comes. I've been holding back until her little brats get home~"

Ari had heard enough and was ready to take the hunter out, but movement from the corner of her eye stopped her. She turned toward the kitchen and saw Serena standing in the doorway. She was swaying slightly from one side to the other, her head hanging forward as if she was sleepwalking. Jacqueline stood up and moved to see what Ari was looking at.

"Damn. Did you let her open a new bag of tea? She normally opens a new one every Saturday. This screws up my time table a little bit."

Serena stumbled forward. "What are you talking about...?"

Jacqueline ducked back into the office just as Serena lunged for her. Ari caught the taller woman's hands and twisted her away, using her own weight to change Serena's trajectory into the living room. They tumbled over the back of the divan, rolling onto the floor. Ari landed underneath Serena, who straddled her waist and wrapped both hands around Ari's throat. Ari's feet were still on the couch and the awkward positioning gave her the leverage necessary to somersault Serena onto the coffee table. It was sturdy enough that it didn't break, but Ari doubted it was very good for Serena's back.

Jacqueline returned with a gun drawn. She aimed it at Serena and cocked the hammer, but Ari slammed into her just before she managed to pull the trigger. They hit the living room wall, arms tangling until Jacqueline pistoned her flattened palm into Ari's chest to knock her back. They struggled for the gun briefly but Jacqueline gained the upper hand by dropping into a crouch and shoving her shoulder into Ari's gut. Ari was thrown back and forced to let go of the gun.

"What the hell are you doing?" Jacqueline growled. "This is wolf manoth."

"You're going to kill her in cold blood."

"It will be self-defense. There's a difference."

Ari shook her head. "No, there's not. If you think there is, you're delusional."

Jacqueline shoved Ari away and focused on Serena again. Their conversation had given her time to shed her bulky sweater and transform into a golden-blonde wolf. The animal was immense, with dark eyes and its deadly-looking fangs bared. The wolf snarled and launched herself off the coffee table, teeth flashing as Jacqueline brought the gun up. Ari threw herself against Jacqueline and let Serena hit her instead. The gun went off, the explosion muffling the sound of shattering glass as Serena closed her jaws around Ari's neck. The sharp fangs hit the leather of Ari's collar and miraculously didn't penetrate or slip. Ari got her arm around Serena's neck and flipped her over, knocking her to the ground. She made sure she landed hard enough to knock the wind from the wolf's lungs, hopefully taking her out of the fight for a few seconds.

She looked up and saw Jacqueline had recovered and was aiming a gun at Serena's head.

"I would move if I were you, Miss Willow. I can't be confident I'd make a clean enough shot to avoid you. I guess it would help the self-defense claim if you were both shot, but the forensics would be tricky. I'd prefer if you stood up and moved aside."

Ari let her wolf have a little slack on its leash. She felt her logical and ordered mind giving way to animalistic rage. She bared her teeth, the flesh around her eyes darkening as she flattened her feet on the ground and pounced forward. Jacqueline's eyes narrowed with confusion as Ari knocked her backward. She slapped the gun out of Jacqueline's hand, closed a hand around her throat, and pushed her down to the floor.

"You're a goddamn wolf!"

"I'm a *canidae*. I will not let you kill this woman in cold blood."

Serena slammed into Ari from behind, trying again to find a place to bite. Ari rolled her shoulder and spun around, holding Jacqueline in front of her with Serena's wolf riding her back. She threw herself against the wall and Serena yelped in pain before the weight fell away. Jacqueline twisted away and reached for her gun, but Ari threw herself on top of her and pinned her arms back.

"She's going to kill us both, you idiot!"

"I won't let you kill her."

"You may not get that luxury. Someone is going to die in this house today." She laughed and twisted to look at the dazed wolf in the corner. "You're thinking it's going to be me. You're thinking I know your secret, and hey, I was going to kill this bitch and her kids anyway. Go ahead. Tear me apart, wolf. Prove that we don't need the wolfsbane to turn you into animals. You're all animals without us intervening."

Ari looked back to see Serena was slowly recovering. The wolf was already back on its feet, swinging its low-slung head around to get its bearings before it attacked again. Ari put her arm around Jacqueline's neck and rolled, using the assistant as a human shield as she began pushing herself along with floor with her feet. Serena looked at the retreating prey, growled in a low rumble, and began to stalk after them. Ari reached the office where she had first found Jacqueline and scrambled inside, kicking the door shut just as

Serena arrived at the threshold. Ari and Jacqueline got to their feet and Ari gave the room a quick once-over for weapons. Serena slammed against the other side of the door and released a querulous whine.

"I suppose you're just going to let her kill me."

"You said it yourself. You drugged her food, you got her husband killed, you got Mark Kurtz killed, and you would have killed her kids if they were here. The way I see it, you've earned your death several times over. Are you ready to die for your cause, Jackie?"

Serena growled again and Jacqueline tensed.

"I'm ready. The plan was to have her attack me before you arrived. I'm ready."

"I don't think you are. I think you're terrified of being hurt, being ripped to shreds. You didn't see Mark Kurtz after Logan got done with him. You think she's just going to gnaw on your arm a little bit? She went for the throat. She'll tear out your windpipe, Jackie, and that will just be to disable you. We're wolves. We don't nip and scratch... we hunt to kill. You hunters are putting yourselves in the crosshairs of a species who has spent their entire existence fighting the misconception that we're killers. Forget what I said about dying for your cause. Are you ready to die slowly and screaming as the wild animal you let off the leash tears you to bloody bits?"

Jacqueline was trembling by the time Ari stopped speaking. "I... can fight her off. I've done it before."

"And you know that because of your hunter training?" Ari asked. "What was it? Some doped, weak, starved animal your father kept in a cage until it was too weak to defend itself? Is that why you think you stand a chance against that rage monster outside?"

Doubt finally filled Jacqueline's eyes, and she looked toward the door. "I..."

"Do you want to survive this?"

Jacqueline looked at Ari. Finally she nodded, quickly and only once, but it was enough.

"Then don't do anything stupid in the next few minutes." She walked to the door and looked at the knob. "This is stupid. This is so stupid. Oh, Dale, why aren't you here to slap me in my stupid plan-making face?" She took a few deep breaths to brace herself and then threw the door open. Serena was startled by the sudden movement but overcame her surprise quickly. Ari threw herself at the animal, closing her hand around Serena's snout and holding it shut as tightly as she could. She wrapped her other arm around the wolf's neck and squeezed. The wolf bucked and writhed to get free, but Ari had the better angle. She managed to wrestle Serena to the ground and pinned her there by bracing her feet against the doorjamb.

Ari felt her own wolf tickling at the back of her mind and closed her eyes. She fought the change, knew that she stood a better chance of winning the fight if she stayed two-legged. She twisted her neck so she could see Jacqueline, uncomfortable having the assassin in her blind spot. She looked conflicted, but she was sitting with her back against the wall and her knees drawn up against her chest. The reality of poking a dangerous animal to the point of snapping was finally dawning on her, and Ari could see her face had become pale behind her makeup.

"Relax, Serena... just settle down. Relax." She kept her voice as calm as she could, her hand holding tight to Serena's golden fur. "Just get through this first bit, okay? Then you can clear your head... and you can put all this behind you. But right now you need to take over for the wolf and realize what you're about to do. You're about to become a killer. I know you don't want that no matter what this woman did or planned to do to your family."

The wolf bucked and squirmed against her but Ari held her tight.

"There's a gun on the floor over there. I could end this right now, or I could let Jackie do it, but I think there's been too much death. I won't make your kids into orphans, and I won't let you go to jail for murder, so you stop. Lie down and let the wolfsbane get out of your system. Think about your kids. Think about who would be left to take care of your kids."

Serena trembled and whimpered softly, but the tension slowly faded from her body. Ari held tightly to her until the transformation was nearly done, then she pulled away and took the throw off the back of the couch. She wrapped it around Serena, who was now fully human and shivering. She looked up, her eyes wide and the pupils dilated. Ari helped her sit up and brushed the hair out of her face.

"What happened? My head is killing me."

"You were poisoned. Stay here." She walked over to Jacqueline, who seemed to have regained some of her aggression. "Now you."

Jacqueline glared at her. "You're going to kill me."

"No. But you're a problem. I can't have you blabbing about what you've found out. I'm working to save lives here. Not just *canidae*, but hunters, innocent bystanders... I can't have you running around threatening that."

Serena said, "There's a room in the basement." Her voice was tremulous but slowly becoming stronger. She clutched the blanket tighter around herself. "We can tie her up down there, keep her until you're out of danger."

Ari wasn't sure she liked the plan, but it was better than anything she'd come up with. "Okay. You have something to tie her up with?"

"Uh. Yes. Yeah, down by the garage, there are some ropes we use for the boat. They should be enough to hold her. I'd get them myself, but I'm..." She gestured at her nakedness.

Ari looked between the two women. "Can I trust you alone with each other?"

Serena didn't take her eyes off Jacqueline. "I suppose you'll find out when you get back."

"Shit." Ari didn't see how she had much of a choice. She turned and jogged out of the house, jumped the railing, and ran to the end of the driveway. The ropes were coiled on the ground like snakes, and she crouched to slip them over her arm before running back to the house. Part of her knew what she would walk in to find, but she was still horrified by the sight of Serena stepping away from Jacqueline's bloody body.

Ari dropped the ropes and swayed on her feet, bracing her hands on the back of the couch to keep from falling over. She closed her eyes, angry at herself for not preventing what had just happened.

"Damn it, you didn't... you didn't have to do that."

Serena's voice was calm and measured. "She poisoned me. She caused my husband to get killed, and she planned to murder my children. That is all the provocation I needed."

"You're not thinking straight. The wolfsbane..."

"That drug fogged my thinking briefly, yes. But you brought me back from the brink." She casually wiped Jacqueline's blood from her hand using the blanket Ari had draped her with. "If this is indeed a war, Ariadne Willow, there will be casualties on both sides. You should either prepare for that, or you should get out of the way. Thank you for letting me know what I was up against, and for saving my life. If you hadn't arrived when you did, I fear I would have been caught completely unawares and there would be a different corpse staining my hardwood floor right now."

Ari tried to take comfort in that, but it was too bleak for her to even contemplate. "What are you going to do now?"

"I'm going to join my children in Ireland and hope the hunters aren't as thick over there. And you? What is your next step?"

Ari shook her head. "I have no idea."

"You very nearly made a grave error this afternoon. You got between a hunter and a *canidae* and tried to save both."

"I could have done it if you hadn't killed her the second my back was turned."

"Perhaps. Or maybe you wanted a reason to turn your back. You're waging a war on two fronts, Ariadne. You're trying to save everyone, and when you fail, you will have saved no one. Choose, and soon, or I fear the choice will be made for you."

Chapter Four

When Ari texted that she would be on Yarrow Point, Dale calculated that she had at least an hour before any client work could be done. So instead she opened the bottom drawer of her desk and took out a file Ari hadn't seen. She didn't know it existed and with any luck wouldn't know about it until she had something conclusive to share. Just before Thanksgiving, during the kidnapping investigation, she and Ari had been trapped in Milo Duncan's house by a blizzard. She had been called to the house to help take care of Ari, who had been dosed with the wolfsbane as some sort of object lesson in the dangers of exposure. While Ari was coming down off the high, Milo had given Dale a sample of the drug.

"Ari's mum brought it with her but we didn't know she'd use it so recklessly. I'm scared to go into my own kitchen. Anyway, if anyone should have it, it's you."

Dale had lifted her hands as if Milo was offering her a live grenade. "I don't want it!"

"No, not for a weapon or anything like that. Have it tested. I figure if you can figure out where it came from, maybe we can cut the hunters off at the source. Really I just want the shit out of my house, and I figure you can keep it as safe as anyone."

Since then Dale had been trying to track down the source during every free moment. The actual sample she'd gotten from Milo was sent off to a lab where it was broken down into its base components. The complete report had taken much longer to finish than she expected, but eventually she'd received the email. The *canidae* knew that wolfsbane was an accidental discovery; no hunter had gone looking for a drug that would turn their enemy into primal killing machines. She'd found a naturally-occurring plant called wolf's bane, but that appeared to have no relation to the synthetic version other than a name.

The synthetic wolfsbane had a high concentration of hyoscyamine, an alkaloid that could cause hallucinations, disorientation, and short-term memory loss but it was cut with something that only set off the side effects when exposed to a *canidae* physiology. She was tempted to dose herself with it just to see what happened, but she was horrified at the thought of having any trace of it on her lips or skin and having it transfer to Ari when they kissed or made love. Her eyes moved guiltily to her to-go cup of tea, and she quickly stuffed it into the trash under her desk.

There were only three labs in Seattle with the ability to manufacture the wolfsbane on a large scale. She hadn't had the opportunity to check any of them out, but the lab report listed the items they would need large amounts of in order to mass produce the poison. She decided the next time Ari went out for a run, instead of going home to sleep and wait for the call, she would choose one of the labs to stakeout and watch for signs of hunter activity.

She hated keeping the investigation a secret from Ari, but she knew it was the best course of action. If Ari knew, she would insist on keeping Dale away from the danger and investigating it herself. Dale wouldn't be able to sleep, certain that something would go wrong and she'd be somehow exposed. She hadn't even witnessed Ari under the full influence of the drug, but sitting by her bedside as she sweated out the toxins, holding her hand as she slept through another hour, another day, was bad enough. She didn't want to relive that uncertainty. Besides, Ari had talked about giving her more responsibility so she could be a true partner at the agency. Dale was fine making appointments and filing paperwork, but she appreciated being seen as an equal.

She went through the file again, checking it against the suppliers of the pharmaceutical labs, marking them down in order of likeliness. Lorne said hunters had day jobs like anyone else, and a lot of them were using those jobs to help advance the cause. Tracking down *canidae*, spreading the wolfsbane, covering up the bloody murders committed by their people... the drug was supposed to make every kill self-defense, but it was good to have people in the legal infrastructure who could make any death look justified. Maybe some of them were chemists with PhDs that qualified them to work at the labs.

It would be easier if there was a way to identify hunters. Some *canidae* could allegedly sense a hunter, but Ari lacked that skill. Milo had said it was just an ineffable sense, an instinct that they were in the presence of someone who meant to do them harm. Ari's lack was due to the fact she'd run away while she was still being trained by her mother. She knew how to transform, how to survive, but she'd missed out on honing the instincts that most *canidae* learned from their parents. It also might have had something to do with the fact Ari was part hunter. Dale still couldn't believe Gwyneth had kept that from her, but how exactly do you sit down your daughter and reveal such a horrific secret?

Ari hated her mother, and for good reason, but Dale sometimes understood where she was coming from. Attacked and raped by a group of hunters simply because they'd discovered she was a wolf, one of them had left her pregnant. Gwyneth made the choice to keep the baby - a decision Dale would forever be grateful to her for, no matter what else the woman did - and quickly discovered she couldn't shift naturally into wolf form. She made another decision, a life-changing choice, to put Ari through an arduous, potentially fatal procedure in which the blood tainted by her hunter parentage was replaced with that of a full-blooded wolf *canidae*.

The procedure worked, in a way, but the transformations hurt Ari in a way other *canidae* didn't have to suffer. Part of Dale's job was to massage that pain away, and it was the part of her job she took very, very seriously even before she and Ari became lovers. Ari had spent most of her life managing an excruciating amount of pain, and Dale was the first person to help ease it. It made her feel needed at a time in her life when that was something she didn't think was possible. Meeting Ari and being welcomed as an integral part of her life wasn't just important; Dale knew that it had saved *her* life in the process. In return there was no line she wouldn't cross for Ari.

Before meeting Milo, she'd never taken the time to really deal with the fact she was dating outside her species. She was aware Ari was technically a *canidae*, and despite the fact she was one-hundred percent human in every other way, her ability to change into a wolf made her something different. She'd dealt with the oddity of knowing her girlfriend might occasionally become a wolf in the middle of the night, and she'd had the bizarre dream or two in which sex became... unusual, but actual waking acceptance was something she'd never had to consider.

She decided she didn't care. Ari could have been a green-skinned, five-eyed bug from Neptune, and if nothing else was different Dale would still love her. She went back to her desk and shrank down the browser so she could see the wallpaper. It was a photo she'd taken of Ari before they realized that using her picture to advertise a *private* investigative services was a bad idea. She'd saved the picture for herself because Ari looked absolutely beautiful in it, and she smiled as she remembered the day she'd taken it.

Whatever happened for the rest of wolf manoth, whatever the road ahead had in store for them, she would be with Ari every step of the way.

Serena went to get dressed while Ari dealt with Jacqueline's remains. She wrapped the body in the blanket from the couch and secured it at either end with the rope she'd gotten from outside. The blood soaked through almost immediately and she reluctantly retrieved a trash bag from the kitchen to cover the reddened end of the blanket.

She was furious with herself for letting it happen, but also for the sense of relief she felt. She didn't like the idea of a hunter walking around fully aware of who she was, especially after name-dropping Lorne. If Jacqueline had survived and somehow gotten free, she could have signed Ari's death warrant. She wished there could have been another way even though she knew Jacqueline wouldn't have hesitated to kill both her and Serena. Hell, she'd coldly discussed killing two children like someone talking about an extermination. In the end, that as all she and Serena were to her. They were pests that needed to be eliminated. She couldn't afford to be that brutal about hunters, but she also couldn't waste too much energy mourning for them.

Serena came back from the bedroom in a tailored blouse and slacks. Her feet were still bare, and her hair was damp and pushed away from her face to indicate she'd splashed some water on her face. She still looked like she was buzzed, and Ari made a point not to turn her back on the woman.

"What do we do now?" Serena asked.

"I don't have a fucking clue." She rubbed her face and thought for a moment. "You said she'd only worked with you for six weeks. Where did you find her?"

Serena said, "I didn't. The gallery where I show my work sent her over. She arrived not long before the blizzard hit, and she turned out to be a godsend. The whole time she was poisoning my family."

Ari tensed. "Your kids... she could have been dosing them. You should call and make sure everyone is all right. If they had the wolfsbane in their system it could make them lose control at any time."

Serena was already dialing her phone. "What do I tell her?"

"Just tell her to keep an eye on them. Let her know what's going on. Jacqueline implied that she was waiting until the kids got home to take you all out together."

"Then why did she kill Logan first?"

Ari shrugged. "He was the alpha. He was bigger than her, stronger, and she eliminated him so he wouldn't be an issue later on."

Serena said, "Shows how much she knows. I was the alpha of this family."

"Obviously," Ari said.

Serena put the phone to her ear and began pacing the length of the room as she waited for an answer. Ari went into the office Jacqueline had been using and searched her desk. She found a wallet that belonged to Jacqueline Ramsey, and she copied down the home address before searching the rest of the wallet's contents.

A small packet of pale brown powder brought her up short, making her freeze for a few seconds before she carefully withdrew it. She recognized it from her own exposure, the cloud of dust her mother had blown into her face to show her the danger they were facing. She placed it on the desk as Serena spoke to her mother in the other room, her voice becoming a low Gaelic growl as she explained the events and revelations of the past hour.

Ari found an envelope for the wolfsbane and folded it into quarters, lessening the chance anything might slip out of the plastic and spill onto her skin or into her pockets. She searched the rest of the office until she finally found Jacqueline's cell phone plugged into a charger on the far wall. She was going through it when Serena came to find her. She looked even worse than she had earlier, gaunt and worn out, and she leaned against the wall as she spoke.

"Mother says that the kids are fine, but she's taking precautions to make sure they aren't infected. Is there anything I should do to prevent myself from getting sick again?"

"Jacqueline said that she'd infected your tea, but she could have spread it anywhere. Silverware, dishes... I suggest having someone come in and boil... hell, forget that, just throw it all out and buy new stuff."

"What are you going to do?"

"Someone's going to wonder what happened to Jacqueline. This will be the first place they look. How quickly can you get out of town?"

Serena closed her eyes and sighed as if the very idea was too exhausting to contemplate. Ari remembered her own reaction to the wolfsbane and felt sympathy for her.

"I can have someone pick me up within the hour and take me to the airport."

"Okay. I'm going to see if I can keep anyone from getting suspicious, but it'll be better if you're not here if they do come looking."

Serena said, "Thank you. And..." She furrowed her brow. "I'm sorry. For what I did. I can't believe you're still helping me after... after I tried to..."

"You didn't try to do anything," Ari said. "It was the wolfsbane. I've been there, I know what it does to people."

"How long do the effects last?"

"In my case, it knocked me out for a good three days. You need to be wary of feeling sleepy and lazy for a little while. But after the initial burst of violence there weren't any more. As long as you can avoid being exposed again, you should be fine."

Serena took a deep breath. "I'm scared to touch anything in my own house for fear of getting exposed again. I can't even take a shower because what if it's in the faucet? And I am dying for a glass of wine."

Ari said, "If there was ever a morning that justified drinking straight from the bottle, I think this is it."

"I think you have a point. But I'll wait until I've driven myself to the airport before I get drunk."

"Solid plan. And after everything that's happened, I haven't had a chance to express my condolences about your husband."

Serena nodded. "Thank you. I don't think it's quite hit home yet. I'm very glad you were here."

"I am, too." In the long run, at least, it was true.

"Do you have any idea what we're going to do with the body?"

Ari wanted to say it was Serena's problem, wanted to walk away claiming she'd been against the killing, but she felt equal responsibility for what had happened. "I don't know how organized the hunters are, but there's a chance she was supposed to report in. If anyone realizes she's missing they're going to come here first. They have people in the police department, and they probably have a presence at the airports. They might be able to stop you from getting out of the country if they know you've killed her." Ari took Jacqueline's phone out of her pocket and scrolled through the sent messages.

"So we cover it up."

"Could be easier than I thought. She's been sending progress reports every day at six."

Serena said, "That's when she gets off work and goes home."

"Okay. So we just have to send a progress report to keep people from getting suspicious. I'll take care of that. As for the body, if no one is going to come looking for her and no one is going to be here, we can just take her down to the garage."

"The garage." Serena looked ill, but she nodded. "Okay. Yeah. Her car is in the first slot, the closest to the house. You can put her in there."

"That, uh, may be easier said than done. I know she looks small, but there's a reason people say something is 'dead weight.' I can't carry her down there by myself."

Serena looked into the living room. "God. This is whole morning has been surreal. Okay. Yes, I'll help you take her down."

Ari pushed up her sleeves. "Which side do you want to take?"

They checked outside to make sure there weren't any boats nearby that could see what they were doing. The fortifications between the Ahearn property and their neighbors meant they didn't have to worry about prying eyes from next door as they gathered Jacqueline's wrapped body and carried it across the deck and down the stairs.

"Have you ever moved a dead body before?" Serena asked, breathing heavily as she backed down the deck stairs to the backyard.

"Can't say I've had that experience, no. Seen a couple, though. Not exactly a fan."

"I can understand why."

They entered the garage through the side door. Ari had taken the keys out of Jacqueline's purse and unlocked the car, then helped place her behind the wheel. She knew that any medical examiner would be able to tell she'd been moved, but she put off that worry until the body was actually discovered. They closed the car door and Ari looked around the dark garage. It was cold enough that the body might be preserved long enough to obscure time of death when the police did become involved.

"If anyone asks, you heard about your husband's death and felt you needed to tell your kids in person. That's why you left so abruptly. As far as you know, Jacqueline is holding down the fort. I'll back that story up when I sent the progress report from her phone."

"These hunters, the ones like Jackie. Do you know how many there are?"

Ari shook her head. "A few hundred, probably a lot more. They're all over the world, but they're converging on this part of the world because the *canidae* population is so high."

"Are they going to just keep hunting us forever?"

"Allegedly this is hunting season. They call January wolf manoth."

"So once January is over they'll leave us alone?"

"No," Ari said. "I think they're finally getting an opportunity to stretch their muscles and they won't go quietly when the month ends. I think the only way they'll stop is if we stop them."

Serena said, "If that's the case, Miss Willow, then you should get over your aversion to killing very quickly."

Dale had just taken out her phone to dial Ari when the office phone rang. She returned the cell to her pocket and lifted the receiver. "Bitches Investigations, how may we help you?"

"Is this Ariadne Willow's agency?"

"Yes, sir. I'm afraid she's not available at the moment."

"Oh. Uh, okay. This is Milhous, I'm the doorman at the Bull and Terrier. It's a bar she comes to every now and again..."

Dale remembered hearing Ari talking about it. "She's mentioned you. I'm her partner, Dale Frye. Can I give her a message?"

"No, we're just calling up the regulars we have numbers for. She needs to stay away from here for the time being. Bartender showed up to get everything ready for opening up tonight and found a couple of people had broken in. He didn't think anything was taken but he found a lot of brown powder on the floor of the back room. We think he was spreading some of that wolfsbane around. We decided better safe than sorry."

"Probably wise," Dale said. "You're going to lock the place up, right?"

"Already done. None of us are getting close to it. We're trying to find a way to clean it up."

Dale chewed her bottom lip for a moment. "Look, why don't I come down and take a look? I won't be affected even if the place is painted with wolfsbane, and I can see just how contaminated it is."

"Oh. Would you mind? I mean, we've been trying to think of someone we'd trust to do that, but the fact is we don't really hang around with, uh..."

Dale smiled. "With people like me? I understand. You may not know me, but you know Ari. And she trusts me. Is that enough?"

"It's enough in my book. We'd really appreciate it."

"I'm happy to help any way I can." She looked at the clock and tried to remember how far away the bar was. She knew it was north of town, but not exactly where it was. "I think I can get there in about half an hour."

"Okay. Thanks again. I didn't expect you to come help us out. I really was just calling to warn Ariadne about what was going on."

Dale said, "I'm happy to help. I might not be *canidae* by birth, but thanks to Ari I'm part of the family. I don't like it when people mess with my family. I'll be there as soon as I can."

"We'll keep an eye out for you."

She hung up and took out her phone. She didn't even try to call Ari in case she was in the middle of something, so she sent a text that explained where she was going and why. The address to the bar was in Ari's address book, and she found the driving directions online. She tucked her hair under a knit cap and put on her jacket before locking the office behind her.

She knew Ari went to the bar infrequently, but she'd never been invited along. She understood why; it was a *canidae* bar, and no matter how close she was with Ari, she would never be one of them. And she knew sometimes Ari needed to be with her own people. It was her version of hanging out with a pack. Dale had her own ways of decompressing and she liked to be alone as much as the next gal. Going to the bar without Ari felt a bit like a betrayal, but she was in a unique position to protect *canidae* from wolfsbane.

She had an obligation to help.

She also couldn't deny that she felt a bit of a thrill from getting a call and running out to investigate a break-in. Ordinarily she just passed the information off to Ari and watched her go off to have the adventures. It was exciting to be on the flip side of the equation for a change.

The bar was in the University District in a cluster of other similar establishments, like a ghetto of drinking holes. Dale eventually found the right one after passing it twice. There was a sign that pointed down a dark flight of stairs that, even upon closer inspection, seemed like the basement entrance of the restaurant on the corner. She parked at the curb and walked across the parking lot to the alley entrance. A small group of men and women standing around the back door, and the largest of them broke away and moved to intercept her. He was massive, black, and the muscles straining his T-shirt made him look like a beating waiting to happen.

"Hey. I'm Milhous... are you Ariadne's friend?"

His voice was gentle, and she found herself smiling as she approached. She took the hand he offered, her small fingers completely enveloped in his. "I am. I'm Dale Frye. What exactly happened?"

Milhous turned and led her back to the group. "Barry, that's the afternoon 'tender, came in to set up and found a van parked here with the back doors open. He went downstairs, found 'em messing around in the back, chased 'em out. He got a partial license plate and he saw they had boxes of that wolfsbane shit Ariadne's been talking about. He already had a tickle at the back of his throat so he didn't want to risk going back in, and he didn't want anyone else going in, either."

One of the men standing near the door glanced up when they got closer, and Dale assumed he was Barry. "Hi. I'm... a private investigator." They didn't have to know she was just Ari's assistant. "You don't have to worry about coming up with a cover story for me. I know what's going on here. How do you feel? Any nausea or strange thoughts?"

"I think I'm okay for now. How long you think it'll be before I snap?"

"I don't know. You may not have been exposed enough to completely lose control. If I were you I'd go home and get some rest, wait for it to blow over. After a couple of days you should be out of danger."

"Me and everyone around me," he said. "People are saying this stuff makes us go berserk. We attack people we love, just tear 'em to bits. Is that going to happen to me?"

"I doubt it," Dale said softly. "Could you tell me where you saw the brown powder?"

Barry pushed away from the wall. "I'll show you. It's easier than trying to explain."

"Are you sure?"

"Hell, I been down there once. Either I'm infected or I'm not. A few more minutes won't make a difference."

"I appreciate it." She took off her cap and ruffled her hair so it would lay flat. Barry stopped moving and stared at her, and she noticed that everyone else was staring as well. "What? What did I do?"

Milhous said, "You have red hair."

Dale furrowed her brow. "Yeah."

"No, it's... I'm not judging. I just didn't know Ariadne went for that kind of thing."

"Redheads?"

"No. Uh. Look, never mind."

Dale looked at the gathered group. "Am I missing something?"

Barry said, "Look, let's just go down and check things out, all right? I don't want to be outside if this thing hits me. The longer we stand here gawking, the longer it'll take me to get home."

Dale followed him inside. The back door led directly to a store room crowded with boxes of liquor. Rows of shelves held crates of glasses, coasters, napkins, and other ephemera that all bars required. Barry turned on the lights and walked to one of the shelves. "This is where I found the powder. One of the guys was in here and he bum-rushed me on his way out. I started to chase him and another guy came out through the main door and knocked me down. That's when I saw the powder here on the ground." He started to stretch his toe out to touch it.

"No, I see it. Stay back."

He retreated and covered his nose and mouth with the collar of his T-shirt. Dale crouched next to the spill and touched a little with her pinkie. She brought it to her nose, smelled carefully, and then used one of the napkins to wrap the finger up until she had a chance to wash it properly. She pulled out one of the boxes near the spill and sniffed again. "Kind of cinnamon..."

"Huh?"

She shrugged. "You or Ari could probably be a lot more specific about its scent, but I smell something like cinnamon. They were dusting the glasses with the wolfsbane." She looked back at him. "So. What's the joke about my hair?"

"Huh?" he said again.

Dale stood up. "Outside, when I took off my hat. It just seemed like it was a weirdly big deal that I have red hair. Is that some kind of *canidae* joke?"

He looked down at his feet. "Oh, that. No. Uh, not-not really. I mean, it's..." He chuckled. "Are you a hood?"

"I don't know what that is."

"They're usually college girls. They know about us, and it turns them on. So they get together and come down here. They find one of us to take home for a screw, and the *canidae*... you know... changes? During the..."

Dale raised an eyebrow. "They become the wolf during sex?"

"Different strokes, right?"

Dale shuddered. "I guess. But... no, for the record, I am not a hood. They all have red hair?"

"Most of them. I'm sure some of them dye it to fit in with the crowd. Milhous doesn't like it, but the management doesn't really care. He says if a human girl shows up with red hair, she gets an exemption and he has to let her in."

"Wow." She shook her head and went to the swinging door between the store room and the bar. "Well, just for the record, that's not me. I'm going to look around and see if I can find anywhere they messed with in the main bar. Hang out here."

"No problem."

She wet a towel in the sink and used it to wipe down any surfaces the hunters may have applied wolfsbane to, checking the color of the towel to see if it was discolored before she moved to the next item. She found a sprinkling of dust near the glasses, and more around the patron-side of the bar. She realized there was a chance she was also wiping away fingerprints of the people responsible, but it didn't seem likely the police would be very interested in a break-in where nothing was taken and the only evidence was a little dust.

"Barry?"

He pushed the door open with his elbow.

"The van that was waiting outside. Were there any identifying marks?"

"It was just a normal van." He thought for a second. "Oh. There was a thing on the side. Like they'd tried to paint over something but it was still visible. It was a... uh." He closed his eyes and held up one hand as if he was drawing it. "Like a bird coming out of an egg."

Dale pictured the image. There was something familiar about it. "Bird coming out of..." Her eyes widened. "Could it have been a dragon with its wings around the sun?"

"I guess. Yeah, it had big wings, so yeah. That makes more sense."

Dale grinned. "That's the logo of a local pharmaceutical company. One of three in town that has the ability to manufacture wolfsbane in large amounts."

"Hope so. Ever since Ariadne started talking about that stuff, people have been afraid to come here. I mean, this is a bar for *canidae* and run by *canidae*, and they still don't feel safe. I guess after this morning I guess they have a point."

"No, they don't," Dale said softly. "Ari loves this place. Everyone needs somewhere they can go without worrying about what they are."

Barry stared at her for a second and then smiled. "Huh. I guess you're not like those hoods. You really care about Ariadne."

"I love her. I'm going to spend the rest of my life with her."

"But you're..."

"Human, human, human, I know. That doesn't matter."

Barry said, "For most of us, it would be. You must have a special one."

"I do." She pushed her hand through her hair and exhaled. "I could spend all day scrubbing in here and I still wouldn't feel confident telling you to come back in. I'd tell you to call a cleaning crew, but then you run the risk of them being hunters and having them make the problem worse."

"You've wetted down the places where you saw the stuff, right? We'll take precautions and vacuum up the rest. If you think you have a lead on where they're making wolfsbane, you should go. We'll finish up here."

"Nope," Dale said. "I'm not letting you guys anywhere near this junk. Besides, I can't do much spying while the sun is still up. Now, you said something about a vacuum...?"

CHAPTER FIVE

JACQUELINE RAMSEY lived in an apartment downtown, and Ari took the opportunity to stop by the office to tell Dale what happened. Unfortunately the office was locked and dark. She checked her phone and found she'd missed a text. "Bull&Terrier infected w/ wolfsbane. Checking it out, sniffing for clues like my mentor. Remember, you have food at my place. -D"

Ari replied with a warning to be safe and stopped by Dale's apartment to pick up something for lunch on her way to Jacqueline's building. The huntress lived near Lake Union, and despite the weather Ari saw a few sailboats out on the surface of the lake. She parked down the street and unwrapped her sandwich, eating with one hand while she skimmed Jacqueline's phone with the other. The contacts list was full of code names - Woden, Low Key, Neith, Jupiter, Sedna, and Orion - along with a few real names.

Her daily reports were usually no more than a few abrupt sentences - "no sign of agrsn, dose upped slightly" - and were always sent within a few minutes of six o'clock and were always sent to the number assigned to someone called Bendis. She prepared the text she was going to send in order to keep the watchers from descending on the Ahearn house. "L dead; S out of reach w/ children until further notice." After a moment she added, "Will follow S overseas to continue dosing." With any luck that would keep anyone from asking why their operative had suddenly dropped off the face of the earth.

When she finished eating she took Jacqueline's keys and approached the building from the south. The lobby was empty so she found the elevators and rode to the third floor without being forced to explain her presence. She didn't know what she expected to find in the apartment, but the chance to root through a hunter's home was too intriguing to pass up. She let herself into the apartment and locked the door behind her.

She had to admit she'd half-expected to find an armory with guns propped up against the furniture and ammo scattered across the kitchen counter. Instead she was faced with an extraordinarily normal home. Four or five business suits hung in dry-cleaner bags on the hall closet, the trash was full but not alarmingly so, and she'd left her dishes from breakfast on the coffee table. There was a laptop on the couch and Ari opened it to be immediately stymied by a password request.

The closet revealed luggage with airline tags still attached to the handle. Jacqueline had flown into town from New York two months earlier, not long before she started working for the Ahearns. Ari carefully went through the bag and found a half dozen small bottles of spices that she could tell were really filled with wolfsbane just by looking at it. She put them aside until she could dispose of them in a safe manner. She was putting the bag back into the closet when her phone rang. She checked and saw Lorne's number on the display and prepared herself before she answered.

"Hey." She made herself sound out of breath, moving into the living room to pace in a circle. "I just left the Ahearn place."

"Oh," he said, a little thrown by her starting the conversation. "What did you find?"

"Nothing. No wife, no kids. But I did find something interesting... apparently the family had a personal assistant. Jacqueline Ramsey? She's missing, too."

"Did you say Ramsey?"

"Yeah. Why, you know her?"

"She's a huntress. I didn't know her personally, but I knew she was in town. She's missing?"

Ari said, "Yeah. Seems like they left in a pretty big hurry."

Lorne thought for a long time before he spoke. "Could be she found out what happened to her husband and decided to get while the getting's good. We've been hearing rumors about the wolves picking up on our presence here. Someone's been sloppy. The guy who trained me said it was going to be a good week or so before they got wise to us. Maybe we weren't giving the animals enough credit."

Ari looked out the window, glad that her warnings were throwing a wrench in their plans. "They didn't survive this long by being stupid," she reminded him as she looked out at the lake.

"Yeah, well, neither did we. We're hunters. We've been training for this day for two hundred years. Now's our chance to prove it wasn't just time well wasted."

"What's our next move?"

"Well, that's what I was calling to talk to you about. A couple of our boys were tasked with booby-trapping a wolf bar this morning, but the assholes got themselves spotted. They called asking for advice and I told them to hang tight. We're waiting to see if the wolves are smart enough to track us down with the info they got and, if they are, we're going to set a trap for them."

Ari struggled to control her breathing. The bar had to be Bull and Terrier, and Dale was the one who would be following the trail of any clues they found.

"So what do you say, Willow? Want to set a trap and catch ourselves a wolf?"

Dale was on her hands and knees with a flashlight so she could make sure there wasn't any wolfsbane in the vents, poised to be ejected into the air as soon as the heater clicked on. Someone had gone down the street to a construction site to borrow a respirator and Milhous donned it to help her with the cleanup without risking infection. The downside was that when he spoke the filters made him sound like Bane from the most recent Batman movie, and Dale had to strain to understand him. While she was crawling around the vents, he was behind the bar checking the glasses and fixtures.

"Sorry 'bout the whole hood thing," he said. "We don't get many non-*canidae* here, and the ones we do get usually have the red hair thing going on so we know what they're after."

"I hope you haven't been admitting many of them lately. Hunters can have red hair, too."

"Oh, we know. Ariadne made sure we were duly warned. That girl of yours has been like a dervish this past month or so."

Dale frowned, certain the mask had garbled his word. "Like a what?"

"Dervish. Whirling dervish. It's an Islamic order..." He waved off the explanation. "Tasmanian devil. That's a better comparison.

Running around, making sure we all know what's going on, warning everybody to be careful."

"Oh. Well, I guess Taz is better than Chicken Little crying about the sky falling."

Milhous said, "A lot of us owe our lives to her, you know. We've been on alert, watching our backs. Hard to say how many lives she's saved, but this whole wolf manoth thing would be a lot bloodier without her sending up the flare."

Dale smiled proudly. "I'll be sure to let her know she's a hero of the *canidae* community."

"Can I ask how you two even got together? Most of us shy away from... I mean, usually it's just easier to find another *canidae*."

Dale sighed. Apparently the more people learned she was with Ari, the more they would be touted as poster girls for interspecies relationships. "I saved her from a group of jerk-ass kids when she was in wolf form. Took her home, she changed into a person, crawled into bed with me, and the shock of having a naked stranger in my bed trumped the whole 'werewolf' thing." She winced. "Sorry. I've been trying not to say that word."

"What, werewolf? We say it all the time. Even if you're just a dawg like me. It's not pejorative."

"Sure feels like it when I hear a hunter say it."

Milhous shrugged. "Well, sure, people who hate us can make anything sound like an insult."

"Is that like telling people it's okay for me to say 'wolf' because I have wolf friends?"

"Maybe not exactly," he chuckled. "But similar."

Dale was about to respond when her phone buzzed. She checked the display and smiled. "Speak of the devil. Hey, Ari. I was just talking about you with Milhous."

"You're still at the Bull and Terrier?"

Dale stood up. There was an unsettling hint of panic in Ari's voice. "Yeah. I wanted to help make sure the barroom was clear of wolfsbane so they wouldn't have to risk themselves. What's up?"

"The guys who were sabotaging the bar told someone they had been spotted. The hunters are waiting to see if anyone from the bar tracks down the truck and follows them."

"Damn. Lorne's seen me. If I show up following the truck, he'll wonder why I'm helping a *canidae* bar."

"Well," Ari said, "yeah, that too. But he's setting a trap for you, Dale. Promise me you won't go anywhere near that truck or wherever it leads."

Dale said, "Who is the alternative, you? It'll be bad if Lorne finds out I'm looking into it, but it'll be impossible to explain if he catches you."

"Did the truck give you any leads?"

"Don't ignore the question, Ariadne. You're working with Lorne, and I'll find a way to investigate without him catching me. Thank you for the warning, but now that you've told me they're setting a trap I can prepare for it."

Ari sighed, "Dale, don't take a stand on this."

Dale glanced at Milhous, who had his back to her so he could studiously check the wall for signs of wolfsbane. "I'm taking the risk for you, Ari. Keep your cover, work with Lorne, and I'll do what I can to stay safe. But I will investigate that truck, because it could lead me to the place where the wolfsbane is being manufactured. I'm not going to just hand that off to someone else because it's not safe. And I'm not sending another *canidae* into a place that might be full of wolfsbane. You do your job and I'll do mine."

"This isn't your job," Ari snapped. "You're just my secretary, you sit behind a desk all day and type up my reports, you don't go out and–"

"Goodbye, Ariadne." Dale disconnected the call with a fierce jab, stuffed her phone into her pocket, and looked at Milhous again. She could feel her blood rising and knew her face was as red as her hair. Milhous finally risked looking at her and she said, "What?"

"Oh, I forgot you were here. I completely spaced out and didn't hear a thing."

"Good." Her anger ebbed, replaced by a sharp twist in her chest. She knew Ari would only have said something so horrible in order to protect her, but it was still a lousy thing to do. A cheap shot to someone who had taken pride in how integral she had become to Ari's agency. To hear the woman she loved call her 'just a secretary' had been the same as being slapped across the face. She felt tears stinging her ears as she turned to examine the room again.

Milhous cleared her throat. "May I say something?"

"Fine."

"Anyone who doubts how real your feelings for that wolf are? They wouldn't doubt it now. You don't get that mad if you don't care."

Dale chuckled and wiped the corner of her eye. "Shut up and

help me look for more wolfsbane."

Ari crossed her arms over the steering wheel and rested her head against them. She was glad Dale had hung up, her only regret being she hadn't done it a few seconds earlier so she wouldn't have heard that hateful tripe falling out of her girlfriend's mouth. In the moment she'd thought it was a necessary length to make Dale see the smart thing to do was step back and let someone else deal with the dangerous stuff. It wasn't because she doubted Dale's capability, it was because she wanted to know Dale was safely back at the office and risking nothing worse than a paper cut. In trying to make that happen, she'd insulted her horribly.

"Slick," she whispered as she leaned back in her seat. "Real slick, Ariadne." She wiped at her cheeks, looked at the clock, and started the car. Lorne wanted her to meet him at the police department so they could arrange their next move. She calmed her emotions during the drive, not wanting to explain why her eyes were red when she showed up. She parked outside the building and took out her phone. She knew if she called, Dale would just send her to voicemail - rightly so - and sent her a text instead.

"Dale. I'm sorry for lying about how important you are. I just wanted to keep you safe. I love you. You're not 'just' anything to me. Ariadne."

She sent it, returned the phone to her pocket, and got out of the car. Lorne was waiting for her in the lobby, forcing her to appear nonchalant as she approached.

"Are you trying to keep me from snooping in your desk, Detective?"

"I've learned to be careful around private dicks like you," he said. "Come on. We have to go make sure the wolves aren't sniffing around the company."

"Which company?"

He led her back outside. "The Orarian Group. We have some people in their research and development lab, and they're the ones who have been churning out wolfsbane for us. The wolves spotted a van with the logo, so we're going to stake the place out to see if they show up."

"They'd have to be pretty stupid to attack a place they know is full of wolfsbane."

They reached his car. "You've never heard of suicide bombers, kamikaze attacks? For all we know they want to get dosed while they're inside. Go berserk, kill our lab geeks, cut off production that way. We're not going to let them."

Ari got into the passenger seat. "What's the plan?"

"We wait until they go in, then we grab them. Take them somewhere nice and quiet and get them to ID some of their friends. That way we don't have to spread the 'bane around and hope we get lucky. We can just target them straight out." He grinned. "And we can make sure there are some hunters nearby when the wolves go rabid."

"Hm. Lorne, you have to..." She pressed her lips together and tried to think of the right approach. "Regardless of whatever else is going on, the whole wolf manoth thing... do you ever stop to think that what we're doing is insane? We're drugging people, real people, and making them do things they would never do otherwise. And we're killing them for it. Why? Just because this is what our great-great-great-grandparents did way back in the Dark Ages?"

Lorne stopped at a light and drummed his fingers on the wheel. "You ever run into any wolves? Seen what they're like when it isn't wolf manoth?"

"No."

"I have. When I was a kid, my mother hated what my dad was teaching me. She told him I was just a boy, didn't need to know self-defense. We would go out into the woods every weekend, sometimes in the backyard, and we'd practice. He taught me how to shoot, how to take care of my guns. The whole time Mom was trying to impart culture on me. She gave me this book about how the hunters and the wolves came to an understanding because in the 1800s because some huntress screwed a wolf. What kind of sick mother reads her kid something like that? Bestiality is an okay bedtime story now?"

Ari's mother had read her that story, the true history of Johanna Brion and Agatha Westreich, and she'd only recently discovered it was all true. She remained silent, however, as Lorne continued toward the drug company.

"One summer we went camping in the Cascades. Dad said I was finally old enough to kill one for myself, so a couple of his pals found one. Took it up into the woods and held it until we were ready. It was my first hunt. Dad let it go, and it took off running. I went after it, but there was no way I could keep up. It got away from me. I searched the woods for hours, even after Dad told me I might as well give up, and we went home.

"A few days later I came home from my friend's house and found the door had been kicked in. Dad wasn't home, but Mom was. Fucking wolf tracked us down, broke into our home, and killed her. Tore her to damn pieces." His voice had grown so soft Ari could barely hear it. "Thing was long gone by the time I got there, and I wasted a lot of time holding her hand, crying, trying not to believe it. When Dad got home, he told me it was my fault for letting it go. Told me I had to avenge Mom's death before he called me his son again."

Ari fought down her nausea. "Did you find it?"

He shook his head. "No way to know. Wolves all look alike to me. Dad passed away a few years ago. He was still blaming me for what happened. But I promised him I'd take out every wolf that crossed my path. When I found out wolf manoth was coming back, I knew it was my destiny. I was supposed to be here, hunting those wolves, killing them for... not for my mother, but for whoever's mother they killed. The kids they killed."

Ari said, "They're not all killers."

"Close enough." He sniffed and looked out the window, rolling his shoulders as he tightened his grip on the wheel. "How about you, Willow? You heard my origin story, pathetic and weepy though it was. What's yours? When did you find out you were a hunter?"

She'd prepared a story in anticipation of just such a question, but his revelation had thrown her. "Uh. Well, it's hardly as traumatic as yours. It was just me and my mother, no brothers to carry on the tradition. So she taught me. Figured the skills I learned would come in handy when I started dating and the boys got a little too adventurous. So she trained me and I realized that everything she taught me would help out if I was a private investigator. Sneaking around, following people..."

"No guns, though."

"No, I don't really like guns."

"What kind of hunter doesn't like guns?"

"The kind that prefers to use her mind."

Lorne scoffed. "That's why there aren't many huntresses around."

"I guess so," Ari muttered.

He drove downtown, following the monorail tracks to Westlake Square. He used his badge to park without paying, then escorted Ari down the street to McGraw Square. It was still early enough that people were at work and kids were in school, so the small park was mostly empty when they arrived. Ari had always thought the circular center of the square looked like a full moon, and she awkwardly crossed it as she followed Lorne to one of the south-facing benches. Her eye was immediately drawn to a building across the street with a cursive sign announcing it as headquarters for THE ORARIAN GROUP written between the first and second floors, the words flanking the logo of a dragon wrapping its wings around a sun. Lorne watched traffic as he settled in, arranging his blazer so it fell more naturally over the weapon holstered on his hip.

"That's where the wolfsbane is being made? Over the Bartell Drugs?"

"Well, not officially. The labs are on the third floor, and we have people in place. They manufacture the stuff and get it out to us."

Ari said, "So we have all kinds of layers through the entire city. Have you ever met the people at the top? The big bosses?"

"The big bosses, no. I mean, there are people who are in charge of the operation here in Seattle. Them, I've met. But the hunter's council? They're still over in England. They were going to come over here for that big ceremony the wolves were going to have, but once it was called off they cancelled their plans. Kind of a shame. It would be nice to meet the guys at the top of the pyramid." He began patting down his pockets and looked over his shoulder at the food cart. "I think I'm going to grab something to eat. I missed lunch. Want anything?"

"No, I'm fine."

"Be right back."

He got up and walked away, and Ari immediately took out her phone to see if Dale had replied to her text. There was nothing new, so she sent a new message to her mother's phone. "Wolfsbane made in Orarian Group labs. Third floor. Hunters on the ground now, may be vulnerable later." She sent it and pocketed her phone as Lorne walked back. He put a drink down between them. "Figured you might want something to drink. If not, I'll just be forced to drink two sodas. And I don't like diet."

"Thanks," she said. She took the flag-like remnant of straw paper off and sipped the drink. She wasn't a fan of soda but she appreciated the thought. Lorne needed to think they were allies for as long as possible. Her phone buzzed in her pocket and Lorne looked over when she didn't reach for it.

"Gonna get that?"

"It's probably just Dale with something about a case. I'll check it later."

Lorne folded back the paper on his burger and took a bite as he watched the street. "Way I figure it, whoever the wolves send to check this place out are going to make themselves obvious if we're paying attention. They won't just walk in and storm the castle, they're going to case the joint. It's our job to spot them. You probably do a lot of that, huh?"

"Yeah, I've done my fair share of sitting and watching. But what if the wolves show up and wonder why we're just sitting here watching the building? We could scare them off."

"Not if they think we're just two people hanging out in the middle of the day. We could pretend like we're on a date."

Ari tensed to prevent herself from shuddering. "Please. I could never date anyone with a beard like that."

He reached up and rubbed his chin. "You don't like the soup strainer?"

"I could live without it."

"I'll keep that in mind."

She bit the inside of her cheek to stop her sneer from forming. "It's hard to date anyone. How do you know they're not a wolf?"

"I have a sense."

"Oh, really." She kept her voice flat, her eyes locked on the building.

He nodded. "Yeah. From the moment I started hunting the wolf that killed my mother... and God, doesn't that sound like a damn Western song... I've been able to tell when there's a wolf nearby. I can smell it on them. It's kind of an earthy, dirty scent."

Ari wondered if he could smell it on her, or if he was ignoring it because he was so obviously attracted to her. As far as she knew, hunters didn't have any valid ways of identifying someone as a *canidae* unless they actually witnessed a transformation. On the other hand, Lorne was a detective who had spent his entire life seeking vengeance on a group of people he'd been raised to see as the enemy. There was a chance he could see things others couldn't. She put down the cup of soda and put her hand on top of his. He looked down at it, then at her.

"Sorry. The cup made my hand a little cold."

"No problem."

She decided that if he didn't feel a hint of revulsion when she was touching his hand, she didn't have to worry about him sensing something more ephemeral like a scent. She took her hand back and resisted the urge to wipe it on her jeans.

"I called a couple of uniformed officers who are on our side, and they're going to keep a watch for any suspicious activity. And the hunters who are working inside are aware of the situation. They're getting ready to move the wolfsbane reserves to another, more secure location, but they have to do it when they don't have bosses breathing down their necks."

"Yeah? You want someone keeping an eye on the transfer making sure no wolves try to sabotage it?"

"Someone like a private eye?"

She shrugged. "You did say you were going to try bringing us on as consultants after the whole Missing Melody thing. That hasn't really turned into anything."

"It's barely been two months! And we've been pretty busy getting ready for this wolf manoth."

"Yeah. I'm hearing a lot of excuses."

He sighed, smiling his surrender. "We'll be moving it tonight. I'll take you to meet the guys who will be in charge so they won't mistake you for a wolf in the dark."

"Wouldn't want that."

Lorne took the final bite of his burger and slipped his hand out from under hers. "Have you ever killed one?"

She looked at him. "A wolf? No."

"I'm still thinking about the one I shot last night. Ahearn. I've killed wolves before, but to kill one during wolf manoth feels different. It feels like I'm part of something larger. You know?"

"No," Ari said. "I really don't."

"We could change that, you know. Tonight you could skip security and come out hunting with me. Find a wolf, chase it down. We make a pretty good team, Willow."

Ari forced a smile. "By which you mean I do all the work and you swoop in to put a pin on it?"

He chuckled. "That's what I call teamwork."

"Maybe another time. I think it'll be important to keep an eye out when the wolfsbane is being moved." She wasn't lying about that part. She knew her presence would make a difference, even if it was just making sure they didn't kill her mother.

"Well, don't wait too long. You keep putting it off, you'll miss your opportunity. Wolf manoth won't last forever."

Maybe not, but sometimes Ari felt like it was never going to end.

Dale ignored Ari's text when it came in, focusing on the last bit of cleanup necessary before she felt confident the *canidae* would be safe inside. She had worked up a sweat and gotten her clothes dirty from crawling around on her hands and knees to check every nook and cranny. When she was finished, Milhous went to bring the others inside. They'd been stationed outside to warn off customers, spreading the word about the wolfsbane outbreak. She was polishing off the counter when Milhous approached with a tall thin man wearing a plaid shirt tucked into his jeans. He looked to be in his seventies but he walked with the energetic stride of a thirty-year old, his eyes hidden behind tinted eyeglasses.

"Miss Frye? Milhous tells me you've spent your whole day decontaminating my bar."

Dale looked at the time and was surprised to see how close that was to being true. "Wow. No wonder I'm hungry. Yeah, I wanted to be sure the place was clear."

He held out his hand. "I'm Harvey. I own the bar. I wanted to thank you personally, and I wanted to make sure you were reimbursed for your efforts."

"Oh... that's not necessary..."

He shrugged. "You're a private investigator and you just spent hours making this place safe for not only my patrons, but for my staff and for myself. I don't care if you just did it to be nice, sometimes niceness needs to be rewarded."

"Sometimes niceness is its own reward."

He ignored that. "What's your hourly rate, and when did you get here?"

Dale hesitated but finally told him. He took a checkbook from his back pocket and bent over the bar so he could fill it out. "If it wasn't for you, I'm not sure what we would have done. I wouldn't feel confident letting people in here tonight, that's for damn sure. So thank you, Miss Frye." She took the check and thanked him. He put his hands on his hips and regarded her for a moment. "Milhous tells me you're in a relationship with a wolf."

She chuckled. "I am. Her name is Ariadne Willow."

"Ah, the *canidae* Paul Revere. Give her our thanks."

"I will."

"Do you need a ride somewhere?" Milhous asked. "I'd be happy to give you a lift."

Dale shook her head. "I have my car down the street. Let me know if you need a human canary to test something for you."

Harvey smiled. "Will do."

She had draped her jacket over the back of a booth and slipped it on as she went outside. She looked at the check once she was outside and saw that either Harvey was terrible at math or he'd given her a heck of a bonus. She decided it wasn't worth arguing about and folded the check to put it in her pocket. She was shocked to find the street was already dark, even though the sun did set pretty early in the winter. She buttoned up her jacket and started toward the street where she'd left her car.

Halfway there she heard the shoe scuffing on the sidewalk behind her. She didn't slow or look back, but she became much more aware of her surroundings as she continued walking. Ari had once told her not to react until she knew what exactly she was running from, and she glanced at storefront windows she passed in an attempt to see behind her.

"Going to granny's?" someone said in a voice lower than a shout but louder than a normal speaking voice. "Gonna take her a basket of goodies?"

"I bet she has some good goodies..."

Dale picked up the pace, not quite running yet. She moved her hand to the pocket holding her phone and kept her breath steady. She had her keys in her hand already, trying to keep herself calm as she approached her car. One of her pursuers picked up his pace and caught up with her, slinging an arm around her shoulder. She twisted away from him only to bump into someone else. She fell back so she wasn't pinned between them. They were wide-shouldered and dressed in layers. The one who had put his arm around her was tall and pear-shaped around the middle, while his friend had his hair gelled into a wave that rose from his forehead.

Dale decided to try for nonchalance. "Hey guys. What's the problem?"

"No problem here, little red."

She bristled. "I'm not a hood. I told Milhous and..."

"Yeah, we know what you said. But look at that pretty red hair. You're a hood."

"I'm not. I just want to get to my car and~"

Someone grabbed her from behind. She fought herself free and spun on her heel, panic starting to rise as she realized there were more of them than she'd expected. She also understood now that she'd only heard the first two because they had wanted her to know they were there. She swallowed the lump in her throat and watched the men as they formed a semi-circle around her. The streetlights weren't on yet, and they were little more than shadowy gremlins.

"Don't do this."

"We're just talking to you, little red," said the one who'd done all the speaking so far. "Been so long since we talked to a real human girl. Least, not one that wasn't trying to kill us."

Another man said, "Yeah, your kind have been really bringing it on the past few weeks. Calling themselves hunters, making us out to be monsters. But you're the monsters."

"Look, I'm not even close to a hunter. I'm not like them."

"No. No, you ain't," the first man said. "You're sweet. Bet you taste sweet, too."

Dale took her keys out of her pocket. "You don't want to do this."

"Oh, I think I know what I want to do. I want to leave a message for these hunters. We're wolves. We're not gonna take this wolf manoth bullshit lying down. So I think leaving them a cute little red riding hood is just the thing we need to show them just what they're up against."

"But we're gonna have a little fun with her first, right?"

The first wolf laughed in a way that made Dale's skin crawl. "Oh, yeah. We're gonna have fun with her all right. C'mere, little red."

He reached for her and Dale brought her hand up at the same time. She had worked her ignition key between two fingers and she dropped under his arm, rolling forward and stabbing the key into his chest. The blade wasn't sharp enough to pierce his skin or even his shirt, but it did make him rock back on his heels and gave her an opening to escape. She continued forward, avoiding the sloppy attempts by the other two to grab her. She looked at her car but knew that if she stopped long enough to unlock the door they would swarm her. She would have to put some distance between it and her pursuers before she could use it to escape.

Her plans didn't have time to advance much farther, for just after she started to cross the street to use the alley as a shortcut, she was grabbed around the waist and knocked to the ground. Her knees were scraped as the man held her down, snatching one of her arms and holding it against her side as she flailed at him with the nails of her other hand. She pulled her leg up underneath herself, rolled on her hip, and kicked. Her sneaker landed on the soft flesh of his thigh and he doubled over on top of her as his friends caught up with them.

"Feisty, for a human."

"We'll take care of that, won't we little red?"

One man lingering at the edge of the group was scanning the street. "Come on, get her out of the street."

Dale fought, but two of them were now working in concert to pin her down. They lifted her and let her feet drag on the ground as she was pulled into the alley she'd so recently seen as her salvation. "No," she grunted as she was dropped, flailing in the darkness for anything that could be used as a weapon. She heard a growl, low and bestial, and her blood turned to ice.

"Who is already changing? God, have some fucking patie~"

The leader's gripe was cut off by a bark that echoed off the bricks of the alley. Something large and furry passed over Dale and tackled the boy who was holding her down. He cried out in surprise as he was knocked to the ground. They grappled, and one of the others tried to pull the wolf off of him. Dale got onto her hands and knees and threw herself at the man trying to help. She knocked him to the ground, he punched her in the head, and Dale got her body arranged to bury her knee in his groin. His body tightened in pain and he went still as she got wearily to her feet.

She didn't know how many had been attacking her, but all the men left standing had taken off down the street once the tide turned. Dale considered chasing them but decided to let the moment end. She was shaking from adrenaline, well aware the crash was coming, and sagged against the wall. The wolf and human-form *canidae* continued to fight on the ground, but the wolf was soon thrown off so the man could get away. Dale heard footsteps as he fled, could see the silhouette as the wolf started to follow but then thought better of it and came back to check on Dale.

There was the sound of dry twigs cracking in a fire, a few quiet grunts and soft exhalations as pain turned into relief, and then there was a person standing in front of her.

Dale ran her hand over a sweat-slicked shoulder, up into the thick hair, and pulled her close. "Thank you, Ari." She kissed her hard, a kiss of gratitude and apology for their earlier fight and passion at the thought that someone would fight so valiantly for her. To her surprise, however, the woman in her arms hunched her shoulders and recoiled backward, breaking the kiss with enough force that their lips made a popping sound.

The woman put her hands on Dale's chest to prevent another forward assault and spoke with a British accent. "Um... yeah. Not Ari."

Dale took out her phone and shined the light into the wolf's face, eyes widening as she saw who it was. "What the hell are you doing in Seattle?"

"Well," Milo Duncan said with an appropriately sheepish grin. "This is a little awkward."

CHAPTER SIX

DALE TOOK off her coat and helped Milo into it. On Dale it reached halfway down her thighs, but with Milo it was just barely long enough for decency. They left they alley and Dale used the light from her phone to scan the street for the keys she'd dropped when she was tackled. Milo silently got into the backseat of the car, and Dale went into the trunk to receive a pair of pants from Ari's stash. She handed them into the backseat once she was behind the wheel and waited as Milo squirmed into them.

"Are you all right?"

"Me?" Dale looked at her in the rearview mirror. "I'm fine."

"Seriously? After what just happened?"

Dale shook her head. "Nothing happened."

Milo sighed and leaned forward between the seats. "Dale, I'm a reasonably attractive woman who spends the better part of her nights running around naked. I've been in situations like that before, and they're never something you can just brush off."

"Oh. That."

"What did you think I meant? Oh. The kiss? Yeah, that was nothing."

"Gee, thanks."

Milo chuckled. "You know what I mean. You thought I was Ariadne. No problem."

Dale twisted in her seat to face Milo. "Which brings us back to the question you avoided answering. What are you doing back here?

I thought you went back to England weeks ago."

"I did. My friends were there, and I wanted to gear up with them to deal with wolf manoth on my own turf. Got there, filled them in about everything that was happening, and we braced ourselves for a flood of hunters. But the flood never came. They were all coming here."

"To Seattle?"

"To the whole Pacific Northwest. Ariadne's mum tracked down cabals in Oregon, Idaho, up in Canada... loads of wolves up in Canada. Hunters decided to come where they had the most chance to spread out and the lushest hunting grounds. There are some making trouble over in Germany and Eastern Europe, but the big show? Nah, the big show is happening right here. So Gwen brought us back."

"Us?"

Milo nodded. "A couple of my mates came with me. We've been helping to spread the word on wolfsbane."

"So what were you doing here? Not that I'm anything but grateful you were around."

"Yeah. Um." She looked down at her hands. "Gwen sort of... asked me to keep an eye on you."

Dale stared. "Me? Why?"

"Because *canidae* are pissed off. Some of them are taking the news of wolfsbane as a warning, and they're keeping their heads down. Others aren't quite so pacifistic. The way they see it, humans are declaring war on us, and we're not going to just take it lying down. Hunters are going after every wolf they find, so now some *canidae* have decided that all humans are fair game. Wolf manoth is turning into an all-out war. Ari's mum didn't want you to be a casualty."

Dale sagged back into her seat. "Damn. I can't believe we're only two days into this stupid month. I feel like everything is just..." She closed her eyes. "The stress is getting to her. She's trying to hide it, but I can tell. She snapped at me earlier, and if she has to go through another four weeks of this I'm afraid she'll crash and burn."

"Need a plane ticket out of here?"

"Where would we go?"

"Somewhere hunters won't be looking for you. Mexico, maybe. You'd have to deal with a couple of coyotes, but at least they're not wankers with automatic weapons and biological weapons."

Dale chuckled. "Ari would never go for it. The offer is sweet, though." She took a breath, held it, and let it go slowly. "Don't take it off the table, though. If I change my mind in a few days, I want to be able to toss Ari on a plane whether she's willing or not."

"Done and done."

Dale turned and settled in the seat again. "And I guess since I know you're here, we can at least be sociable. Ari and I have some safe food back at our apartment. It's not much..."

Milo shook her head. "Gwen's got us all sorted. Thanks though. How about you? Feel like meeting the troops? A couple of 'em are really interesting in meeting you."

"Sure," Dale said. "Sounds like fun. And it'll be nice to be surrounded by *canidae* I can trust if it's open season on humans. On the way I'll fill you in about why Ari's hanging out with a hunter."

Milo said, "Not necessary."

"You're following her, too? I don't know if that's safe, what with Lorne being a detective. He could spot you."

"Oh. No, we're not following her. It's just that Gwen's been filling us in."

Dale frowned as she pulled away from the curb. "Wait. How does Gwen know what Ari's up to?"

"Ari's been keeping her informed."

Dale focused on the street ahead. "For how long?"

Milo became very still, then hung her head. "Shite. Look, if she didn't bring it up..."

"How long?"

Milo sighed. "Gwen said it had been a few weeks."

Dale tightened her grip on the steering wheel. "Huh."

"I'm sure~"

"Milo, do me a favor and don't say anything else unless it's to give me directions. Can you do that for me right now?"

After a few seconds Milo pointed. "Turn left up here."

Dale nodded. "Thanks."

Ari and Lorne stayed at McGraw Square until a squad car pulled up to take over surveillance. They had called Orarian to let them know they had reason to believe someone was intent on sabotaging a shipment of their drugs. Security had been beefed up, and the wolfsbane was set to be moved at six-thirty. It gave Ari plenty of time to run by the office and hopefully catch up with Dale. There was still no reply to the apology text, and she felt enough time had passed that the apology had to be given in person. Lorne offered to swing her by and wait for her, but she refused as politely as she could. He took her back to her car and she drove the short distance to her office.

Her hopes of reconciliation were immediately dashed when she saw the office lights were off. She unlocked the door and went into her office, unloading the items she had taken from Jacqueline Ramsey. She kept the phone so she could send the progress report at six, but the packet of wolfsbane went into an empty tea tin and into the wall safe. She didn't want to risk spilling even a particle of it in the office. Once she'd relieved herself of the incriminating evidence, she used the bathroom. When she was finished she stood in front of the mirror and lifted her shirt to see if her brawl with Jacqueline and Serena had left any bruises. Her entire left side was sore, and she could feel her right ankle beginning to protest at being used too much, but for the most part she had survived intact. Her collar didn't have any evidence of Serena's bite, for which she was immensely grateful.

She put her shirt back on and went out to the front office. The streetlight shone through the glass and illuminated the Bitches Investigation printed on the glass.

Just a secretary. How could she have spouted such bullshit, even if it was a Hail-Mary pass trying to keep the woman she loved out of danger? It was nowhere near the truth. She'd been a private investigator when their paths first crossed, just starting out and stumbling through case after case trying to turn a profit. She sat in Dale's chair and thought about the days before they found each other. She had finally found stability working for a private investigator named Glory, who pulled the rug out from under her by relocating. Ari was left behind with her own license and an agency she had no idea how to run.

At that point in her life, everyone seemed transitory. She left her mother, her mentor left her, and every woman she took to bed ended up leaving because she couldn't figure out when or how to reveal the truth about her dual nature. She didn't know which date called for the "by the way I can change into a wolf" conversation.

Then Dale showed up. She began their relationship by saving Ari from a group of hooligans and giving her a hamburger, then took her home. That night Ari was disoriented enough that she changed into human form and crawled into Dale's bed. The screaming subsided quickly enough, and the conversation turned to practical things like what Ari did for a living and Dale's current unemployment situation. Dale had taken a few business classes before dropping out of college, and she offered to get things on a smooth track in exchange for a little rent money. Somehow it had turned into a full-time job, not just setting up client meetings and filing, but filling stashes of clothes, giving Ari post-change massages, and renaming the agency something that actually attracted clients.

"Just a secretary," Ari muttered, rubbing her face. When it came down to it, Dale was Bitches Investigations and Ari was just the employee who did the majority of the legwork.

She took one of the business cards out of the drawer and placed it on the blotter. Her name was underneath the embossed name of the agency, and she picked up a pen to add Dale's name underneath it. Dale was her partner in every sense of the word. She was going to stop taking that for granted and start making sure she knew just how vital she was.

The wolfsbane was set to be moved at six-thirty, which gave her an hour and a half before she had to be in position. She used Dale's desk phone to call her mother so she could fill her in on everything that had happened since that morning.

Gwyneth answered on the second ring. "Ariadne?"

"Mom. I know where they're making the wolfsbane. It's a place called the Orarian Group." She gave the address. "They have a lab on the third floor, and that's where the drug is being manufactured. Lorne is afraid the location has been compromised, so they're moving it tonight. Six-thirty. I convinced Lorne to let him join them in the transfer, but I thought you'd want to get someone else moving on it. Someone from our side."

"I'll see who is available."

"Do you know anything about what happened at the Bull and Terrier?"

There was a hesitation on the other end of the line. Not much, but enough to make Ari nervous. "Yes, I've been filled in. Miss Frye did a superb job cleaning the place up this afternoon. Everyone is still being cautious, but they feel they've averted catastrophe. We owe Miss Frye a debt of gratitude."

Ari smiled even as she wondered where Dale was. If she had already finished cleaning up the trap, shouldn't she be there? Her pride overwhelmed her anxiety. "Yeah... she did well today."

"Are you all right? You sound weary."

"Just a long month." She looked at the desk calendar and saw how many days were left before the sanctuary of February. "I found a hunter this morning. Jacqueline Ramsey. The wolf she was targeting killed her, so we had to cover things up. I have to send a progress report to her boss at six, but after that no one should try finding her for a while."

"You were complicit in a murder?"

Ari closed her eyes. "I didn't have much choice, Mom. Serena Ahearn had been dosed by this hunter, the same hunter who had killed her husband. She was under the influence of the drug and... I guess she went a little feral. There was nothing I could have done to stop her."

"Or so you're telling yourself now."

"You would have done the same thing."

Gwyneth said, "Yes, I would have. For the record I'm not condemning you for this. You did the right thing. Leaving the hunter alive would have been a ridiculously dangerous move. I'm just surprised to hear you say we're at all alike."

Ari pressed her thumb against the bridge of her nose. "I just called to fill you in. If you have anyone who can sabotage that shipment, I would appreciate it. Barring that I'll call you tomorrow to let you know where the wolfsbane ended up."

"Take care of yourself, Ariadne."

"It's what I've been doing since I was fifteen. Not planning to stop now." She hung up and rubbed her face with both hands. She was tired, and she would have given anything for a nap, but she needed to be alert and ready for the transfer. It bugged her that she didn't know where Dale was, but the odds were that she was angry about their argument and had gone straight home. Ari decided she would swing by to pick up a change of clothes, make a face-to-face apology, and hopefully get her head on straight before she was due to meet with Lorne for the transfer.

"Your girlfriend is worried about you."

Dale looked at Ari's mom and then quickly looked away. She had been ignoring the phone call, but she knew Ari had been on the other end of the line. "Yeah, well. Hopefully she won't have to worry very long. What did you say about a murder?"

"A *canidae* dosed with the wolfsbane attacked and killed the hunter who had poisoned her. Ariadne helped cover it up."

"God," Dale said. She suddenly understood why Ari had been so tense on the phone earlier. She wasn't being overprotective for the sake of it, or because she doubted Dale could handle herself.

She had been given a reminder of what wolfsbane could do, of what it could make someone do, and she'd overreacted. Dale suddenly felt like the biggest jerk in the world for letting it get to her. "Poor Ari..."

Milo sensed the tension in the air and decided to change the subject. "So, Gwen. You said something about being available. We're here."

"Yes, indeed you are," Gwyneth said.

They were in the living room of her house, the curtains drawn on the windows that faced the street. Dale had gotten a quick introduction to all of the British *canidae* currently stationed around the room, and a few of them were still giving her wary looks of distrust despite the fact Milo had vouched for her. Dale was trying to appear as non-threatening as possible while also trying to keep their names straight. There were six in all, not counting Milo: the pretty brunette was Paige, and she had joined Dale and Milo on the couch when they finally decided Dale was harmless enough to join them; Paige's husband, a muscular man named Owen; an Eurasian woman named Hannah and her stern-faced partner, Mia; a black man named Benji; and the youngest of the group, an Indian man named Tarun.

They'd been staying at the house Milo still technically owned, but they were using Gwyneth's house as a base of operations. Dale felt bizarre being in her girlfriend's childhood home without her girlfriend actually being there. Then again, apparently Ari had been there several times in the last few weeks without bringing it up, but she had her reasons for secrecy. She closed her eyes and pressed her fingers against the closed lids.

"You all right?" Paige asked softly.

Dale looked at Paige and smiled. "Yeah. Just a rough time right now."

Gwyneth said, "Hopefully Ariadne has found something to make the rest of the month a little easier. We now know where the wolfsbane is being manufactured. It's being moved in an hour and a half, and she believes we can hijack the shipment. There will still be some wolfsbane out there, of course, but if we can cripple the hunters' ability to resupply their forces with this drug, we can even the playing field."

"And then what?" Tarun asked. "We take away their weapons so we can attack them on even ground? What happened to Miss Frye tonight was done by us. By our side. That is... that is not okay with me. I don't care if they started this, if this is just some month-long hunter celebration. I will not allow myself to be dragged down to their level of violence just to survive."

Owen said, "You may not have a chance, Tarun. Right now the world out there is kill or be killed. Even if we strike first, it's still self-defense. They're turning our people into weapons. All we're doing is taking that weapon away from them. If a hunter gets hurt in the process, I think they brought that on themselves."

"Yes, but where does it end?" Benji said. "An eye for an eye, a death for a poisoning... they hijacked a *canidae* bar, do we drive a truck into their hunting lodge or whatever the hell they call it?"

Gwyneth said, "We do whatever is necessary to protect ourselves and our species. This is not a war we declared, but we will gain nothing by hiding our heads in the sand. We attempted a peaceful resolution, and it failed. The hunters believe they have an advantage over us because they've been training in secret these past two hundred years. They think they are prepared because they are rested. But our kind hasn't had the luxury of a rest. For a *canidae*, every day is a war. Every day we wage war against discovery, exposure, and death. The hunters chose to fight us, and we gave them the opportunity to back down. They did not take it. So now we will do what wolves have done since the beginning of time. We will defeat our enemies and we will survive."

Milo scooted forward to the edge of her seat. "Okay. Rah-rah and all that. But we've got less than an hour to sabotage the labs and stop the shipment from getting wherever it's going. And we have to do it without any of us getting exposed to the wolfsbane that we're trying to capture. Do we have, I don't know, a plan of some sort?"

Gwyneth nodded slowly. "I have a plan. But I doubt anyone here will like it very much. Especially you, Miss Frye."

"Can we cut all this 'Miss Frye' nonsense? My name is Dale." She sighed. "And if it gets wolfsbane off the street, I'll suck it up and do what needs to be done."

Gwyneth nodded her thanks. "Very well. Tarun, do you have your computer... thing?"

"My iPad." He turned it on and handed it to her. She examined the screen and turned it so the others could see a map grid of downtown Seattle. "The wolfsbane is being manufactured in a drug lab here. Ariadne says that at approximately six-thirty this evening, it will be moved to an unknown locale."

Mia, who Milo mentioned was a cop back in England, moved

to the edge of her stool and braced her hands on her knees as she looked closer at the screen. "What all is around there?"

"We've got the Westin Hotel, Westlake Square, it's just down the street from the start of the monorail. It'll be heavy-traffic by the time the truck is moving. They're probably counting on that to help camouflage the transfer."

"We can corral them," Mia said. "We stage an accident there, and there, and we can guide them down the road we want."

Dale said, "Fifth Avenue is one-way. If we put an accident here..." She stood up to point at the map. "That would force them to use Westlake if their destination was north of the lab."

"And if it's south, they would be forced onto sixth?"

Dale shook her head. "Sixth is one-way, too."

"Christ, does this town have any streets that aren't?" Mia nodded.

Gwyneth said, "For now it's working to our advantage. We stage an accident on Olive, forcing the transfer to take either Westlake to the north, or continue on to Seventh if they plan to go south. There are enough of us here to cover both possibilities."

Dale said, "Or we could increase our odds. We could find out for sure the hunters don't use Seventh Street."

"How would we do that?"

"I could call Lorne and tell him that I heard a rumor you guys were setting up an ambush. I could say there's something planned to guide them onto Seventh Street, they'll see the car accident and assume that's it, and they'll avoid it."

Milo said, "It's risky."

"Lorne knows me, but he thinks I'm just Ari's secretary. He thinks I'm completely oblivious to this whole hunter-versus-wolf thing. If I tell him what I know, he won't suspect anything is up. He'll take the information at face value."

Paige said, "His reaction will tell us a lot, too. Dale should tell him that both Fifth Avenue and Seventh Street are both going to be out of play. If he dismisses it casually, it means going south isn't on his agenda. We'll know for sure they're heading north and we can focus all of our energy on Westlake."

Benji said, "His guard will be down. By taking Westlake, he'll think he's avoiding the trap we've set for him on Seventh."

Gwyneth nodded at Dale. "Make the call."

Ari was incredibly anxious as she rejoined Lorne at McGraw

Square. This time they met across the street in front of the drugstore, within view of the squad car that had been watching the building. Ari had gone to Dale's apartment for a placeholder apology, but the apartment was empty. She had tried to think of anywhere else she might have gone instead and came up empty. She called and didn't receive an answer, and panic started to set in as she composed her text.

"Be mad at me as long as you want, but please tell me where you are. I'm worried. Let me know you're okay." She sent it, then used Jacqueline's phone to send the progress report to whomever was on the receiving end. She waited five minutes for Dale's reply, then drove to meet with Lorne so she wouldn't be late. Her mother was counting on her to be there in case the wolfsbane was relocated to a second location.

The sky had grown pitch black since their last visit to the square, but the buildings made up for the lack of sunlight by glowing from seemingly every window. Ari looked into the lobby of the building that held the lab. If push came to shove, she could wait until the lab closed and break in. She'd done some shady things in the past, including stealing confidential records to verify a teacher's health insurance claim. Sometimes the law had to be bent for the greater good, and destroying an entire batch of wolfsbane, if not their means of producing it, had to fall in that category.

Lorne walked back from the squad car after being briefed by the officers. "No one unauthorized in or out of the lab all day. I think maybe we're in the clear on this one. Wolves may have been too busy sniffing each other's butts to pay attention."

"Is the product still being moved?"

"Yeah, we figure better safe than sorry. We..." His cell phone rang and he fished it out of his coat. "We have a fallback location all set up, the lab has been compromised however minimally, so we're going to protect our assets." He answered the call. "Kyle Lorne." He looked at Ariadne. "Yeah, I know who you are. Why are you calling me instead of her? Oh. Well, I'm standing right next to her." Ari looked at him with an eyebrow lifted. He moved the phone slightly away from his ear. "You don't answer the phone when your secretary calls?"

Ari had to fight her natural reaction and instead grabbed her phone to check for missed calls. There was nothing from Dale, but she acted as if there was. "Oh. I must have had it on silent." She took the phone from him. "Dale?" Ari tried to keep her voice steady and casual. "What's up? Are you okay?"

"Say you're going to put me on speaker so you won't have to repeat yourself."

"Dale, I'm going to put you on speaker so I don't have to repeat everything." She did so, and held the phone in front of her face. She glanced at Lorne as he leaned in, hoping Dale knew what she was doing. "Is everything okay?"

"Everything is fine. Listen, I don't know what's going on lately, but I know you and Detective Lorne have been working on something big. I just got a tip from one of our informants. Duncan. You remember Duncan, Ari?"

The only Duncan Ari knew was Milo, and she was in England. "Yeah. What did he say?"

"He didn't know much, but he said there's something big being planned on Fifth Avenue and Seventh Street tonight near Westlake Square. Does that mean anything to you?"

Lorne looked at Fifth Avenue, then turned to look north. "Yeah," he said. "It means someone's trying to make a move on this place. Looks like the dogs are smarter than I was giving them credit for."

"They may have just been waiting for night," Ari said.

"Sounds like a wolf to me," Lorne agreed. "Thanks for the information, Miss Frye. This informant of your give you anything else that might be useful?"

"No. I was lucky I got that from him."

"All right. Thank you."

"Happy to help. Ari...?"

Ari said, "Yeah, Dale."

"Be safe."

Ari bit down hard on the inside of her cheek and hoped Lorne wasn't paying attention to her expression. "Thanks. You too."

Lorne hung up and turned in a slow circle. "Fifth and Seventh. Why not Sixth?"

Ari was still trying to get over hearing Dale's voice. "I don't know. It's one-way?"

"So are..." He pointed. "Sixth is a one-way street that goes north. The other two are one-way going south. They're blocking the south routes trying to box us in."

Ari wanted to feign helpfulness, but she didn't want to compromise whatever Dale was planning. "Why just the south routes? Are they trying to force us north?"

"No. They expect us to go south for some reason. They're setting up roadblocks to catch us en route. We're heading north on Westlake so they'll be left scrambling. We'll have to watch our ass but we'll leave them in our dust soon enough."

A van rounded the corner and pulled up in front of the labs. Lorne motioned for Ari to follow him over as the driver climbed out.

"Everything ready?" the driver asked as he shook Lorne's hand. Ari kept her hands in her pockets and used her thumb to spell out a text message.

"They're packing up the stuff. They'll start bringing it down soon. This is Ariadne Willow. She'll be keeping an eye out for anyone trying to mess with the shipment. We just got word that the wolves are setting something up on Fifth and Seventh. Shouldn't affect us, but just in case."

The driver nodded a greeting at Ari as she sent her text. He turned to watch the traffic. It was fairly light for that time of day, and none of them seemed to be slowing suspiciously near the labs. "We kept our eyes peeled for anyone who was trying to follow us. Looks like all clear behind us."

Lorne clapped the man on the shoulder. "Then let's go see if they're ready to start loading us up."

Dale looked at her phone, surprised to see she had missed two texts from Ari. She looked at the most recent, the one that had drawn her attention to the phone, and read the message out loud. It just says "Birth if waste land."

Milo snorted. "Don't look at me. She's your girlfriend."

They were in the backseat of a rental van, with Gwyneth driving and Paige in the passenger seat. Hannah and Mia were in the middle row, while the boys were driving Gwen's car to cause the accident that would serve as the distraction. Dale had borrowed a heavy black jacket from Gwyneth so she would be less conspicuous if they were forced to get out of the vehicle.

Mia had taken her phone out and, after a few jabs at the screen, said, "Is there a street in that area called Westland?"

"Westlake," Gwen said.

Mia held up her phone. "She was typing a text without looking at the screen. Auto-correct turned it into 'birth if waste land,' but she typed 'north on Westlake.' That's the route the hunters will be taking."

Dale grinned. "Good girl, Ari." The seatbelt pulled tight across her chest as Gwen pulled out into traffic and headed toward the brightly lit towers of the Westin Hotel.

Ari stayed in the doorway of the lab, hands in her pockets, controlling her breathing as much as she could. Inside the room, Lorne and his courier goons were loading up the completed batches of wolfsbane into red coolers so they could be transported. If any spores, just the lightest dusting, got on her skin, she would lose control and go berserk. She would tear Lorne limb from limb, turn on his friends, and go looking for more victims before she regained her senses. She was fortunate in that her sole exposure had occurred when she was among friends, even if they were friends in the loosest sense of the word, and she didn't have a chance to truly harm anyone.

Lorne noticed her hanging back. "What happened to women's equality in the workplace? You too good to get your hands dirty?"

"Someone has to supervise," she said, "and I don't trust any of you guys not to get distracted by all the shiny surfaces in here."

"They are shiny," Lorne admitted. "All right, that'll do it. The chemists told us they would pack up all the chemicals and crap themselves. Afraid we might actually mix the wrong things and blow ourselves up."

Ari said, "I've seen smarter guys do dumber things."

"Your girlfriend is a real laugh riot, Kyle."

"Well, it's not like I keep her around for her sparkling personality."

Ari started rethinking her aversion to ripping the men apart. Lorne picked up the last box and led the procession outside with Ari bringing up the rear. Once they were downstairs in the lobby, Lorne called the current uniformed babysitters across the street to see if anything had happened while they were inside. He got the all-clear and motioned for the troupe to walk out to load the truck. It didn't take long; the latest batch of wolfsbane for the entire Pacific Northwest only took up five coolers, which easily fit underneath the benches in the back of the van. Lorne secured them and motioned for the others to get in.

When he held the door for Ari, she smiled indulgently. "I'm supposed to keep my eyes peeled for wolves, right? Kind of hard to do that from a windowless backseat."

"True. All right, ride up front with Chase."

Ari winked at him and walked around the van. She was about to get in when there was a sudden squeal of tires from nearby, but the acoustics of nearby buildings made it hard to tell the direction. Lorne jumped out of the truck again, gun drawn as the sound of crunching metal pinpointed the location of the accident. A white Fiat 500 had just attempted to turn onto Fifth Avenue and met a truck coming head on. Three men had climbed out of the car and were yelling at the other driver, who was pointing over his head at a sign indicating it was one-way.

"This is the wolves." Lorne said, "Get in the truth. Go. Go!"

Ari and Chase got into the cab of the truck, and the engine roared as he twisted the key in the ignition. Ari took the time to fasten her seatbelt, not bothering to warn Chase as he took the corner onto Westlake and surged north. The squad car that had been watching the Orarian Group rushed forward to deal with the accident. Ari twisted to look out the window before the disturbance was out of sight, trying to see if she recognized anyone in the scuffle.

"See anything, Willow?"

"Nothing," she said truthfully. "Could've just been a traffic accident."

Lorne shook his head. "No, your girl warned us about this. We should have a squad car over on Seventh, too. Just to be sure there aren't any innocent bystanders caught in the trap."

"Good pl~"

She was cut off by a sudden sideways shift of gravity, held in place by her seatbelt as the safety glass of the window shattered and cut her forehead and cheeks. The tires skidded as the van was pushed into the lane next to it, and Ari could hear squealing tires of the cars behind them slamming on their brakes. Lorne, who had been crouching between the front seats to talk to her, had taken the brunt of the collision and lay flat between her and Chase. Chase was still conscious and pulled his gun free, kicking open the twisted metal of his door and falling out onto the street.

Ari heard the bark and howl of wolves and got out to see what was happening. The van that hit them was parked blocking traffic, the side door thrown open. Three wolves were running across the pavement, which was crisscrossed by the headlights of stalled vehicles and glistened with broken safety glass. With the wolves were two women Ari had never seen before, both brunette and masked, and they were holding guns. Chase used the crushed back of the van for cover as he opened fire, and one of the wolves jumped into the air to tackle him. The wolf bit the arm holding his weapon and twisted, and the weapon clattered to the ground.

Ari was so stunned by the violence of it that she nearly missed the wolf leaping at her. She brought her arms up to protect her face as she was knocked onto her back. The wolf snarled and snapped at her face and then, much to her surprise, licked her from chin to forehead. She looked into the animal's eyes, ignored the predatory noises and gnashing teeth, and recognized the person behind the mask.

"Milo...?"

Milo scratched Ari's face, pushed off of her, and turned tail to run back to the van. One of the human-form wolves pulled open the back door of the van. She immediately ducked as a shot rang out, and its ricochet seemed to echo until it transformed into the wail of dozens of sirens. Milo and one of the women jumped into the back of the van. Ari got to her feet as she heard Lorne scream in pain, wobbling on her feet as she lurched forward.

In seconds the human women had all five coolers out of the van. They ran back to their getaway vehicle as Lorne fell out of the van cradling his bloody arm to his side. He brought his gun up and fired, and the legs went out from under one of the wolves. She yelped in pain, but neither of her human companions could abandon the coolers to help her. Ari felt a clutch of anguish that she couldn't help the poor bleeding *canidae*.

The clutching feeling intensified a moment later when Dale appeared in the doorway of the van and dropped to the pavement.

The breath left Ari in a rush as Dale ran to the fallen wolf. She gathered her comrade in her arms and began to backpedal as quickly as she could without toppling over. Lorne opened fire again and Ari couldn't stop herself from lunging at him.

"Don't!"

Her voice was an unrecognizable shriek, her mind filled with the moment two years earlier when another bastard with a gun had shot Dale in the head. Ari slammed into Lorne hard enough to knock him off-balance, and she flailed her limbs to make it look as if she had simply stumbled and lost her balance in the confusion. She looked over her shoulder, dreading the sight of her girlfriend lying sprawled on the pavement. Instead she saw Dale crouched in the doorway of the van. The sirens of responding police cars were so close the sound echoed off the surrounding buildings. Ari could see the squad cars speeding down the street as her eyes locked with

Dale's. Time seemed to stop, a kaleidoscope of red and blue reflected off shattered glass, and then Dale pulled the van door shut. The van was thrown into reverse, turning so sharply that for a moment it looked as if it might topple over.

"Willow! Get behind the wheel. Get after them!"

Ari barely heard Lorne's shouts over the cacophony of sirens, but she knew she had to comply. She ran to the front of the van and climbed into the vacant driver's seat, glancing into the back to see Lorne and Chase were secured before she did anything. Both men looked horrible, covered with blood that Ari could only assume had come from bites.

"Don't let those fucking dogs get away!"

Ari faced forward and dropped her hand to the gear shift. She left it there without moving it before she stepped on the gas and sent them careening forward instead of back. The van jumped the curb and drove across the sidewalk until it impacted a concrete planter. She was thrown against the steering wheel before collapsing back into her seat. Squad cars filled the road behind them, inadvertently cutting them off from pursuing the getaway van, and Lorne shouted in frustration.

"Sorry," she managed, "sorry... I didn't... I wasn't thinking..."

Lorne seemed not to hear her, but he growled, "Someone is going to pay for this clusterfuck."

Ari didn't care if he blamed her, didn't care if she took the brunt of his frustration for driving forward instead of pursuing. All that mattered was Dale, and the fact she had been conscious and unhurt when the van door shut between them. Everything else was incidental.

CHAPTER SEVEN

DALE HAD never experienced chaos like the kind that unfolded inside the van. She tried to keep tabs on everything that was happening while also giving directions to Dr. Frost's office. Hannah transformed immediately after the door was closed, blood pouring from her in such amounts that her whole hip was slick with red. Mia had pulled her up into the bench seat in the center of the van, one hand tightly pressed to the wound as she demanded Hannah stay with her and stay awake. Milo and Paige were in the backseat holding onto the coolers of wolfsbane so they wouldn't tip over and spill due to Gwen's panicked driving. Sirens echoed through the streets, some responding to the chaos they'd left in their wake while other cars were dedicated to their pursuit.

Gwyneth had taken the time to squirm into a shirt, but she was still naked from the waist down following her transformation. Milo and Hannah were both naked as well, but Paige and Mia were still fully-clothed as they remained human to provide cover fire during the assault. Dale glanced down at her clothes and saw Hannah's blood covered her shirt, and she felt a twist of nausea before she focused on the task at hand. They had to get Hannah to a doctor, and Ari's *canidae* physician was the only one she knew who might be able to save her.

"Turn right at the next corner," Dale said, and Gwyneth cut through traffic so she would be in the proper lane, ignoring the screech of brakes and howling horns she left in her wake. Dale held tightly to the arm rest until the van settled again. "I didn't mean immediately."

"For the next few minutes, let's pretend 'immediately' is implied," Gwyneth said with unnatural calmness. Mia was sobbing behind her, and Dale turned to see Paige and Milo were struggling with their own emotions.

"Yeah. Okay, immediately is good. We're almost there."

They reached the end of the business district and soon found themselves speeding through a residential area. Dale wanted to warn Gwyneth to slow down and be careful, but she doubted that suggestion would go over very well in the van's current environment. She focused her thoughts and tried to remember where the doctor lived. He had a veterinary practice in town but he also treated *canidae* as an alternate source of income. He was one himself, thought Dale didn't know if he was a wolf or some other subset species.

She had her phone open as she pointed Gwyneth in the right direction, guiding her around the corner as she called Dr. Frost to warn him about an incoming patient. When they pulled into his side driveway it felt as if hours had passed, but the dashboard clock insisted it had only been three minutes since she pulled Hannah off the pavement. Dr. Frost's porch light was on and he came out to meet them on the driveway in his bare feet. His shirt was unbuttoned at the collar and there was a sauce stain on his upper lip as he opened the driver's door and leaned inside.

"If this is about someone going berserk, I can't help. It's this wolfsbane shit~" He looked past Gwyneth and saw the gore in the backseat. "Good Lord. Open the door. Now!"

Mia opened the van's door as Frost ran around and clambered inside. He scanned the women in the van before he found Dale. "Miss Frye, my bag is inside the house underneath the coatrack in the foyer. Get it, now, please."

Dale went to retrieve the bag. As she burst into the foyer, a woman with brown hair that had started fading to an elegant pale silver appeared in the kitchen doorway. "Aaron... oh my God..."

"I'm a friend," Dale said, unable to think of anything else to say as she grabbed the bag and ran back outside. The others had thrown on clothes and gotten out of the van to give the doctor a chance to work, with Mia sagging against Milo and sobbing against her shoulder. Dale delivered the bag and saw the woman had followed her outside. Frost reached back for the bag, saw the woman, and gave an apologetic shrug.

"Sorry about this, Caroline. Not exactly the most romantic evening in the world."

"Shut up and tell me what you need," the woman said as she climbed into the van with him.

Gwyneth moved to stand next to the door. "Do you have an office inside where we can take her?"

"I don't feel comfortable moving her any more than necessary."

"Did you see the damage on the front of this van? Trust me, you don't want it sitting in your driveway any longer than necessary."

He grimaced and looked over his shoulder. "All right... someone go inside and open the garage door. I have an emergency room in there. And I'm going to need blood donors. Are any of you matches?"

Milo and Paige raised their hands.

"Congratulations, you've just been nominated as canteens."

Dale had been inside the house before, so she ran for the garage. She turned on the light and found a neatly-appointed medical center with wood paneling and a glass case full of beautiful medical equipment. She punched the button and the door began rising as Frost and his date-slash-assistant began preparing Hannah to be moved. Caroline came to retrieve a gurney, and together with the wolves they transferred their fallen comrade onto it and carried her into the garage. He gently lowered her onto the bed and then looked at the group gathering around him.

"Out. Unless I need to suck your blood or you're helping with the surgery, I need you out of here."

Milo hooked her hand on Mia's arm. "C'mon..."

Mia shrugged her off without looking. "I'm not going anywhere."

"You're not going to be any good to her here. You'll just get in the doctor's way, and he's already working in less-than-ideal conditions. Give him a little space. Paige and I will be right here for her. She'd want you to take care of yourself."

Mia looked down at her partner. "Her name is Hannah Milsap. She..." Her voice caught in her throat. "Her name is Hannah."

Caroline looked up sympathetically. "We'll take very good care of Hannah for you, dear. But now you should go and let us work."

Mia reluctantly allowed herself to be led into the house by Dale and Gwyneth. They put down the garage door and left the doctor to his work, then focused on their own emergency. The police were looking for the van at that very moment, and the backseat of the van was full of a poison that would turn every person in the house, with the exception of Dale and possibly Dr. Frost's date, into homicidal maniacs.

"We need to get rid of the van," Gwyneth said. "And the wolfsbane."

"That's easier said than done," Mia said, her voice still shaking. "We don't know how to safely dispose of the stuff, and I for one am not eager to experiment. If we burn it, the smoke might still affect us. We can't dispose of it in the water because then it might get into the water supply. If it doesn't get filtered out..."

Gwyneth held up a hand to stop the speculation. "We have a time bomb on our hands. Getting rid of the van is job one. We might not know how to get rid of the wolfsbane, but losing a vehicle should be easy enough. Mia, any suggestions?"

Mia was staring at the closed garage door.

"Detective Cohen!" Mia's shoulders jumped and she finally faced them. "I understand what you're feeling right now. You're not going to help her by standing there catatonic. We need to find a way to get rid of the van."

Mia nodded and pushed her hands through her hair. "Is there, um. Is there any sort of construction site nearby?"

Dale had to think for a moment and then nodded. "Yeah. There are a few."

"Then we should get there as soon as possible. We can dump the van, use bleach to take care of any physical evidence we might have left behind, and hopefully it won't be discovered for a while."

Gwyneth went down the hall, turning on lights as she went. She returned in a few minutes with two buckets of laundry bleach. "Will this be enough?"

"It'll do," Mia said.

Gwyneth said, "Okay. Let's go."

Mia shook her head. "I'm not going anywhere. I'm staying right here until Hannah wakes up."

"Mia..."

"Stop being selfish." Mia and Gwyneth both looked at Dale. "Your girlfriend was hurt badly, but you know where she is. She's right through there being tended to by a doctor. Ariadne is... Ari was there, too. She was amid all the gunfire and she was surrounded by hunters the last time I saw her. If they happened to see me, they are going to have a lot of tough questions for her. I doubt they'll ask nicely. But I'm not going to help her by sitting here wringing my hands together. Hannah is in good hands. Her friends are here. You'll do her more good by coming with us and covering our tracks."

Mia nodded slowly.

"Excellent," Gwyneth said. "We should go soon. We don't want to run into any roadblocks."

Dale held up two fingers and closed her eyes as she thought about the neighborhood. "When we leave here, we should go north. There are roads that go through the park. We can take one of those to the nearest construction site without running into any cops."

Gwyneth said, "Are you positive?"

"I don't want to get caught in a blood-drenched van any more than you do. I'm sure." She put her hand on Mia's arm. "Dr. Frost will call me as soon as he knows something, or Milo and Paige will call you. But the longer we stay here, the longer we keep this van here, the better chance we'll be caught."

Mia nodded. "Okay. Yeah."

They went outside and Gwyneth checked the street for signs of police. When she declared it clear, they climbed into the van. Mia didn't want to sit on the blood-soaked middle seat, so she crouched between the driver and passenger seats. Dale gave Gwyneth the first few turns and closed her eyes as they reached the park and drove into the dark tunnel created by the canopy overhead. Her heart pounded as the adrenaline of the past hour was beginning to wear off and leave her weary. She slumped against the door and tried breathing exercises to calm herself.

"I saw what you did back there," Mia said softly.

Dale opened her eyes and looked at her. "Me? I just tried to talk some sense into you. I hope I didn't come off as cold or bitchy..."

"No, not that. And it was fine, by the way. It was exactly what I needed to hear. Hannah would have cheered." She smiled weakly and looked out the windshield. "I meant that I saw what you did during the ambush. You ran into the line of fire to save her. To pull her into the van. You didn't have to do that."

"Milo and Gwen were in wolf form, and you and Paige had your hands full. I was the only one who could get her to safety. You would have done the same for Ari."

"Yeah, because she's a wolf. I don't know if I would have done the same for you. I'm a cop, and I think I would have just kept running if it was you." She met Dale's eye. "I wouldn't now, though. No matter what happens in that garage, whatever small chance she has of surviving is down to you. Thank you, Dale." She held out her hand, her slender fingers shaking from emotion or an excess of adrenaline.

Dale took her hand and squeezed. "I'm just glad I was there."

"You said you saw Ariadne there as well," Gwyneth said. "I didn't."

"She was okay so far as I could tell. She was the only one not bleeding when they got back in the van."

There wasn't an obvious reaction from Ari's mother, but Dale thought she saw a lessening in the tension around Gwyneth's lips. She looked out at the road, grateful for the lack of traffic as they drove through the dark streets of quiet neighborhoods with only the rattle of the van's engine breaking the silence. Dale looked over her shoulder at the coolers stacked on the back seat of the van and realized the sad truth of the night's events. Despite her shell-shock, despite Mia's near catatonic worry over her partner, and Hannah's touch and go condition, in the end they had won.

It was a hell of a victory march.

Chase had gotten back into the van in time to promptly pass out, and Lorne pulled a first-aid kit out of the glove compartment as Ari drove. She had taken two wrong turns, been 'forced' onto a one-way street, and ended up hopefully miles away from wherever Dale and her mother had fled. Lorne cursed and punched the seat with his uninjured hand with every turnaround and reversal, and Ari helplessly lifted her fingers off the wheel.

"Look, if you think it's easy to chase one car while avoiding every police officer in Seattle, be my guest."

"I told you, I can deal with them if we get stopped. It would have wasted less time than you driving all over creation."

Ari bared her teeth. "I'm trying, all right?"

Lorne grunted. He had taken off his bloody jacket and had wrapped his right forearm with gauze. One of the wolves that had jumped into the back of the van disarmed him by trying to take a chunk out of his wrist. He looked up and caught her staring. "Eyes on the road, Willow. It's just a flesh wound."

"It's a *canidae* bite." Ari didn't have to hide the concern in her voice.

"Doesn't mean anything. Not every bite kills. Just keep your eye on the road."

Ari knew the truth. A bite from a *canidae* infected the victim and confused their biology enough that it tried to transform. The urge could be fought for a while, but eventually the need became too strong and the transformation took over. The eventual surrender was partly to blame for the 'full moon' myth that got tossed around werewolf stories. A fully-grown person trying to transform for the first time was a messy sight to behold; there was a reason *canidae* underwent their first change during puberty. Their bodies had to be taught how to shift out of one form and into the other without leaving them crippled or deformed.

Judging by the amount of blood on Lorne's clothes, the bite was deep enough and bad enough that he was infected. It was only a matter of time before his body lost the fight against the infection and he tried to transform into a wolf with dire consequences.

"Damn it, we're not going to find the bastards." Lorne grunted and pulled his sleeve down over the bandage. "Look, Willow, when we get to where we're going... Chase is the only one that got bitten. Understand me?"

She glanced at him. "You can't hide that."

"Watch me. Broken glass all over the place, damn dogs were shooting at us. I can explain away a bandage easy enough."

"Lorne..."

"Ariadne. Look, by the time I give in to this, wolf manoth is going to be over anyway. If I tell the big guy I'm compromised, he's going to lock me in a room. I'll be useless to the fight. Let me go down doing what I'm supposed to do, not locked up in a room with a bunch of doctors waiting for me to twist myself into a pretzel, okay?"

She slowed at a red light and finally nodded. "Mum's the word."

"Thanks."

"How bad is Chase?"

Lorne looked into the back. He sighed and his voice took on a note of sadness. "He's not going to make it. The wolves tore him to pieces."

While he was trying to kill them, while he was transporting a poison... She wisely kept her mouth shut and focused on the road ahead. "Where are we going?"

"Drive toward Safeco. You know where that is?"

"Why, because a woman can't be into baseball?"

"That's not what I meant."

Ari said, "Come on, Lorne. Don't give up flirting just because you have a little scratch."

He chuckled weakly. "All right. And yeah. In my experience, I'd be much safer using dress shops as landmarks than the Mariners."

Ari said, "I'll have you know I love the Mariners. I'm a big hockey fan. They're the hockey ones, right?" She decided to take advantage of his weakened condition to see how much he had noticed during the fracas. "I didn't get an accurate count on how many wolves hit us be there. You?"

"Ah," he grunted and shook his head. "Five, I think. Can't be sure. Two of them were still wearing their human suits."

"So two humans and three in wolf form?"

"You got a different count?"

Ari shook her head. "That fits with what I thought I saw. One of them knocked me on my ass. Don't know why it didn't rip me to pieces like it did you and Chase."

"Maybe it thought you were too pretty to mess up."

Ari scoffed. "Sure."

"You are, though," he said, resting his head against the glass. "You're very pretty, Willow."

"You're very pretty yourself, Detective Lorne. You could lose the beard, though."

He reached over with his free hand and patted her leg, his hand lingering on her thigh long after the time had come to move it. She looked down at it, looked at him to see he'd passed out, and sighed. She moved the hand before she smacked his arm to wake him up.

"I still need to know where we're going. You can sleep when we get there."

"Right." He shifted in his seat and sat up straighter.

He gave her directions into the industrial district, past warehouse stores and tall electrical transformers connected by wires that hung between them like thin strands of ivy in a technological forest. He guided her to the parking lot of a taxi company and told her to park the van behind the fleet of blue-and-green cabs. She parked nose-in next at the end of the row and climbed out. Lorne put his jacket on to cover the bandage on his arm, then he and Ari checked on Chase to find he hadn't survived the trip.

"Damn. All right, one more thing for Huxley to be pissed off about, I guess. Come on."

They left Chase's body and Ari let him lead her to the side entrance. The interior was a sprawling garage with a half dozen of the Alki Emerald Cab vehicles in the midst of repair work filling the space. Ari realized how easily the backseats could be coated with wolfsbane. Any *canidae* that caught a ride would end up catching something else. She added cab rides to the list of luxuries she could put off until February.

An office was attached to the top of the wall where the owner could literally oversee his fleet, and the man who had been sitting inside of it quickly descended the stairs to meet them as soon as they came in. He was at least in his sixties but he looked as solid as a retired football player. When he reached the floor he charged toward them with his fists balled at his sides, and Ari braced herself for an attack despite being half the man's age.

"What the hell happened out there, Kyle?"

"The wolves fucking hit the transport. They were waiting for us. I don't know how, but they were on top of us as soon as we left the building. We saw one trap, but the other..."

The man looked at Ari. "Who is that?"

"Ariadne Willow. She's the private investigator who has been helping us the past few weeks. Ari, this is Patrick Huxley. He's in charge of the Pacific Northwest."

"Where's Chase?"

"Dead. Wolves got him."

Huxley grimaced. "And the wolfsbane?"

Lorne reluctantly shook his head. "They got it. All the coolers."

Ari expected anger and thought she had anticipated violence, but she was still unprepared for the roundhouse punch the man threw. Lorne was also unprepared, taking it punch on his chin and dropping as if his legs had been cut out from under him.

"Do you know how long we've been stockpiling that shit? How long it's taken us to get the amount we had in that lab? We moved it on your word, exposed the entire operation because you said it was compromised, and now all we have it whatever our boys are carrying in their pockets? You'd better give me a damn good reason not to cut my losses and put a bullet in your head right now."

Lorne stayed down, one hand rubbing his jaw where he'd been punched. "I saw the wolves who took the 'bane. I can track them down and get it back."

"You really think they're going to keep it around?"

"I think they're going to have a hell of a time disposing of it without risking exposure. If we move fast enough this doesn't have to be a total loss. In addition we'll find out who the hell these wolves are working with. They were far too coordinated for it to have just been dumb luck. They had the attack all thought out."

Huxley snorted. "That doesn't sound like any wolf I've ever seen."

"It is what it is, boss."

Huxley looked at Ari. "You, I don't know. How do I know you're not working with the wolves?"

"She's unaffiliated." Lorne worked his jaw back and forth. "She was trained by her mother so she didn't get brought into any clubs." He looked at her and explained. "Membership goes through the father."

"I guess that's another reason there aren't many huntresses."

"That, and the fact women make lousy hunters," Huxley said. "Let me see your phone. I don't want you contacting anyone about this place."

Ari rolled her eyes and took out her phone, arching her eyebrow when she realized Milo's tackle had indeed caused some damage. She showed the shattered screen to Huxley and shrugged. "Looks like I won't be contacting anyone for a while even if I had your permission."

Huxley said, "Where did you leave Chase?"

"He's in the back of the van."

"Are you hurt? You have blood on you."

"I had to get Chase up into the van. Plus I managed to wing one of the wolves as they were getting away. I think it was a kill shot."

"Oh, good. 'You think'. Well, as long as you think you got one of them, it all evens out perfectly." He sighed and shook his head. "Go home, Kyle. We'll clean up your mess. Call tomorrow and let us know if you've tracked down the wolves or if you've decided to go one more day without putting one in the win column. Get out of here."

He turned and went back up the stairs. Lorne turned and walked out, and Ari hurried to catch up with him. "Wow. That guy knows how to win loyalty, huh?"

"It's not about loyalty, it's about the war. I failed."

"You lost a battle."

"It was a big fucking battle, Willow. That wolfsbane they took, that took us a year to make it all. There's still a lot out there, but once it dries up we've got no reserves."

Ari said, "We could get word out that there's a shortage. Tell people to start being a little more economical with the wolfsbane they have."

"And let every hunter in the city know how monumentally I fucked up? No thanks." He rubbed his jaw again. "I know I shot that wolf. We need to check out all the places the wolves could have gone to get medical help. Know of anyone who treats two-legged dogs?"

Dr. Frost. "No one comes to mind. I could have Dale look into it tomorrow."

"Yeah, speaking of Dale." Ari tensed. "Thank her for the warning. It didn't exactly end up helping us, but she tried. I hate to think what the wolves would have gotten away with if we hadn't gotten the red flag. Be sure she knows I appreciate it."

"I will."

"Have a good night, Willow."

He started to walk away so she said, "Hey, Lorne. I don't have a car here. You expect me to walk all the way home?"

"Oh, right. Come on. I'll give you a ride. My car is over here."

Ari followed him past the dark cabs. "You want me to drive? I may suck at hot pursuit, but I can at least get you to your door. And it would give you a chance to rest your arm even though I know it totally isn't hurt at all."

He flexed his fingers and grunted. "Yeah, you know what?" He tossed her the keys. "Drive me home. It's not far from here."

"I knew you lived in some artsy warehouse loft near the stadium. If you're nice I'll even change the bandages for you."

"Wow, it's true what they say. Get your ass handed to you in front of a woman, and they'll treat you nicely for the first time since you met them."

Ari grinned. "Never underestimate pity, Detective." The truth was that she wanted to check out his wound to see how dire his situation was. There were stories about people being bitten without changing, and she hoped whoever Dale and her mother were working with had the self-control necessary to pull their punches, but she would much rather see the injury than just cross her fingers and hope for the best.

Lorne's personal vehicle was a red pickup, and Ari smiled as she got behind the wheel. "This is very redneck of you. I didn't expect it."

"What did you think I would drive?" He settled on the bench seat next to her, cradling his wounded arm now.

"I don't know. Something small and fast."

"First car was a '68 AMC Rebel convertible."

Ari hissed through her teeth. "Red?"

"Yellow."

"That's an acceptable alternative. So you got muscle cars out of your system early?"

He shrugged. "Sort of. You'd be amazed how quickly a muscle car loses its cool factor when you go off-road at ninety miles an hour and flip four times. I was fine, but my girlfriend was in the hospital for a while. Trucks are safer. Sturdier."

"Wow. The girl ended up okay?"

"Oh, sure, she mended and kicked my ass to the curb. Rightfully so. I may technically have dumped myself come to think of it."

Ari smiled. His building had street parking and he directed her into a spot half a block away from the front door. The lobby was lit brightly enough that it hurt her eyes when she walked inside, and he was stopped four times by other residents who had questions about their locks or suspicions of other residents stealing their mail. By the time they reached his apartment on the third floor Ari was afraid they would never reach their destination.

"You're pretty popular around here, huh?"

He shrugged. "People like having a cop living nearby. That's why they let me get away with my wild parties and loud disco music at all hours of the night."

Ari chuckled. "Sure."

"I'll have you know I'm a wild man, Willow."

"Oh, really."

"Yep. I once flaunted the no-pets rule and had a Chia Pet."

"I don't think that counts."

"Pet. It's right there in the name."

He turned on a lamp next to the couch and illuminated an apartment that, while not exactly tidy, was at least a few steps above most apartments occupied by single men. He took off his jacket and inspected the blood on the sleeve before he detoured into the kitchen and threw it away. "Want something to drink?"

"No, thanks. You have a first-aid kit here?"

"Yeah, in the bathroom. Down the hall, first door on the right."

Ari went down the hall, retrieved the kit, and came back as Lorne was sitting on the couch with a bottle of beer. She sat down next to him and opened the kit as he began undoing the quick and dirty bandaging job he'd done. He hissed as the dried blood was peeled away from the skin and Ari looked down at the wound.

"Ouch. That looks pretty bad."

"Looks worse than it feels."

Ari said, "Are you trying to be macho for me, Detective?"

"Maybe."

"Let's see how you handle this." She cleaned the wound with alcohol swabs, and Lorne gave up the attempt to look stoic and manly after the third stinging touch. Ari was glad he didn't know she had experience with bites like this, because if he asked her opinion she would have had to be honest. Her honest opinion was that he should give up being a hunter, walk away from Huxley, and get his affairs in order. He sipped his beer in the hopes it would numb the pain, and stomped his foot once on the carpet as she cleaned the edges of the wound.

"Sorry you had to see that."

She shrugged. "I've seen bloodier things."

"No, I mean... at the cab company. That wasn't exactly my finest moment."

Ari said, "Oh, that. Hey. You should see me with my mother. One sharp word and suddenly I'm twelve years old and I forgot to clean my room."

"You know, if this does turn out bad, I'm glad I've gotten to know you, Willow."

She widened her eyes. "Whoa. Now I know it's bad. You're delirious. Are you forgetting all the times you've cursed my name or that I've gotten in the way of an investigation? Why on earth would you be glad you met~"

He cut her off by kissing her. Ari stiffened and pulled back as gently as she could, but Lorne moved with her and prevented their lips from parting. He turned his head to the side and parted his lips, and Ari reluctantly applied pressure to his arm just above the bite. He hissed and recoiled, and she took the opportunity to get up off the couch.

"Whoa."

"Sorry."

"Yeah." She cleared her throat and scratched the side of her neck. "That was... not welcome."

He had grown suddenly sheepish. "I'm glad we met because you're attractive, and I thought we had a..." He chuckled. "You know what, forget it."

"Look, it's not that I'm not..." She pushed her hands through her hair and decided to go with the truth. "Kyle, I'm gay."

He looked up as if she had admitted to being a wolf, then closed his eyes. "Oh, my God. Dale."

"Yeah."

"Oh, God. Of course you two are a couple."

She nodded. "Sorry. The night you just had, this is the last thing you need."

He smiled. "Hey, this is nothing new to me. I'll just get back on the horse again once wolf manoth is over. If I'm still around."

Ari sighed and sat down again. "Kyle, this is a bad bite. I've seen a couple in the past few years, and I've seen bites much smaller than this turn people. You want my advice? Fuck Huxley and everyone else. Turn in your badge and take a long vacation. Go whale-watching. Enjoy the time you have left. That's what I would do."

"Yeah. But we've never established I'm anywhere near as smart as you are, Willow." He smiled at her and nudged her knee with his. "Now, if you're really not interested in me, then you really came up here to tend to my wounds. So get to it before this thing becomes infected and I have two problems to deal with."

She smiled and focused on tending to his wound. She hadn't really expected him to go for the early retirement, but it would have been infinitely easier if he had taken the offer. It was going to be hard enough taking down the hunters if she didn't have to worry about actually liking one of them.

It didn't take them long to spot a fenced-off construction site. Gwyneth circled the block until she found the entrance and Mia got out to unlatch the gate and let them in. Gwyneth drove across the rough gravel lot and pulled behind a row of trailers that likely belonged to the construction company executives. She cut the engine and then helped Dale spread the bleach across the bloody backseat and anywhere one of them might have left fingerprints or DNA evidence. When they had done everything they could, they ran back to the gate where Mia had kept an eye out for police. She reattached the lock she had picked and Gwyneth tried to call the boys to come pick them up.

"No answer," she finally said. "I imagine they're dealing with the fallout from the accident."

"I don't suppose we could take a bus," Dale said.

"We shouldn't risk it," Mia said. "If the van is found tomorrow, the cops will get cameras from all the buses around here. How far is it back to your home, Gwen?"

"We should stay off the main roads as much as possible, so... three miles, give or take."

Dale said, "It would probably be easier for you on two legs. If you want to change, I can take your clothes."

Gwyneth said, "I've given Ariadne enough reasons to hate me in her life. I won't add to the list by leaving her girlfriend to walk home alone at night." She looked over at Dale. "It will give us an opportunity to get to know one another."

"Great. Well, I've been meaning to walk more..."

They started walking, Gwyneth leading the way with Dale and Mia hanging back to brood over the fates of their respective partners. Dale looked at Mia, with her button-down blouse tucked into a pair of slacks. She was a far cry from her tattooed punk of a girlfriend, and eventually curiosity got the better of her. She matched Mia's pace and in doing so gained her attention.

"Sorry. I just figured if we're going to be walking across the city, we might as well make conversation."

"Sure. What do you want to talk about?"

"How did you and Hannah meet?"

Mia couldn't help but smile. "We don't really match on paper, do we?"

"Nothing wrong with that," Dale said. "It's just that when two people as different as you two end up together, I figure there's a story behind it."

"It's not much of one, I'm afraid. I went with Owen to get a tattoo, and Hannah owned the shop. She was cute, she made me smile, and I thought what the hell. She was nowhere near my type. Covered with tats, slovenly, sleeping until noon on work days. Ordinarily I'd have run screaming from her. But I helped straighten her up a little and she helped loosen me up a bit." She looked down at her feet. "If I lose her..."

Dale put an arm around her shoulders. "That won't happen. Dr. Frost is amazing. He's helped Ari a lot over the past few years."

"Speaking of great stories," Mia said, "I bet there has to be quite a tale behind a human and a wolf hooking up. I don't even have any real human friends."

Dale chuckled. "Well, we started as friends. She gave me a job when I really didn't have any other prospects and I helped her make it work. I guess we're kind of like you and Hannah. Neither of us was doing too well on our own. We're better together."

Mia said, "I'll wager you have quite a few stories."

"Oh, there are a couple." She chuckled under her breath. "There was this one time, there was a poodle..."

She continued the story as they walked, ducking into the shadows whenever one of them spotted a police car. Eventually they reached the wealthier side of town and they were able to let their guards down a bit. Dale was breathing hard by the time Gwyneth let them into her home, but both *canidae* women seemed none the worse for wear. They gathered in the kitchen where Gwyneth poured a glass of water for each of them.

"There are guest rooms upstairs if you'd like to claim one before the others arrive. There are toiletries in the hall closet."

Mia shook her head. "I'm not sleeping. I want to be alert in case there's news of Hannah's condition."

Gwyneth looked like she wanted to argue but thought better of it. "Then you can stretch out on the couch. Dale..." She seemed to consider what she was about to say next before she decided on it. "The room at the top of the stairs is Ariadne's former bedroom. If you wished to spend the night in there, I doubt she would object."

"Thank you, Miss Willow."

"Gwen, please."

Dale nodded. "Good night, Gwen. Night, Mia."

She went upstairs and used the bathroom, eyed the shower with desire, and reluctantly left it behind. Instead she went into her girlfriend's childhood bedroom and shut the door behind her. The ceiling was sloped to follow the angle of the roof, with a bed tucked into the small side of the room. There were no pictures of pop singers or actors on the wall, and the curtains were pale enough to catch the moonlight and cast it across the floor. It was like seeing a ghost, some snippet of the past stuck in amber. She looked for remnants of what had created the woman she loved.

Dale took off her shoes with a sigh of relief and wiggled her toes in her socks. Three miles in just under an hour had left her sore and tired. Looking down at herself she saw that she was still wearing clothes stained with Hannah's blood. She cringed at the thought of what would have happened if they'd been stopped by the police.

She stripped down to her underwear, emptied her pockets, and dumped the ruined clothes in the trash. Her phone was almost entirely dead so she turned it off to save what minimal charge remained in case of emergency. She opened the closet and discovered at some point Ari's mother had transferred the clothes her daughter left to vacuum-sealed storage bags. Dale opened one and took out a T-shirt that was big on her and would have been gigantic on teenage Ariadne. She chuckled quietly as she put it on. "Looks like this time you left a stash for me, puppy."

She peeled back the blankets and crawled into the bed where Ari had spent her formative years. She curled on her side and hugged the pillow to her chest. It was ludicrous to think any scent remained after so long, but the action allowed her brain to think it was smelling Ari. She closed her eyes and let her exhaustion pummel her adrenaline into submission and she was asleep in seconds.

Ari hung up the landline after her call to Dale finally went to voicemail. She rubbed her face and hoped Dale was just busy or had her phone turned off. "Be okay, Dale," she whispered. "Just be okay."

She had left Lorne with a fresh bandage and a second apology for rejecting his kiss, but he assured her he was okay. He offered to drive her back to her car, but she was so tired that she didn't even remember where she had parked it. She lied and told him she would take a cab home but after discovering who owned Alki, she doubted she would ever take a cab again.

Instead she walked a half mile to a park, stripped, and put her clothes into a plastic grocery bag that had blown against a tree. She hooked the handles of the bag around her collar and transformed into the wolf. She let the wolf's brain focus on home and let it go, hoping it had energy reserves that she lacked in human form. She was vaguely aware of running, the soft grass underneath her paws and the flash of headlights passing by on the street. The wolf always knew to be wary of roadways and police cars, but tonight the warning was stronger than usual. Whenever a car passed close enough to see her, the wolf ducked under whatever was nearby until it was gone.

She regained consciousness with her forepaw scratching at the wall next to the elevator in her building. She transformed back into her human form, dressed, and went upstairs with pain radiating out from every joint from her quick shift. She let herself into the apartment and collapsed on the couch. She tried calling Dale and knew she would find the strength to go wherever she was if she answered. But the phone just rang, and she resigned herself to the fact they would be spending the night apart.

She told herself that Dale was okay. It had been a long and crazy day, and they could reunite in the morning once they had a chance to rest. The idea of sleep put the image of a bed in her mind, and she rose as if hypnotized to stumble down the hall. She stripped naked and went into the bathroom to find Dale's perfume. She dabbed it behind her ears, made a cross with it over her upper chest, and rubbed it into both wrists.

Enveloped by Dale's scent, Ari finally went to bed and stretched out on top of the blankets. She was asleep before she found the wherewithal to actually pull them over her.

Her last conscious thought was, "Two days down of wolf manoth down. Twenty-nine to go."

CHAPTER EIGHT

January 3

AFTER SUFFERING through strange wolf-centric nightmares for a few hours, Dale finally gave up on sleeping and got out of bed. It was still the middle of the night, but she knew there was no chance she would get back to sleep. She went into the closet to see if there were any other clothes she could borrow, and she found a pair of pants that fit her. She was bustier than Ari was as an adult, so none of the teenage-size shirts would be appropriate for her. Instead she kept on the oversized nightshirt and tucked it into her jeans until she could change into something better.

Her exploration of the closet made curious as to what other treasures there were to be found. There was a desk across from the bed, and she turned on the lamp as she took a seat and scanned to find the best place to start snooping. She opened the top desk drawer and found a school book on top of a wild mess of papers. She laughed as she lifted the garbage to peer underneath it.

"You are going to need a filing system, Miss Willow."

Ari said, "I have a filing system. Everything I need is in that drawer."

"That's not a drawer. That's a branch of the city landfill."

"Fine. If you want to add filing to your tasks, knock yourself out. And it's Ariadne. Or Ari. Don't call me Miss Willow."

"Okay, fair enough."

She brushed at her cheek as she pushed the drawer shut and continued to explore. She and Ari had never planned to have a proper employee-employer situation. When she walked into Willow Investigative Service, which she still thought was an atrocious name, she expected to spend two weeks getting things organized in order to grab a paycheck that would hopefully satisfy her landlady. But the two weeks ended and she couldn't bring herself to leave Ari alone.

"So I guess, um. We never said if this was going to be long-term."

"No... and you have the Shepard case that's on-going. If you need some help with the research, or um... God knows you won't be able to find the right files if it goes to court. I could stick around at least for a little while."

"That could be months."

Dale shrugged. "Where else do I have to go?"

"Excellent. Then, uh, I guess we should talk salary."

Four years passed. Cases came and went, girlfriends came and went. She and Ariadne were close friends but there was always something deeper under the surface. They fought it for the longest time, for reasons she couldn't remember anymore. Things finally changed when they were close to losing everything. Ari was framed for a murder and went on the run, and Dale had gone with her. There was no question in her mind that she would, no alternative beyond running when Ari ran. The first time they made love, they were fugitives. Everything had been taken from them - their jobs were at risk, their homes were too dangerous, and someone was trying to kill them so they would never tell their side of the story - and it didn't matter as long as they had each other.

It was then that she remembered the two missed messages from Ari. She retrieved her phone and turned it on, ignoring the battery warning as she read them.

"Oh, Ariadne." She wiped at her cheeks and chuckled. She composed a quick reply: "You're my puppy. Forever. I love you."

She was still sitting at the desk when there was a soft knock on the door. "Miss Frye?" Gwen said. "Are you awake?"

"I am. Come in."

She opened the door and stuck her head inside. "I saw the light was on and thought you would want to know. Dr. Frost called, and Hannah made it through the surgery. She lost quite a bit of blood, but she's going to survive."

"Oh, thank God. Thank you for letting me know. I assume Mia already knows."

"The only message Hannah had before passing out was 'tell Mia to get some sleep.'" Dale laughed and Gwen smiled. "I told her and then ordered her to bed. You should do the same. You've had a rough day."

"I will. Thanks for letting me know."

"You're welcome."

"The other girls are sleeping over at Dr. Frost's, I guess?"

Gwen shook her head. "They went to Milo's home. As for the boys... I haven't heard from them."

The tension that had faded from Dale's posture returned. "Do you think they're in trouble?"

"We've no way of finding out tonight without tipping our hand. If we inquire, and the police are aware they were involved in the catastrophe we caused, we'll be exposing ourselves. I'll be checking the news for updates. For now, sleep."

"Yes, ma'am."

"Gwen. It's Gwen. Goodnight, Dale."

"Night."

Gwen left, and Dale turned off the lamp. She kept her phone in hand so she would be woken if Ari responded to her text. She crawled under the blankets and rolled on her side, pretending that Ari was lying behind her. She'd spent plenty of nights sleeping alone since they became a couple, what with Ari's evening runs as the wolf. Somehow this night felt different, and it was the first night she would have given anything to feel Ari's arms around her. She held the phone to her chest and closed her eyes, focusing on the relief about Hannah's condition to drift back to sleep.

Ari woke and stretched her hand across the mattress, momentarily confused to find it empty despite the fact Dale's scent was all around her. Slowly she remembered applying the perfume and opened her eyes to the disappointing sight of an empty bedroom. She'd dreamt of Dale, real moments from their relationship and a few fantasy ones that got thrown in for good measure. She took a moment to adjust back to reality before she got out of bed and took a shower. When she was finished the perfume was still strong enough that she could smell it, but she added another dab behind each ear just to make sure it was there for the entire day.

She found the food Dale had stocked in the fridge, everything safely packaged and delivered, and she felt a tug of gratitude as she prepared her breakfast without fear that someone had messed with it. "Come on, Dale," she whispered. "Where the hell are you?" She called her mother while she was cooking breakfast, but there was no answer. Most likely they were still trying to cover their tracks from the night before. She wondered what the hell Milo Duncan was doing in town. Who were all those other wolves? Who had been shot? All those questions paled in comparison to her concern that her mother was currently in possession of ninety percent of Seattle's wolfsbane. The idea terrified her, but not as much as the idea of leaving it with the hunters did.

She ate slowly in the hopes Dale would come home for a change of clothes, but Lorne arrived first. He knocked, and hollered through the door before she could have possibly replied. "Willow? You in there?"

"I'm here. Just a second." She put her dishes in the sink and ran the water over them and reached for her phone before remembering it had been crushed. She wasn't even sure how to get a replacement; Dale handled all that stuff for her.

"I tried your place and there wasn't an answer. So I looked up your, ah... your girlfriend..."

"Yeah, just a second." She turned off the light and picked up her jacket. He looked a bit haggard but otherwise none the worse for wear. Physically, at least. There was something off about his demeanor, a sullen and defeated feel to how he barely straightened his posture when she opened the door. "Morning, Detective. How's the arm?"

He nodded a greeting. "It's doing a little better. Itches. Anyway, come on. We're going to have a babysitter today. He's waiting downstairs."

"A babysitter?"

"Huxley thought it was prudent to make sure we didn't have another situation like yesterday. Thought I needed someone to keep an eye on me."

Ari sighed. "The more the merrier."

She locked the apartment and followed him downstairs. He had parked on the street and Ari could see someone sitting in the backseat of the car. The babysitter looked up when they came outside, his eyes locking on her as she walked around the car. He wore a blue suit over a black shirt open at the collar, his black-and-silver hair cut short and center-parted. He had sharp features, the sort of perfectly-aligned face that would been perfect for a coin. His mouth remained a solid scratch underneath his nose as Ari got in and fastened her seatbelt. She twisted to look at him and saw he was staring at her.

"Hi, Butch. I'm Ariadne Willow. Friends call me Ari. You can call me 'ma'am.'"

"I'm Mr. Keighley. You look familiar, Ariadne Willow."

Lorne said, "She's a private investigator. She's worked with me on a few cases."

Keighley kept his eyes on her. "I didn't ask you, Mr. Lorne, I asked your friend. Have we met before?"

Ari shook her head. "Doubtful. I'd probably still be getting over the creepy feeling. Who is this guy?"

"This guy is the one deciding whether or not you get to stay in this group," Keighley said. "Both of you are the last ones standing after a failure of the most epic proportions. Every hunter in this part of the world was crippled last night because you two couldn't do your jobs properly. Huxley thinks you can salvage this disaster by finding the wolfsbane. I'm the one who is going to make sure you succeed."

"I'm going to call you buckets-of-fun, because that's what you are."

Lorne said, "Willow... just don't."

"Fuck that." She twisted in her seat. "I'm not a hunter, okay? I have the genes, but I didn't grow up with this bizarre cult-in-waiting mentality that everyone else seems to have. And to be entirely honest with you, I'm glad the wolfsbane got stolen. I'm glad it's off the table. It was dirty pool. You want to convince the world wolves are dangerous? Don't stack the deck by making them act dangerous. You don't teach kids that fire is hot by sticking their hands over a candle." She scoffed. "Scratch that. You probably did teach your kids that way."

Keighley's gaze never wavered. "Are you finished?"

"Yeah."

"Then turn around and shut your mouth."

Ari faced forward and dropped into her seat. Lorne started the car and pulled away from the curb. Ari glanced in the mirror and saw Keighley was still staring at her, though at the moment he only had a view of the back of her head. She resisted the urge to flip him off. It was going to be a long enough day without further antagonizing the man. She would have to choose her battles carefully.

Dale was able to borrow some of Gwen's clothes so she didn't have to look like a thrift-shop refugee, but the result was an ensemble that made her feel like she was going to a job interview or maybe standing trial. She ate a banana for breakfast since it had the smallest chance of dripping or staining the borrowed blouse. Gwen was on the phone the entire time they were at the house, pacing through the living room as she discussed the wolfsbane with various *canidae* across the city. Watching her work, Dale realized that Ari hadn't been taking the burden entirely upon herself. She'd shared part of it with her mother. In keeping that collaboration secret, she'd been protecting Dale from shouldering any of the stress on her own. *"I'm struggling to protect every wolf in Seattle from this drug, and oh, I'm working with my mother whom I haven't seen or spoken to since I ran away from home, but seriously, don't worry."* She would have worried. She would have been a nervous wreck, and Ari's choice, however misguided, had been made to protect her.

Mia finally joined them, her hair still wet from the shower, and Gwen told them Dr. Frost was waiting for them. The plan was to visit Hannah, then reconnect with the rest of the pack at Milo's house. They listened to the radio in the car and other than a brief mention of a car accident where gunfire was exchanged, there was very little discussion of the accident. As far as they could tell the press was considering the entire mess a road rage incident. The police would likely be another matter.

Dr. Frost most likely hadn't slept, but he still seemed perky and wide awake when he let them into the house. He had changed clothes but they already looked slept-in due to the rolled-up sleeves and the three buttons open at the collar. He led them through the house to the recovery room, knocked softly, and held the door open for Mia. "She needs her rest, but she insisted that she had to see you before she would sleep. Try to keep it as brief as possible."

Mia nodded. "Thank you."

Dale stepped back. "I'll be in the living room."

Frost held up a hand to stop her. "No, she specified that she wanted to see both of you."

Mia said, "Yeah. Trust me, she'll want to thank you in person."

"Okay..." Dale went into the room behind Mia, feeling awkward and out of place as she shut the door behind them.

Hannah was lying on the bed under the window, sheet pulled up to her stomach. She wore a tank top that had obviously been donated from Dr. Frost, the scooped neck showing off even more of the tattoos that ran up and down her arms. Dale had briefly seen the extent of her artwork when she stripped down to transform, but for obvious reasons hadn't let her gaze linger. Mia knelt next to the bed and took Hannah's right hand in both of hers, and Hannah's eyes fluttered open. The corners of her lips curled up in an automatic smile that made the lines around her eyes wrinkle.

"There's my worry-wolf."

Mia took Hannah's hands in hers and kissed her knuckles. "I think I earned it this time. You scared the daylights out of me, woman."

"I was a little scared myself there." Her voice was rough and weak. "Tell me you got some sleep last night."

"Fifteen minutes or so," Mia said.

"I guess that's good enough." She looked at Dale and smiled. "Ah. My hero."

Dale smiled nervously. "Hi. I'd ask how you're feeling, but..."

"I feel alive," Hannah said. "That bullet hit me, and I went down, and I... accepted it. Milo and Gwen, they were wolves. Mia and Paige had their arms full, and I would have bitten their heads off if they got sloppy with the wolfsbane just because of me. So I went down and I knew deep down I was gone. And then a human with nothing to gain jumped down and grabbed me. You saved my life. I can't repay you enough for that."

Dale shrugged. "This is my war, too. The hunters are attacking Ari's people, then... then it's my war, too."

Hannah shifted with a grunt, moved the blanket, and lifted the shirt. She lightly tapped the gauze over her wound, a shockingly small square of white just below her ribs. "When this heals, there's going to be a scar. I'm going to tattoo your name over it so I'll always remember you."

"I think your partner might have issues with you tatting another woman's name on your chest."

Hannah laughed, then winced at the pain. "Ow. If she has a problem with it, she can just deal."

"No problem whatsoever. I think it's perfect." Mia bent down to kiss the skin right next to the bandage, and Hannah stroked the back of Mia's head with such tenderness that Dale felt like an utter intruder. She backed up a step toward the door.

Hannah said, "I know you have to go, but I'm glad you stopped by."

"No," Mia said. "I'm staying right here."

Hannah said, "Why, so you can watch me sleep?"

"Yes. Exactly that, yes."

Dale said, "I don't think anyone will blame her if she sticks around. Besides, if we need backup later on, it'll be nice to have someone in the reserves."

Mia kissed Hannah's lips and stood up. "I'm going to walk her out and explain to Gwen I'm staying. I'll be right back."

"I'll be here."

They left the room and Mia gripped Dale's arm to keep her from walking down the hall. "I have a confession to make. When Milo first mentioned you and Ariadne, we all made a lot of jokes. We called you a hood. Milo insisted it was different but we wouldn't listen. We couldn't fathom one of us actually falling in love with a human, and we looked down on Ariadne for it without even knowing the situation. I understand now, and I couldn't be sorrier for treating you so poorly."

"It's fine."

"It's not. You may not feel it necessary to offer forgiveness, but it's definitely necessary for me to show remorse."

Dale nodded. "Thank you."

Mia, absolved, let go of Dale's arm and led her outside. She told Gwen that she planned to stay, which Gwen accepted without surprise or argument. "The boys have finally turned up. I sent them to Milo's house and we'll meet up with them there."

"Sounds good. Tell everyone to be safe. I'm here if you need me."

"Go... be with your partner," Gwen said.

They waited until she was inside before Gwen started the car and drove away from the house.

"Have you given any thought about what to do with the wolfsbane?" Dale asked.

Gwen shook her head. "It's far too dangerous to risk it falling into the wrong hands. By the same measure, it's too risky to destroy it since we don't know what effect it will have on the drugs. If we burn everything we may just release a cloud that will expose every *canidae* in the Seattle area. It would be a massacre."

Dale nodded. "If you come up with someone and you need a human, let me know."

Gwen looked at her. "You would take that risk for us?"

"I keep saying this... you're Ari's people. That makes you my family, too."

Gwen kept her eyes on the road for a long moment. "We don't have the kind of relationship where I think this would matter to her, but regardless... if Ari ever wishes for my blessing to be with you, assure her that she has it."

Dale smiled. "Thanks. Who knew all it would take is running into a gunfight and offering to deal with hazardous waste to get my girlfriend's mother to like me?"

Gwen actually laughed; Dale was surprised to find she and Ari had a very similar laugh and it warmed her to the woman. She knew how much bad blood there was between the Willow women, but she couldn't help but admit she sort of liked Gwen.

"Yes, I'd say you have the whole in-law thing down pat, Dale."

They arrived at Milo's house seconds after another car pulled into the driveway, and Dale was relieved to see Owen, Tarun, and Benji had all made it through the evening unscathed. The boys waited as Gwen parked, still standing next to their car as Paige and Milo came out of the house.

Gwen greeted the men in the driveway. "Where were you last night?"

Tarun said, "A black man and an Indian man with unusual accents were involved in a car accident seconds before all hell broke loose, all a few blocks away from the Space Needle. Where do you *think* we were last night? Cops finally let us go this morning when everything checked out. Thanks for that, Miss Willow."

"Of course, Tarun."

Owen had kissed Paige when she came down the drive, and he slipped his arm around his waist. "How did everything else go? Hannah's okay, right? She's out of the woods?"

Gwen nodded. "She'll need some time to recover, but she's in one piece. The biggest issue right now is what we do with our spoils. I'm not exactly keen on holding five coolers full of wolfsbane in my garage indefinitely. But let's talk about it inside."

The group filed into the house and Gwen waited until they had taken their seats in the living room before she spoke. "First things first. Boys, you weren't present last night so you missed one rather large development. As far as we're concerned, Dale Frye is as much a *canidae* as the rest of us. She put herself in harm's way to save one of us when she could have just as easily kept herself safe. I'll not hear one word of her being 'other,' even as a joke. Am I understood?"

The men nodded. Benji said, "She saved Hannah's life. Far as I'm concerned that makes her a member of the pack for life. Welcome." He held out his fist and Dale bumped her knuckles against it.

"Now that we have that settled... we can't discount the hunters as a threat just because we took their secret weapon. We have no way of knowing how much wolfsbane was already distributed through the city. There's still a threat out there."

"Not to mention the fact the hunters saw us," Paige said. "They may not know what we look like, but they have a lot of information I'd prefer they didn't. The van..."

"We ditched the van."

Paige said, "Yeah, but you didn't evaporate it. If they find it, it'll lead them to us."

"The van's rental records lead to a shell company that will lead them to a defunct corporation. They'll go around in circles before ending up with nothing. The same with the van itself. It's safely tucked away. Even if someone finds it and connects it to the events of last night, it won't get the police anywhere."

"If they find even a speck of Hannah's blood and test it," Tarun said, "they'll trace her and find out she entered the country with three people who were overnight guests at their lovely precinct last night. I'm just pointing out we may not be as protected as we hope to be."

Milo said, "They might still make the connection from you three to what happened last night. Are you sure you weren't followed here?"

"Positive," Benji said. "We parked for fifteen minutes at a car wash, we stopped to get breakfast from three different fast-food restaurants - which is still out in the car if anyone wants something - and then we drove around like confused tourists for thirty minutes just to make sure we didn't see anyone following us."

"We should still err on the side of caution," Gwen said. "Your personal information was so iron-clad because it was for the most part true. If they decide to look into you again, they'll find you regardless of whether they followed you this morning or not. Hopefully Ariadne will find a way to give us warning when they're on the way, but if she's not able or not privy to the plans, we'll be working blind."

Owen held his hands out. "So where does that leave us?"

"It puts us in a place of power," Gwen said. "You were a pack in London, and now that you're here I'm temporarily your Alpha. Do you have any problem with that?" The group shook their heads. "So we're a pack, and we've struck a blow against the hunters. That means they're going to be coming after us hard. It's only a matter of time before they put together all their evidence and come looking for us."

"How is that good for us?" Owen said.

"We know they're coming eventually. We can be ready when they show up."

Lorne was called into his captain's office immediately upon his arrival at work, leaving Ari waiting at his desk with Keighley. She took the opportunity to observe the unknown quantity. He was still even while waiting, seated behind Lorne's desk with his hands folded in his lap. The sole concession he made to comfort was tilting the chair back so he was at a slight incline rather than sitting up straight. It was the perfect position for napping but he kept his eyes open to silently scan the bullpen. Other detectives scurried around on jobs and cases that had nothing to do with the war, oblivious to wolves and hunters. At the moment Ari envied them.

"So what do you know about me?"

She very nearly flinched at the sound of his voice. He hadn't seemed to move before speaking, but afterward he looked a challenge at her.

"You've been watching me for fifteen minutes. Surely you've come to some conclusion."

"You're a hunter."

He sighed and returned his attention to the room at large.

"You don't believe in wasting energy or time. You make every move, no matter how minor, worth the effort it takes to make it. Conservation of energy, sure, but it also manages to make you incredibly easy to overlook. It pulls you into the wallpaper and lets the eye drift right over you. You make yourself invisible so the prey never sees you coming."

He pushed out his bottom lip a little and nodded his head.

"And you have a bad back."

Keighley looked at her, something almost like surprise in his icy blue eyes. "On what do you base that conclusion?"

"The way you were sitting in the car, the way you're sitting now, and the way you stood in the elevator on the way up here. You try to hide that you're doing it, but you rotate your hips every now and then to stretch out your spine."

"Nicely done."

Ari dismissed him with a lifted shoulder. "I'm a private

investigator. It's what I do."

"Would you like to know what I've observed about you?"

"Not particularly."

"You strive to make people underestimate you. As a woman, you have to outwit men rather than besting them in a toe-to-toe fight. It's your secret to success. You call your business 'Bitches' to counter anyone who might be dismissive of a female private investigator. Laughing at yourself before they can laugh at you, as it were. The collar is an interesting choice. You wear it without irony, yet you lack the other accoutrements of the sub-culture that is most-often associated with that accessory. That tells me you wear it for a reason, that it has meaning, but I'm not sure what that meaning is. Everything about you is defensive. Secretive. It makes me wonder what you're hiding from Detective Lorne, and what secrets you're keeping from us all."

Ari covered her discomfort by smiling before she realized she had just done exactly what he'd accused her of. "Well. Thanks. I'll try to work on that." She tapped her finger on the desk and glanced over at the captain's office. "You know, on TV this is the point when Lorne would come out so we wouldn't have to sit awkwardly together in silence."

Keighley leaned back in his chair and resumed scanning the room.

"Right."

It was another ten minutes before Lorne returned. He looked at Keighley, who made no move to get out of his chair, and pulled an empty chair over to sit next to Ari.

She said, "What did the big man have to say?"

"Basically that I should be suspended for everything that happened last night. It was my operation and it went sideways as horribly as possible. Orarian is pissed because we lost their shipment. They might not have known what the wolfsbane was, but they knew we took boxes out of their top-secret lab and those boxes were stolen on our watch. So they're livid. They're threatening to sue if any of their proprietary information is compromised."

"Never mess with a Big Pharma," Ari said.

Keighley said, "What of the accident reports?"

Lorne said, "They have witness reports and we're working to gather as much security camera footage as we can so we can piece things together. That first accident at the intersection of Fifth has to be involved. I wanted to talk to the three guys who took blame for what happened, but they had already been released."

"Their names?" Keighley said.

"Owen Kiernan, Benjamin Wood, and Tarun Conrad. They came into the country a few weeks ago. We're looking into it."

Keighley said, "You should have kept them."

"We had nothing to hold them on. They were issued a citation, but they weren't under the influence. The arresting officer even tried to connect it with what happened to us, but it all dead-ended. We had to let them go."

"The police had to let them go. You should have had hunters in place to detain them before they left the building. We are beyond legalities right now. What about the van?"

"We're still looking. We don't have a license plate, and the description of a black passenger van isn't really narrowing things down very far."

Keighley stood up and subtly stretched his back. "Then perhaps you should get to work. Every moment wasted is another moment the wolves may have destroyed the wolfsbane."

Lorne slipped past him and took his seat while Keighley stepped out from behind the desk. He scanned the room again before his eyes settled on Ari. "Get to work, you two. Let me know if you require any help with your search. I won't be far."

"Yeah, I bet you won't." She watched him walk away and looked at Lorne. "Just curious. What happens if we don't track down the wolfsbane?"

"Then Keighley tells Huxley that I screwed up beyond repair, and Huxley decides what to do with me." He rubbed his sleeve above the slight rise created by the bandage. "Let's just say being a hunter doesn't offer a very attractive retirement plan."

Ari sighed and picked up the files Lorne had put on the desk before he went to be verbally assaulted by his boss. "Right. So let's see if we can find ourselves a specific black van in all of Seattle."

CHAPTER NINE

FROM THE camera posted outside Bank of America: *The van (driven by Chase) appears at the lower left-hand side of the screen and progresses north at the posted speed limit. In a flash of headlights from a passing car, Ariadne Willow's face is visible through the windshield. At the center of the screen, another van (driven by an unknown woman) appears from the bottom sector of the screen. It impacts the hunter van in the rear quadrant, lifting the passenger-side wheels off the ground as it is pushed out of its lane. The side doors of the wolf van slide open. Two women climb out with guns drawn, masks over their face. Seconds later, a pair of wolves emerge and race past them.*

Ari watched the confrontation again, then held her breath as Dale appeared. She ducked down, grabbed the wolf that had gone down in a spray of blood, and hauled her up into the van. Lorne had fired again while Dale was exposed, and Ari felt a surge of anger. If he'd accidentally hit her, if he'd even winged her arm, Ari knew she would have gone feral without the help of wolfsbane. Then there was the question of who had been shot. It wasn't Milo, and neither of the masked women - whoever the hell they were - had her mother's height or build. That meant one of the two unidentified wolves was Gwyneth Willow, and there was a fifty-fifty chance her mother had been the wolf that Dale rescued.

Her mother might very well be dead.

Of course it could also have been another stranger, one of Milo's friends, but would Dale have gone into the line of fire for a stranger? Or would she have taken the risk because she knew how much it would mean to Ari? The more she thought about it, the more likely it seemed. She expected to have conflicting feelings about that, but in truth all she felt was sadness. She didn't want her mother to be dead, didn't want to be an orphan. She had gone half her life without even laying eyes on the woman, but the thought of losing her this way...

"Are you okay?"

She nearly jumped. She had forgotten Keighley was sitting at the next desk, and his voice had seemed to come from right next to her head. She blinked rapidly and gestured at the screen. "Too long sitting here staring at a screen. This is why I have a secretary."

"Hm."

She stamped down her emotions about what might have been and started the next video.

From the camera at Starbucks: *The hunter van progresses from left to right. In the slowest possible speed, the wolf van is visible accelerating toward the intersection from Lenora Street. Gwen's face is visible through the windshield, but the image is blurry enough that no amount of zooming or enhancing will be able to identify her. Ari is only sure because she's so familiar with her mother's face. In this angle, the hunter's van blocks the view of the assault.*

She leaned forward and rubbed her eyes with the video paused. She was stunned at how many angles they had of the same scene, impressed and violated at the same time. It seemed impossible that none of her many transformations or half-naked traipses across city parks hadn't ended up all over YouTube. She was watching the tapes on a police-owned laptop, exhausting her eyes and boring her silly so the real cops could spend their time on actual police work. She moved the mouse and clicked on the next icon, the footage from the car dealership.

Lorne came back from retrieving his warrant for rental records from Enterprise. "Hey. Find anything?"

She remembered her anger at the video version of him, but fought past it. "There are two sides to every story, and eighty-nine thousand angles to the same damn street corner."

"Welcome to the glorious day of a police officer. Paperwork and squinting at blurry images on a computer screen. Just be grateful you don't have to sit in a room with a VCR trying to find pertinent info between wiggly lines because some shop owner decided to reuse the same tapes over and over again for the past decade. I'd have loved for digital files back in those days."

"I'll kill someone for you if you watch this footage for me."

He smiled and waved his paper like a white flag. "Sorry. Gotta call and check out every black van that got rented last night. You're finally getting that fancy consultant paycheck on this job, better start earning your keep."

"Yeah, yeah..." She rubbed the bridge of her nose, widened her eyes, and went back to the well for the next repetition. This time the hunter van seemed to be coming straight toward the camera. She took a deep breath and rested her chin on her hand as she watched everything happen again. Van One, Van Two, Impact, Masked Women, Wolves, Dale, Escape. Ari paused on the escape and backed up the footage. One of the wolves came around the front of the van: her mother. She jumped into the back of the van. Ari progressed the footage forward a frame at a time.

Her mother left the back of the hunter van. She cut a wide circle around the front of the wolf van, back to the driver's side. Lorne's bullet hit the other wolf.

Ari pushed away from the desk and stood up so quickly that even Keighley seemed unsettled. "I need something to drink. Anyone else need something?"

Lorne said, "I'll take a~"

Ari turned around before he could finish speaking and walked out of the bullpen. The break room was a small windowless closet just across the hall. She went inside and, after a quick scan to make sure she was alone, sagged against the door and covered her face with both hands. She didn't sob, her eyes didn't even become wet, but the emotion churning through her needed an outlet and she refused to do it in front of Lorne or Keighley. She was trembling, and her face burned red as she repeated the fact over in her head until she accepted it was true.

Her mother was alive. Dale was alive. She hadn't realized how little she believed those facts until she was presented with the hard evidence. Being unable to reach either of them on the phone had sown seeds of doubt in her mind that had now been eradicated. They were both alive, and when she found them she would tear them apart for not answering their goddamn phones.

Someone tried to open the door and she pushed back against it. "Just a sec."

"Willow?" Lorne said. "Everything okay?"

"Everything's fine."

"Good, because we just got more security footage. Whole Foods is on a side street, so we may be able to see where the wolves went after they blindsided us."

"I'll be right out."

He walked away and she pushed her hair behind her ears, took a calming breath, and fanned the heat out of her face before she went back out to resume her duties.

Milo's house was essentially a fortress waiting to happen. It backed up next to a wooded park where she could run and roam to her heart's content, but those woods also provided access to any hunter that wanted to sneak up on the house from the rear. Gwen sent Milo, Owen and Benji to set up some early-warning security so they would know if anyone approached the house from that direction. The front lawn was small and stepped, with the street two levels below the front porch. Paige and Tarun were stationed at upstairs bedrooms on opposite ends of the house, one facing east and the other west.

Dale and Gwen, meanwhile, set to securing the downstairs. They blocked doors and covered windows so there would only be one point of ingress or egress, both easily defendable if it came down to that. Gwen carried a sheaf of plywood from the garage into the living room and propped it up against the wall next to the piano. Dale was almost finished covering the picture window and nodded her thanks before she took another nail out of her mouth.

Gwen watched her for a moment before she spoke. "They were right, you know. This isn't your war, Dale. I know you consider Ariadne family, and I think that's very sweet. It's a romantic notion. But odds are that this is going to be a bloody business sooner or later. We nearly lost Hannah, and we may not be so lucky next time."

"You would have lost Hannah if I hadn't been there," she said, speaking from the corner of her mouth so she wouldn't drop the nails she was holding. "I grabbed her, and I told you where to find a doctor. You're going to be fighting an army with, what, five people? I'm not going to leave you down another soldier."

"Dale..." Gwen's voice was softer than she'd ever heard it, so she turned to face her. Gwen was looking down at the carpet. "I've taken so much from my daughter. My decision when she was a baby changed her entire life. My admission of that action threw her out into the world before she was ready. The decisions I've made have destroyed my daughter's life, regardless of the success she's been able to salvage from the ruins. If I let you remain here when the violence begins and I'm unable to protect you..." Her voice trailed off and she looked up at Dale. "I can't be responsible for Ari losing you."

"This is where I belong. Here, or by Ari's side. Since that doesn't seem to be an option, then I'm staying here. I'm not going home and watching TV until someone calls to tell me how everything went down. So just... you know... save it."

The back door opened and Milo came in. "We've got the forest pretty well covered. We'll need someone to keep an eye on the backyard to see if the floodlights come on."

"Dale will do that," Gwen said.

"I..." She caught Gwen's look and stopped herself. "I guess that's something I could do."

"Thank you, Dale."

Milo looked between them but decided not to investigate. "Uh, yeah. Okay. We got a call from Mia while we were out there. Hannah wants to be here."

Gwen said, "Out of the question."

"Yeah, you can be the one to tell her that. She says that she's lying on her back, but she can still hold a gun or look out a window to let us know if someone's coming. It would free up Paige or Tarun to be more useful elsewhere. Plus if Mia was here, that would be one more body. And a cop to boot. Look, she's going to be flat on her back anyway. Might as well give her a view that will be useful to us."

Gwen thought it over for another moment. "Fine. If Dr. Frost says she can be moved safely, then we'll bring her over. Before nightfall. I don't want anyone on the road if the hunters make their move."

"I'll have Owen and Paige pick her up on their way back from lunch. Everyone okay with a bag of burgers?"

"Sounds good. Thank you, Milo."

She nodded and left the room.

Gwen walked to the couch and sat down. For the first time Dale saw vulnerability in her, and in it saw a resemblance to a side of Ari that she tried hard not to show. Like mother, like daughter, she supposed. She put down her hammer and nails and walked over to sit next to Gwen.

"You tried to end this peacefully. The hunters wouldn't let that happen." She took Gwen's hand. "You did everything you could. And this is just an extension of that. You're trying to protect everyone."

"Before the... assault, I had no idea hunters even existed. My parents died when I was very young, so I wasn't taught about our history. Afterward I tried to figure out everything I could about the bastards who had done this horrible thing to me. I discovered the story about Johanna and Agatha, the history of wolves and hunters that stretched back so far. We were supposed to be at peace, but it was obvious people aren't as white-and-black as all that. Treaty or no, the hunters had seen me as a thing instead of a person. I knew it was only a matter of time before something like this happened. And even though I've spent the past thirty years waiting, I still feel unprepared."

"Those *canidae* out in the woods and the ones upstairs... they were a pack long before they came here. They have history together. But the second you declared yourself their Alpha, they agreed. They fell in line behind General Gwyneth not because you just happen to be older and available. They trust you. They've seen you in action and they're confident enough to let you call the shots. Plans are useless. We make plans to keep our minds limber so we can think on our feet when the shit goes down. The fact that Ari has been coming to you for help says loads about how much she respects your opinion."

"I wasn't sure if she'd told you about that."

"She hadn't. Still hasn't. But there are bigger things to worry about now. I understand why she did it so I'm not going to hold a grudge. I'm glad you were there to help take some of the load off her shoulders."

Gwen squeezed Dale's hand. "Are you this good with Ariadne?"

Dale grinned. "Well, you two aren't as different as she'd like to believe."

"Good to hear. Thank you, Dale. We should finish these windows. We have no way of knowing when the hunters will arrive."

"Yeah. I was thinking we could have them on a hinge of some sort, so we could leave them open until we spot the danger and then just drop them down in a hurry for security."

"I'll see if Benji has any construction experience. It's a good idea, Dale."

Dale nodded and said, "Well, it's my first siege situation. I'm trying to make it a good one."

Gwen smiled and stood up. "We'll take a break for lunch. But for now..."

"Right. Back to work." She went back to her hammer, hoisting it and swinging at the air a few times to test the weight. "You know, it's too bad I don't have a hard hat and a tool belt. Of course it's not much of a fantasy if Ari isn't here to appreciate it."

"Dale?" Gwen cleared her throat. "I'm still her mother..."

Dale blushed. "Right. Geez. Sorry."

Gwen chuckled and left the room, and Dale focused on the windows rather than her growing humiliation that she'd just said something so sexual in front of Ari's mother. She took comfort in the fact that, had Ari been there, she would have definitely been laughing her ass off.

Television had lied to her about so many aspects of her private investigation job, and she was discovering it had lied in equal measure about police work. Lorne was slumped at his desk with his fist against his temple like a kid counting the minutes until the bell rang, talking on the phone with someone to get warrants for yet another security camera. They were trying to track the wolf van through the city to its point of origin but they were running into roadblocks. Instead of lunch she got a plastic-wrapped sandwich out of a vending machine and forced it down as she checked rental statements against real people. Eighteen black vans had been rented in the week leading up to the accident, and she was starting to judge people's taste. Seriously, a black van, out of all the options available? Who would make that decision unless it was tactically necessary?

One thing television had gotten right, however, was the horrific coffee. She grimaced as she sipped it, held it on her tongue as she looked for a place to spit it out, then finally and with great reluctance swallowed it down. She took the mug out to Lorne's desk and placed it next to his keyboard. "It looked like you could use a drink. I couldn't find anything stronger, so this will have to do."

"Thanks, Willow." He took a sip and swallowed without problem, and Ari figured he'd been slowly working up a tolerance to the toxin. "We're not getting security footage from Whole Foods. I thought those guys would be more laid back."

"They are laid back. They turned you down because you're The Man, and this is where having a private consultant comes in handy. I could go by, see if they're more amenable to a private investigator." She looked around the room. "Where's Keighley? Think he'd give me a hall pass to go wandering around the city unchaperoned?"

"He went to the bathroom. If you hurry you might be able to

slip out unseen."

Ari took her jacket off the back of the chair. "If he asks, tell him I'm downstairs or something. I'll call you if I make any headway."

"Good luck."

She walked out of the bullpen and started for the stairs. Keighley appeared at the end of the hall and she resisted the urge to roll her eyes. He slowed as they met up, stopping her by raising his hand.

"Where are you off to?"

"I've been looking at those tapes so long I think I'm going cross-eyed. I wanted to head out and get a look at the actual scene. Plus Lorne couldn't get anywhere with the Whole Foods crowd, so I thought I'd try a little badge-less intervention to get their tapes."

"I'll come with you."

"That's really not necessary."

"Detective Lorne drove you to work this morning. Do you have your own vehicle?"

"I... don't live far from here. I was just going to walk..."

"Why? When you have the offer of a perfectly willing chauffeur?"

Ari felt her freedom slipping away. "You sure you want to leave Lorne here without anyone to supervise him?"

Keighley put his hand on her elbow and turned around to escort her to the stairs. "Oh, you're far more interesting to watch than Detective Lorne. Come on, it'll be fun. A little fresh air will do us both good. We can get to know each other a little better."

"Oh, yay."

Keighley sent a text to Lorne explaining where he would be and then returned the phone to his pocket. "So, Ariadne Willow. That's quite a peculiar name. Not exactly a hunter name."

"I was raised by my mother, like I said. She used her maiden name. As for Ariadne... I don't know. Maybe she just liked labyrinths."

Keighley laughed. "Seems reasonable enough I suppose. This is my car."

"Really? The non-descript sedan? Consider me shocked. Am I driving or are you?"

He gestured at the passenger side of the car and she got inside. "So I'm an open book to you, Keighley. You know I'm a private investigator, my sordid parentage, you know I'm gay..."

"I actually didn't know that."

"Well, that's one more for the checkbox. You, though, I don't even know your first name. Why is Lorne answering to you? Are you some bigwig with the police department?"

For a moment she thought he wasn't going to answer. Finally he exhaled sharply and said, "I suppose it's only fair that you get to know something about me if we're going to be spending time together. My first name is Jacob, but I would prefer if you continued to call me Keighley. It's the name I prefer. I'm not associated with the police department. I own K1, the outdoor equipment agency. I donate heavily to the police fund, and in exchange, I'm granted leeway in certain hunter-related matters. It helps to have hunters in high places."

Ari had heard of the company. It made sense for a hunter to own a company that outfitted people for weekends in the great outdoors.

"I'm also an investor in Orarian. I helped fund that wolfsbane that went missing, so you can understand my irritation with everything that happened last night."

"So one thing that hasn't been explained to me," she said. "What happens when February rolls around? Is there a bell that goes off, and we all put down our guns and go back to ignoring the wolves?"

"No. This is just the renewal of hostilities. We're honoring wolf manoth by taking out as many of them as we can, and once the month ends we'll focus on more long-term plans."

Ari tried not to react to the news. "Great."

There was a parking lot next to the accident site, a location Ari felt she knew extremely well from all the times she'd seen it that day on various recordings. He parked facing the road, which had been cleaned up and reopened at some point in the past sixteen hours. Keighley took out his phone and accessed photographs that had been taken at the scene. Broken glass, blood, tire marks, but no vehicles.

"Lorne's boss was probably pretty angry he left the scene of the accident."

"He wrote it off to hot pursuit. Slap on the wrist." He looked up and scanned the street. "The wolves had to have been lying in wait. But even then, how could they have known when we were coming? How could they have even known which van was ours?

Ari assumed the men involved in the traffic tie-up on Fifth

Avenue had texted the information to her mother. If witnesses saw one of the men tapping on his phone, they would assume he was calling 911 or a lawyer. A quick description of the van with a warning of when to look out for it was all it would take. She didn't feel like suggesting it to him in case that string ended up leading them to Gwen and Milo.

"Your assistant... secretary? Whatever she is. She called you with a warning about that car accident not long before it happened. How did she know?"

Ari shrugged. "No idea. I haven't spoken with her since yesterday. My phone got busted in the accident. I didn't have time to swing by the office this morning since someone decided to be an early bird. I'll be sure to ask her the next time I see her."

"Hm." He rubbed his top lip. "She's not a hunter, right?"

"No. I've been keeping her out of this thing as much as I can."

"And yet she stumbled over a vital piece of information mere moments before it became relevant. Maybe the reason you haven't spoken with her is because the wolves have her. There's a chance they discovered your true nature and they're using her against us."

Ari shook her head. "I find that hard to believe. Dale would have found some way to warn me."

"I suppose so. Still, it's very peculiar." He shifted in his seat and reached into his jacket pocket. "Do you have a theory? Some idea how the wolves got the upper hand on someone like Detective Lorne?"

"I think they're smarter than we give them credit for. We like to pretend they're animals, but they're people the same as we are." He looked at her and she was forced to shrug. "Okay, maybe not. But they definitely aren't dumb animals. They have the same instincts and the same analytical mind we do. They plot, they plan, they create contingencies. The only real difference is they can smell us and we can't smell them."

Keighley nodded. "True. Although there are ways to spot a wolf in human's clothing."

"Oh? Lorne hasn't mentioned any."

"Ah, Lorne's young. The ability comes with experience. You start to notice things that you would normally discount as eccentricities. A pretty young woman who wears a dog collar, for instance." Ari looked at him but he kept his face forward to look out the windshield. "A woman who is referred to as a werewolf over a police wire, who calls her detective agency 'Bitches.'" He looked at her and raised an eyebrow. "Everything about you screams 'wolf', Ariadne."

She met his gaze without blinking. "And how exactly does one prove they aren't a werewolf? Not changing into a wolf? I'm proving that right now. I've been proving it every second I've been in your sight." She smiled sweetly. "I think you're just a hammer, Mr. Keighley. You've been looking for nails so long you're starting to see them everywhere."

"That might very well be true. And I would like to think Detective Lorne hasn't worked with you for over a year without noticing some of these traits. He would have to be a piss-poor detective and a pathetic excuse for a hunter if he was going around fawning over a wolf. Can you imagine?" He laughed. "It's very difficult to prove a negative. But there are ways to confirm something you know to be true. Lots of things are genetic, Miss Willow, so I just have to ask... how is Gwen?"

Ari reached for the car door, but Keighley was faster. He shoved something against the soft skin of her side and pulled the trigger. Every muscle in her body went rigid, her feet kicking out against the floor as her shoulders pressed back against the seat. Her head rocked back as he held the Taser against her, taking away her ability to move or think about anything other than the pain and fear as she realized she was being electrocuted. When he pulled the weapon away she collapsed, helpless and dazed, her senses swimming as she struggled to stay awake.

"I noticed it the first time I saw you," Keighley said, his voice echoing as if she had a glass bowl over her head. "You look just like your mother did at your age..."

It was the last thing Ari heard before she hit her head on the window and let herself slip into the darkness.

CHAPTER TEN

MIA AND Hannah arrived at Milo's house a little before dark. They took Hannah to the upstairs bedroom, which they had rearranged so that the bed was near the window. She propped herself up on pillows, wincing as her stitches pulled, but she assured everyone she could handle herself. It was Milo who suggested driving Dale home to get a change of clothes, and Dale gratefully accepted the offer. She didn't know how long Gwen planned to hold the fort, but she would need a few outfits regardless of how long they ended up in the house.

She chuckled as Milo drove her across town. "You know, this is the second time in the space of a couple of months I'll be staying at your house."

"Damn, you're right. Wow. I've had girlfriends who didn't live with me as much as you do. Have you tried calling Ari again? It's only fitting that she moves in with you."

"I tried before we left. Still no answer."

Milo said, "I'm sure she's just..."

"Yeah," Dale said. "Probably fine. Just hectic and busy..." She looked out the window and then had an idea. "Do you mind swinging by the office if there aren't any messages at home? She may not have been able to get through to my phone, but she might have left a message there."

"Sure thing."

Milo waited in the car while Dale went upstairs. To her relief, the bed was slept in and there were dishes in the sink. Ari had been home, had spent the night in her own bed, and that was telling enough to put her mind at ease. She was looking for a note when she spotted the shattered phone sitting on the coffee table. Suddenly every missed call made sense, and the anxiety she'd been nursing flew away like a startled bird let out of the cage.

With her worries slightly abated, she focused on preparing for her sleepover at Milo's. She tossed a few random outfits into an overnight bag, retrieved some toiletries from the bathroom, and found a piece of paper that would stand out when she hung it on the bedroom door.

"Ariadne: Your poor phone!! I'll get you a new one ASAP. We're at Milo's house. Please come stay with us. Your mother is there, but don't let that keep you away. Love you, puppy. Dale."

She turned out the lights and went back downstairs. Milo watched her cross the sidewalk and offered a hopeful smile. "You look chipper."

"Ari spent the night here. She hasn't answered her phone because she left it upstairs with a shattered screen. It's almost like someone, or some wolf, tackled her to the asphalt last night."

"Whoops."

"Yeah, whoops. It's okay. Better than the alternative, I guess."

"Do you still want to stop by the office?"

"Yeah. I should probably go through the messages and check the mail. I was kind of hoping we could get back to a normal caseload despite wolf manoth, but it's not looking likely. I'm starting to think normal is something we passed a long time ago."

"Things will calm down. The hunters are just... running a little wild."

"You call drugging every wolf in the Pacific Northwest and inciting all these horrific murders is just running a little wild."

Milo shrugged. "It's horrific, yeah. But they've been cooped up all their lives. We just have to hold our own through this first little bit and then we'll have a chance to make up our losses."

"You really believe that?"

"I have to," Milo said softly. "Because otherwise it means we're prey, for now and forever, and I don't know how I'd handle that."

That left Dale at a loss for words, so she let the car fall into silence. Milo turned the corner toward the office and parked. Milo elected to come in rather than waiting in the cold car, and Dale found the right key as they went inside. She was looking down at her key ring, so Milo was the first to see the message. She grabbed Dale's arm and stopped her from getting closer to the door, and Dale froze when she saw what had alarmed her.

The word WOLF was painted across the Bitches logo, still wet and dripping down the glass. Something was hanging on the doorknob, and Milo moved closer to take it off. It was a simple loop of brown leather with a silver clasp, and she frowned as she held it up. Dale's eyes were wide, her face pale, and she swallowed the lump in her throat.

"It's Ari's collar." She hugged herself to try the tremors from being obvious, but her knees betrayed her. She swayed to one side and Milo caught her before she could fall. "They have Ari," Dale said. "They have Ari, they know she's a wolf. They have her, Milo."

Milo guided Dale's head to her shoulder and held her tightly. "They do. But we're not going to let them keep her."

The genial atmosphere in Milo's kitchen vanished like a switch had been flipped as soon as Milo reported what had happened. "They have Ari. They left her collar at the offices and painted 'wolf' on the door. They found her out and they're letting us know."

Gwen looked at Dale and then held out her hand for the collar. Milo handed it over, and Gwen stood up. She walked to Dale, placed the collar in her hand, and then forced her to close her fingers over it. Dale watched with detached interest and then looked up to meet the disarmingly bright eyes Ari had inherited.

"You are going to give this back to my daughter. Understood?"

Dale nodded. "Yes, ma'am."

She turned to Milo. "What else do we know?" Before Milo could respond, Gwen's cell phone rang. She took it out of her pocket and saw it was from a blocked number before she answered. She put the call on speaker. "Who is this?"

"You made it very easy for me to find you, Gwen. Phone listed under your maiden name, unless of course you never married. How sad. And you should tell those girls of yours they should be better about spotting a tail the next time you send them out on an errand."

Milo mouthed a curse and ran back to the front of the house. Tarun and Hannah hadn't sent up an alarm but they couldn't be too careful.

Gwen had become rooted to the floor, her eyes locked on the far side of the kitchen, her jaw tight. The voice came back and Gwen flinched, then grimaced at her reaction.

"Are you there? Do you recognize my voice, Gwenny?"

Her eyes were cold, and her words were clipped. Hearing it, Dale was reminded of how cold and inhuman Gwyneth Willow had seemed when they first met. The woman who had frightened her was back in full force, and whoever the mystery caller was, Dale almost pitied him if Gwen ever got her hands on him. "I'm here, Jake."

"Good. I'm sure your girls found the little message I left. I'm very upset, Gwen. I can't believe you never told me."

"Well, I couldn't be certain."

"Of course you could. I was the only one in the proper position that night, as it were. You would have known the second you knew you were pregnant. And then once she was born... I mean, she's the spitting image. The jaw is definitely mine. You must have seen me every time you looked at her. There's no doubt this girl is a Keighley. We made a beautiful girl, Gwen."

Dale covered her mouth and Gwen closed her eyes. Milo came back and shook her head, reporting that the street outside was clear.

"Shame that she took after her mama, though. I was hoping she'd be spared those disgusting dog genetics. But that's all right, I guess."

"If you've hurt her, so help me..."

Keighley said, "Don't threaten me, Gwen. Right now, Ariadne is resting... well, not comfortably, but she's in one piece. If you start making me angry I might take it out on her. I always suspected I would be a strict father. I wish you hadn't deprived me of finding out for myself."

"She's not your daughter. You were just a deliveryman for genetic material. Ariadne is mine. I raised her, I..."

"She hates you. I can see it in her eyes when she talks about you. Even if the stories about her parents were lies, the emotion was true. So don't play the super-parent whose child is in trouble. I saw the house where you and the wolves are holed up, and I know I wouldn't have made much progress trying to break in on my own. I could always come back with my friends, I suppose. But I could also make things easy for us both.

"You have the wolfsbane. In terms of price and rarity, that is worth far more than the life of one girl. Bring me the coolers, every single one of them, and I'll trade you. Ariadne for the wolfsbane. I promise you won't come to any harm during the transfer."

"Go to hell."

Everyone in the room looked at Dale, who stepped closer to the phone.

"Was that Miss Frye?"

"Yeah," Dale said, stepping closer to the phone. "And I said go to hell. Ari would never agree to that plan. In fact, you know what? If you're asking us to choose her over every wolf in Seattle, I think she would gladly take whatever you're threatening over a swap. She would give her life to protect her people, and we're going to honor that choice. So fuck you. Fuck you and your fucking graffiti. No deal."

Keighley chuckled without humor. "Gwen, are you going to let this little human girl gamble with our daughter's life this way?"

"She was never your daughter," Gwen said, eyes locked on Dale's. "And the truth is, Ariadne ran away from me and ended up in Miss Frye's arms. Her decision takes precedence. So fuck you, Jake. Give our love to Ariadne."

She disconnected the call.

Dale took a deep breath and closed her eyes. "I need to throw up."

Milo guided her to the kitchen sink. When she was finished purging, she cupped her hand under the water to splash her face and rinse out her mouth. Milo stayed by her side and rubbed between her shoulders until she pushed up off the edge of the sink.

"What did I just do?"

"The right thing," Gwen said. "I believe that's exactly what Ariadne would have said. Never doubt that, no matter what happens."

Dale whispered, "No matter what happens." The phrase of course prompted her to think of all the possible outcomes, none of them attractive. "What if they dose her with wolfsbane?"

"We'll cross that bridge when we get to it," Owen said. He had stood up during the phone call and still hadn't sat down. "I think it's up to one of us to say this since we don't know Ariadne, but we have to consider her a loss. Either they'll kill her outright, or drug her with wolfsbane and use her to make a point. We can hope for a best-case scenario, but I think it's more likely she's already gone."

"Christ, Owen," Paige muttered, glaring at her husband. "You could sugarcoat it a little. This is Dale's girl we're talking about. She's the one who saved Hannah's life..."

"And I'm grateful to her for that. Truly, I am. But just because she risked herself to save Mia's girl doesn't mean it'll work out for her."

Benji said, "You might could be a little more diplomatic in front of her fucking partner and her mother."

"This is war," Owen said softly. "And we're not going to gain any points by crossing our fingers. If we can save Ariadne, great, we should try. But that shouldn't be the goal. The hunters know where we are now. They know we have the wolfsbane. We don't have the luxury of distracting ourselves with rescue plans when we could have the entire brunt of the hunter's army falling down on our heads."

Dale pushed away from the counter. "I need some fresh air."

"Backyard," Gwen said. "Just to be safe."

Dale nodded as she went outside, followed quickly by Milo. Dale crossed the back porch and left the halo of the security light's glow, then dropped to her knees in the grass. Milo waited closer to the house, arms crossed over her chest and her eyes on the tree line to watch for anyone sneaking onto the property. Dale let herself cry, accepting that she had just made the decision to let Ari die. Not just die, she had been the deciding vote to let some madman rapist kill Ari however he saw fit. It didn't matter if she knew in her heart that it was the right decision, that it was exactly what Ari would have told her to do, all that mattered was that she'd said the words and delivered Ari's death sentence.

After a few minutes, when she had moved her hands to her thighs and was hunched forward like a lawn ornament of a praying angel, Milo finally crossed over to stand behind her.

"We'll get her back."

"No. Owen was right. We can't waste energy on that, not right now." She sniffled and wiped her cheeks. She looped Ari's collar around her wrist, using the first hole to make it as snug as possible. It fell down around the meaty part of her hand like a slender bangle. "We're not going to focus on rescuing her because she's got that covered. Anything we do would just get in her way or screw up her plans. Ari doesn't need us distracted."

Milo chuckled. "Sounds like her." She offered her hand. "C'mon. Let's go back inside. Owen will feel terrible if he thinks you're out here crying because of him."

"Can we let him feel terrible for a few more minutes?"

"Yeah." Milo withdrew her hand and sat down in the grass next to her. "Hell, let's give him a half hour. Bastard deserves it." She put her arm around Dale's shoulders, and Dale rested her head on Milo's shoulder. "Ariadne is tough. And when she comes back, she's going to be proud of how brave you were just now. Hell, I'm proud. I couldn't have done that."

"I still can't believe I did it."

Milo nodded. "I'm fucking sick of this war."

Dale took a deep breath and sat up. "Then let's go figure out a way to end it. Ari's doing her part. We can't just sit around moping in the grass all night." She held out her hand, Milo took it, and Dale hauled her up. They brushed the grass clippings off the seat of their pants and walked back to the house to resume their plotting.

Ari woke without a clue where she was or why she hurt so badly. She was lying on the floor, that much she knew, and she could feel the wall against her right foot and her outstretched left arm. Her mouth was dry enough that she smacked her lips and tried to work up some saliva before she risked pushing herself up. She made it halfway and then dropped. One more thing worked out, then... she was not only hurt, she was weak as well. And she couldn't remember a damn thing beyond watching the endless loop of identical car accidents on a laptop at the police station.

She finally managed to sit up, though her head vehemently opposed the change in orientation, and she looked around to see she was inside of a cage that was bolted to the cement floor of an empty garage.

"Ah, hell, not again." She gripped the bars and shook them to see how much give they had. Most cages designed to hold an animal were surprisingly sturdy, but some of them could be knocked apart by applying pressure at the right spot. When the cage refused to collapse at her whim she focused on the garage itself. The room was freezing, and she could tell, either from intuition or some subtle clue that her conscious mind couldn't identify, that it was nighttime. She rubbed her side and lifted her shirt to see a light burn mark.

"Ow," she whispered.

A quick inventory followed. Her pockets were empty, and oddly she was also missing her collar. She assumed her captors were elsewhere in the building, probably close by so they could hear if she raised any ruckus. The cage door was held tight with a padlock, and she didn't even bother trying to pick it. She moved into a crouch since the cage didn't allow her space to stand and turned in a slow circle to survey the area.

She had been at the police station. She was reviewing the tapes.

She remembered the rancid coffee, the horrible sandwich... Her stomach growled at the thought of food and she wished she had finished the sandwich. She hadn't had anything to eat since breakfast, and by the strength of her hunger it had to be at least an hour past dinner time. She reached up to touch her neck again, surprised at how naked she felt without the collar.

There had been a car. She was driving to the scene of the accident. No, she was being driven to the accident site by...

"Keighley." The cold wave washed over her again as she remembered what he'd said when he was shocking her with the damn stun gun. He knew her mother, knew her by name.

The door to the main building opened before she could follow the thought down the rabbit hole. Keighley stepped into the room and smiled at her as he closed the door behind him.

"Hello, Ariadne. How are you feeling? That was a nasty bump you got when you hit the window. And I suppose the Taser didn't help things much."

"Keighley. A dog cage... really? That's the best you could do."

"Sorry if it's not up to your standards."

She gripped the bars. "It's actually not my first. Wolves like me have to deal with the occasional wiseass who thinks it's clever to put us in a cage like this. So. This is how you treat your daughter?"

He raised his eyebrows. "You remember that much, do you?"

"You said I looked like my mom did at her age. She was actually about ten years younger when you raped her, but I doubt she looked much different. I've aged well. So, Daddy, what's the verdict? Must be pretty disappointed in your little princess."

"On the contrary. You lived on the streets and avoided drugs to make something of yourself. You built your own business from the ground up, and you're in a happy relationship. Any father would be proud to have you as a daughter."

Ari sneered at him. "Yeah, but that pesky 'wolf' thing throws things off the rails for you, huh?"

"It does. We've often wondered what would happen if a hunter and a wolf had a child. The only couple of record was a homosexual pair, so naturally there was no resolution there. But you... you've proven it can be done."

"And the wolf DNA won."

He smiled. "Nice try. We did some digging once we learned the truth. You underwent a procedure when you were a baby. Nature made you normal, but your mother made you a freak. That's why you ran away from home, isn't it? She made you a monster. I'm very sorry for that. If I had known about you, I would have come back and taken you from her. You would have been raised as intended, as a hunter."

"No use crying over spilled milk." She looked around. "So what, were you waiting until I woke up to make me snort some wolfsbane?"

Keighley shook his head. "No, I was thinking we could approach this from an entirely different angle. Your mother did something reprehensible. She stole your birthright and turned you into something you were never meant to be. You were born of a hunter, Ariadne, and we can still make that right. Work with us. Wolf manoth is only just beginning. You can make your mother pay for what she did to you. And Dale, your girlfriend? She's working with the wolves, isn't she? That's not natural, either. She should be working with us. Humans, other people like her. You can be our secret weapon. Infiltrate the wolves and help us destroy them from within."

"So now non-hunters are your allies? I thought you just wanted them for cannon fodder."

"We do as we must. That requires sacrifice."

Ari said, "Sacrifice is willingly giving your life for a cause. These people are innocent and you're arranging their murders. There's nothing noble about that."

"Will you please listen to reason?"

Ari said, "When you feed me, are you going to put it in a bowl? It would be keeping with the motif, but it would be a little humiliating. I don't really think my mental well-being is high on your list of priorities." She blinked. "Sorry, you were babbling about something, but my mind was just so fixated on whether or not you'd be feeding me from a bowl or not."

He worked his jaw and stood up. "Fine. I didn't want to play this for you, but..." He took out his phone and touched the screen. "This is an excerpt from a phone call I recorded earlier."

She heard Dale's voice, and something inside her threatened to break, but she kept her face emotionless as she listened. *"I said go to hell. Ari... fuck you."*

And then her mother spoke: *"... the truth is, Ariadne ran away from me. Her decision takes precedence. So fuck you, Ariadne."*

"Oh, God." Ari covered her face. "Okay, Daddy, I'll do whatever you want, I'll kill all the wolves and I'll make rugs for you out of their pelts and woe, everyone is against me." She took a deep breath and let it out as a sigh. "One, if you're going for realism, you might want to actually use full sentences. And sentences with phrases they'd actually say. Two, wolf hearing, dumb ass. Even if I believed Dale and Gwen said those things, I could hear the break in the recording. Sloppy as hell, man."

Keighley closed the phone. "Just one more tactic I thought I would try. You never know what will work. But we do have one foolproof plan. If all else fails, we won't just kill you. We'll hold you down. We'll fill a bag with wolfsbane and cinch it shut over your head, and then we will throw your dear girlfriend into that cage with you. We'll record whatever happens next so you can get the full experience. Either way, Ariadne, your part of the war ends in this room in that cage. And no matter which side you choose, you'll end up striking a blow for the hunters." He smiled. "Sweet dreams, darling. If you have nightmares, Daddy will be right down the hall."

He turned off the lights as he left the room, leaving Ari alone in the dark.

Milo's furniture had been moved so that anything not blocking an entrance was positioned with a view of the street. Dale was seated in an armchair, arms crossed with her hands on the opposite shoulder, focused on the bend in the road so she wouldn't think about where Ari was or what she was going through. She was so intent on her goal that she jumped when someone touched her elbow. Gwen held up her hands in apology, backlit by the hallway as she moved to sit on the edge of the couch.

"Sorry."

"No, it's fine," Dale said. "What's up?"

"We're taking shifts sleeping and keeping watch. I volunteered you for the first sleep shift."

Dale shook her head. "No. I can't sleep right now."

"I know you think that, but you're the one who needs it most. You've been very stressed for the past two days, and it's capped by this news about Ariadne. You'll be a nervous wreck if you don't give yourself a chance to process it all. Please, for my sake, go upstairs. Get some rest. Just a few hours, and then I promise I'll send Milo to wake you up so you can take your shift."

Dale looked out the window again. "You called me 'the human.' Last time we met, in the offices. Ari showed you the collar and you said I'd marked my territory."

Gwen nodded slowly. "I didn't understand why my daughter chose you. I've never been with any who wasn't a wolf. Well, with the one glaring exception. I suppose it was a bit ironic. I had no issues with the fact you were a woman, which is most people's experience. But the fact you weren't *canidae* was mortifying. I was a little... disgusted by the idea, frankly."

"And now?"

"I wouldn't care if your parents were hunters. If you care this much for my daughter..." She sighed. "You've cared for my daughter more than I have in recent years. You've been there for her when I was absent. I meant what I said on the phone, about your choice taking precedence. I just had to get to know you in order to discover you're exactly the person I hoped Ariadne would find."

"Thank you. And just for the record, Daddy is a dentist and Mom was a teacher. Neither one of them showed any interest in hunting."

Gwen smiled. "Good. Now go get some sleep, Dale. If only so Ariadne won't scold me when we get her back and she finds out I kept you awake all night."

Dale slipped off the chair and stretched. She did feel completely spent, but she wouldn't bet on actually sleeping. Still, she would make the effort for Gwen. She stopped next to the couch and held out her hand, and Gwen took it.

"We'll get her back, Miss Willow."

"Good night, Dale. Milo said you could take the bedroom at the top of the stairs, first~"

"First one on the left. I remember it well. See you in a few hours."

Dale went upstairs and pushed open the door to the room where she and Ari had spent a few days during the blizzard that shut down Seattle. She didn't bother undressing beyond her shoes and socks, crawling under the blankets and propping up the pillows before she lay down. She curled on her side and looked at the empty spot on the bed next to her. In a way, those blizzard days had been some of the best in their relationship. No cases to pull Ari away, no late-night runs or middle-of-the-night rescues... Dale smiled as she remembered the first time it had happened.

Dale fumbled with her glasses, putting them on before she grabbed her phone and looked at the display. She didn't recognize the number so she nearly hit ignore before she decided it could be an emergency. The phone didn't let her ignore the fact it was fifteen minutes before four in the morning. She grunted and then cleared her throat. "Low," was the only part of the word she managed to enunciate. She tried to remember her name. "This is Dale."

"Dale. Uh... shit. You're asleep."

"Ariadne?" She pushed herself up. "No. I mean, what? What's up?"

"I sort of need some help. I went for a run, and now I'm up in freaking Windermere. The wolf tired me out and I don't think I'd have the energy to run all the way home even if I changed. I managed to get some clothes out of one of those Goodwill donation bins, since I don't have any stashes up here, and I'm using the phone at this all-night diner with the promise whoever comes to save me will pay for at least a cup of coffee and... shit. Why did I call you? Go back to sleep."

Dale heard the tremor in Ari's voice and imagined how terrified she must be. Almost ten miles from home, probably barefoot, tired and sore. She pushed back the blankets and sat up, leaning down to retrieve her shoes.

"Where exactly are you?"

"Dale, don't come..."

"I can't leave you out there. I'm glad you called me. Now tell me where you are." She found a pen on the nightstand and wrote the address of the diner on her arm. "I'll be there in twenty minutes. Maybe thirty."

"This isn't in your job description..."

"It is now. I just added it." She decided not to change out of her nightshirt and pajama pants and just put on a robe. "Don't worry, I'm on my way. I'll be there soon."

"Thank you, Dale."

"If you need me, I'm here."

Ari had exhaled sharply into the phone and then laughed. "Wow. I'm not used to that."

"Better get used to it. Tell whoever let you use the phone that I'm on my way."

She stroked the pillow. For the past five years, whenever Ari had needed her, she was ready. She had seen all sides of Seattle at all hours of the night. She knew how bizarre it could be to fall asleep next to someone only to be woken by a phone call saying they needed to be picked up halfway to Bothell. She knew what it was like to not be woken by a phone call, to instead wake up to pee and discover her girlfriend had simply vanished without a trace. On those nights she would sometimes surf the internet or watch TV just in case Ari called and needed help.

Sometimes Ari apologized for the burden or felt the need to make up for it with lavish gifts. Dale would take the half-days with pay so she could catch up on sleep, but beyond that she didn't feel the need for reimbursement. Late-night retrievals were just part of being in Ari's life, and it was a price Dale was more than willing to pay. She stroked the pillow.

"Don't worry," she whispered. "I'm on my way. I'll be there soon. I'll find you, Ariadne."

She closed her eyes and settled her mind, trying to force herself to sleep, wishing more than anything that she would be woken by a dead-of-night phone call summoning her across town to give Ari a ride home.

Chapter Eleven

January 4

ARI WAS on her back, hands laced over her stomach, staring at the ghostly image of the bars above her head. There was enough ambient light for her eyes to adjust to the garage after a few minutes, but she couldn't see details to the point where she could formulate an escape plan. Her hunger had ebbed about an hour earlier when her body decided food wasn't forthcoming. Now it was barely more than a constant gurgle low in her gut. The sound of the door being unlocked alerted her to another guest, and she closed her eyes so she wouldn't be blinded by the flood of light when they came inside.

"Sit up."

She cringed inwardly at the sound of his voice. Part of her hoped that he'd be kept out of it somehow, but that was just foolishness. She pushed herself up on her elbows and watched as Lorne unfolded a metal chair in front of the cage and sat down.

"Hi, Detective. You look pissed. Was there something I forgot to mention?" She pretended to think. "It's not the wolf thing, right? I'm seventy-five percent sure I told you about the wolf thing."

He glared at her. "Are you done?"

"Nah." She lay back down. "I could go all night. But what's the point?"

"Is it true?"

She laughed. "I'm sitting here in a dog crate, Kyle."

"Keighley could be wrong."

"Nah. A daddy knows."

"A... what?"

She sat up again, this time bending her knees to cross her arms over them. "Oh, he didn't tell you that? Yeah, it's a really romantic story. See, thirty years ago when my mother was a student, she met a dark and mysterious man. They had a quick and aggressive relationship, just one night really, and it resulted in a bouncing baby girl named Ariadne. Mama raised me alone because Daddy didn't leave any contact information when he was done raping her. You know how these whirlwind romances are."

"And your mother was..."

"*Canidae*. Yep."

He leaned forward and pushed his hand through his hair. "That's not possible."

"What, a hunter wanting to bang a wolf? Sure it is. You wanted to bang me, remember?"

"That was... God. I've never been happier a woman rejected me. I can't believe I kissed you."

"Well, now. That's just hurtful, Kyle."

He stood up and walked toward the cage. "The attack. You did that, didn't you? Told your mother and her mangy friends where we'd be. It was all you."

"Wolfsbane is a tool of biological warfare. It's heinous, and yeah, I was willing to do whatever it took to get it off the streets."

He paced for a moment before he settled in front of her cage. "I want to see it."

"What?"

"I want to see you change into a wolf."

Ari laughed. "Did you hear that I have to be naked? Go look at tits on the internet like everyone else."

He crouched. "No. I've spent the past few years getting to know you. I liked you, Willow. I trusted you. I thought we were partners. And now this asshole comes strolling in and says he kidnapped you and he's holding you prisoner in a cage because you're a werewolf. I'm having a little trouble believing that, so yeah. I need to see it."

"I'm not getting naked, and I'm not shredding through the only clothes I have here. Looks like you'll just have to take my word for it, champ."

"What did your mother do with the wolfsbane?"

"I've spent the entire day with you, Detective. How would I know what they did with it?"

"You're telling me you haven't been in contact with your mother or your girlfriend all day?"

Ari shrugged. "It's almost like they're trying to fly under the radar after causing a big car accident last night. This city is full of hunters who packed their pockets with shit to make her go crazy and kill whoever happens to be inside chomping distance. She's hiding, you idiot."

"And your girlfriend? I guess she's a wolf, too?"

"Dale? No. She's... blissfully normal."

Lorne stared at her. "That's disgusting."

She held her hands out. "Well, you guys gave us same-sex marriage, and you all said it was a slippery slope to people marrying their house pets. Who knew? I've got a question for you, though. You and Keighley are hunters. I'm a wolf. And this isn't me advocating the plan by any means, but you can understand why I'd be a little confused by the fact I'm still breathing. You guys aren't really known for your imprisoning skills."

"Keighley has plans for you."

"That sounds ominous. What kind of plans?"

"The kind of plans you don't have to worry about. You just have to sit in this cage and wait until we're ready to use you. You're a weapon, Willow. Now that we know what you really are, we've been digging around. Seems like the entire time you've been working with me, you've also been working with the wolves. Warning them, telling them to beware. Once we knew the right places to look we realized that you were making quite a name for yourself. The Chicken Little of the *canidae* community. We're going to make sure you get known as a butcher of wolves. The biggest serial killer your kind has ever seen. We're going to make you kill your mother, your girlfriend..."

Ari lunged at him, but Lorne was anticipating the attack. He grabbed her arm and pulled her tight against the walls of the cage, then put his arm through the bars and cupped the back of her head to keep her from pulling away.

"You're going to regret threatening my people," Ari growled.

Lorne smiled. "Maybe I get to see the wolf after all."

She bared her teeth at him. They held the staring contest for a long moment before Lorne pushed her away and stood up. He turned to leave, but Ari couldn't let him get the last word.

"How's your arm?" He stopped but didn't turn around. "Did you tell Keighley about that? Does he know you're a ticking time bomb waiting to go wolf on him?"

"He knows what he has to know. And I won't 'go wolf' until wolf manoth is over anyway."

"That's how you want to spend your last few weeks? Fighting this insane war, killing innocent people?"

"There's no such thing as an innocent wolf."

"We've been around as long as you have," she said. "We have the same rights you have. We've done nothing wrong, we just want the chance to live."

Lorne walked back to her. "This isn't your world. Your kind was supposed to be exterminated a thousand years ago. You were a... a wrong thing that hunters were supposed to put right. You're a branch of evolution that should have been pruned before you had a chance to fake civility. When the going gets rough, you're animals. We're the dominant species in this world, Willow."

"Why don't you let me out of this cage and we can put that theory to the test?"

He walked away and turned off the lights. "Get some sleep while you can. Pretty soon you're going to be so busy you won't have a second to rest."

The door closed and Ari's eyes, which had gotten used to the light, saw only darkness when the door was closed behind him.

Dale was startled to find someone hovering over her when she woke. She recoiled into the pillows as she tried to disentangle her arms from the blankets. Mia shushed her, hands on her shoulders, and then whispered, "I didn't want to wake you early, but Gwen insisted. Boylston Avenue... does that mean anything to you?"

Dale was still half asleep, but she recognized the address immediately. "Ari lives there. Why?"

"Come on."

Dale kicked back the blankets and followed Mia through the house. The lights were out save for a few lamps in the living room that created a surreal, dream-like glow to the house. Gwen was seated on the couch with a laptop open in front of her. She looked up as Dale approached.

"The eighteen-hundred block of Boylston?" she asked.

"Yeah. What's going on?"

"There's a fire. Ariadne's apartment building is on fire."

Dale crossed to sit next to Gwen on the couch. She was on a website with a live feed to police, fire, and EMT scanners. Next to the computer was a notebook where she had taken down times, addresses, and possible connections to the war. The last entry was Boylston Avenue and Dale tensed. Gwen reached over and massaged her shoulder.

"We think Keighley had people search her apartment to find out what she knew. Her contacts in the *canidae* community, anything that could lead them to me or where I hid the wolfsbane. Then when they were done, they just... they just burned it."

"All of Ari's stuff," Dale whispered, trying to think of everything that was being destroyed at that moment. There were some clothes in Dale's closet, and some of her books had migrated over in the past few months, but it was devastating to think of how much was being turned to ash. "God, that's just cruel."

Mia was standing off to one side with her arms crossed. "It could also be an attempt to draw us out. Right now they know where Ariadne lives, and they can likely find Gwyneth's house without much effort. They don't know we're here."

"Unless they followed us back from the office."

"That was a bluff," Gwen said. "They wouldn't have taunted us with the phone call if they knew where we were. They would have gathered up an army and broken down the doors so they could torture us until we told them where the wolfsbane was. I think Mia is right. This is a signal flare trying to get us to show our hand."

Dale said, "Where is the wolfsbane? I'm not entirely sure I was told what happened to it."

"Mia and I took care of it last night. It's a temporary solution, but it's safe for now."

"How long ago did the fire start?"

Mia said, "The fire department was called about ten minutes ago."

"So what do we do?"

Gwen said, "There's nothing we can do. Whether the fire is a trap or not, there's nothing to gain by going to check out the site. We'd only be risking Keighley or another hunter spotting us. We sit tight and wait."

"No." Dale rested her elbows on her knees, hands on her lips, and then pushed herself up. "No, screw that plan. Screw all of this."

Gwen said, "Dale, what..."

"We're going to sit here and hide while we wait for them to come find us? We're going to let them burn down Ariadne's apartment just because they found her out, and our solution is to cower and hide? Ari is sacrificing everything and I'm sick of letting her be the only one risking her life. I'm not going to sit here in this fortress and cross my fingers and hope she finds a way out of it. They threw wolfsbane in your faces and you took it. They kidnapped Ari and we're taking that, too. They burn down her apartment? That's the line. I'm not going to just sit here anymore."

Gwen stood up. "Where are you going?"

"I'm going to get dressed and then I'm going to find Ariadne."

Mia looked at Gwen, then followed Dale back to the bedroom. "I'd like to come with you."

"You don't have to do that. Your girlfriend~"

"My girlfriend is recuperating because you took a risk you didn't have to take. I'm a cop back in England and I'm a fair-to-middling bodyguard if push comes to shove."

Dale considered it for a moment and then finally nodded. "Okay. Let me change clothes and then we can go." She went into her room and shut the door, trying to calm her shaking hands as she undressed. She put on a black T-shirt under a dark blue blouse. She didn't know if she would be forced to blend in with the shadows, but she decided it would be best if she didn't stand out. She tied her hair back rather than dealing with a brush, placed the olive-drab hat Milo had given her on top of the mess, and stepped outside.

Milo and Owen had joined Mia in the hall. She looked at the wolves and said, "What is this?"

"You're a member of our pack now," Owen said. "We're not going to let you go off alone."

"What about the house security?"

Milo said, "Tarun and Benji are still here, as are Paige and Hannah. That's more than enough to raise an alarm if things go tits-up. We're not leaving the house unprotected, but we're not leaving you unprotected, either."

"Thank you."

Owen said, "I'm just doing it to meet this Ariadne once and for all. She must be quite a lady if so many people are willing to risk their skins for her."

"She is," Dale said. "And thank you."

They filed back into the living room, where Gwen had apparently been filled in about the plan. She looked up from the computer and stood, brushing her hands over her slacks before she said, "This is the plan I should have come up with in the first place.

Hiding was a knee-jerk reaction. I'm embarrassed that I offered it at all. Go. Bring my girls back in one piece."

"Your girls?" Dale said.

"I wasn't talking to you. Milo... bring both of my girls home."

Dale blinked back her tears as Milo promised. Gwen rounded the table, pushed up Dale's cap, and kissed her forehead.

"Be safe, Dale."

"I will, Gwen."

"The same goes for all of you. This pack has sacrificed enough for this war. It's time the bloodshed ends."

Owen led them into the garage where they'd stored their weapons from the van siege. He offered her a pistol and she fought the urge to refuse. This was a war, and she needed to be armed if she was going to be effective. But the very idea of holding a gun was repulsive to her. Fortunately she was saved from making a choice when Mia took the gun instead. Owen looked at her and Mia shook her head.

"I'm not having someone out there without training. She can stay behind us if there's any trouble. And if there's a lot of trouble, she can pick up the guns when we wolf out."

Dale said, "I'm completely okay with that plan."

"All right," Owen said. "Have it your way. Where are we going first?"

"They hit Ari at home. We're going to do the same to them," Dale said. "She's been working with a hunter named Kyle Lorne. I know I can get my hands on his address, so we're going to pay him a little visit. We'll see if we can convince him to tell us what happened with Ari."

"And if he can't be convinced?"

Milo said, "Then we convince him harder."

Owen raised an eyebrow and shrugged. "Works for me. Let's go."

Despite being less than a mile away from Ari's building, Dale knew she had to resist the urge to drive by to watch the fire. They could see the smoke as they drove through downtown to the office so Dale could access her programs to find Lorne's home address. It was still an hour before rush hour, but the sky was pink and purple with the coming sunrise. It was the fourth day of wolf manoth, and Dale felt as if they were already stacking up the casualties. The time had come to wound the hunters a little.

Mia went in first to make sure no one was setting a trap for them, and a quick scan and sniff told her the offices were empty and unmolested. Owen eyed the office door and smirked when he read the name through the graffiti. "You really named your agency Bitches?"

"Yep." Dale booted up her computer. "It tells people right away that we're not messing around and we don't play with kid gloves. We can be just as tough as a male investigator. Tougher, if necessary." She opened a search program and entered Lorne's name. "He's unlisted, but that shouldn't be too tough for me. Mia, should you turn around...?"

"Not in my jurisdiction. What do I care?"

Dale entered her password and searched again. "Here we go. He doesn't live far from here."

Milo said, "So we go over there and ask this guy very nicely to let our friend go?"

"I doubt he's keeping Ari at his place." She had typed in another query. "Wow, Keighley is, like, cartoon duck rich. He lives on Mercer Island. I'm going to see what Street View can tell us about his house." She worked the keyboard again. Milo came around behind her seat and watched as the screen transformed into a bird's-eye view of a property shaped vaguely like Idaho turned on its side.

"Wow. This is kind of creepy. You can zoom in that close on anyone's property?"

"Yep. And yeah, creepy is a good word. But when we're abusing it for our own purposes, I like to call it morally ambiguous." Dale zoomed in closer. "If we were on the street, all we'd see is this little outbuilding by the street. The rest is at the end of a curved driveway and blocked behind tall hedges. But now we can see the main house here, and then what looks like a guesthouse with an attached garage. If I were him, I'd be keeping Ari there. Less chance of her overhearing something she shouldn't, plus it would be better for him to have her isolated. Unfortunately the hedges mean we only have one way in or out, and he'll probably have that covered with hunters. If only we had a wheelbarrow, that would be something..."

Owen missed the reference. "I don't know what a wheelbarrow has to do with anything, but we have something better. We have a trio of wolves." Dale looked at him and he shrugged. "People can't climb through those hedges, but wolves can. We can provide enough of a distraction that you can get in and grab Ariadne."

Dale said, "It's a big risk."

"Like you said. We've done enough sitting around. It's time to put our money where our mouth is. We're not going to just start attacking people without provocation, we're getting back one of our own. If the hunters have to bleed, well... that's their choice."

Dale stood up. "Okay. But we're losing the advantage of darkness. It's going to be dawn before we get to the house so we'll be doing all this in broad daylight. Not ideal, but I'm not going to let Ari wait until tonight."

Mia said, "She's waited long enough. Let's go get her out of that place."

Based on her hunger and exhaustion, Ari figured it was around dawn when the door finally opened again. She refused to sleep just in case her captors took advantage of her unconsciousness, but it was getting harder to keep her eyes open. Keighley entered carrying a dog dish and dressed in a new charcoal-gray suit. She could smell his aftershave, but it had little to do with her enhanced sense of smell; he was practically swimming in it. He waved the bowl and Ari smelled the freshly-cooked hamburger meat wafting from inside. Despite herself her mouth watered at the possibility of eating even as she knew she wouldn't risk swallowing anything a hunter gave her.

"Brought you a little breakfast."

"In a dog dish. Looks like I inspired you."

"Well, you're in a cage. The motif needs to be carried through to the end." He bent down and put the bowl outside the cage, then took a seat in the chair Lorne had left behind. "Detective Lorne tells me he requested you transform for him. You refused."

Ari shrugged. "Not really an exhibitionist when it comes to that sort of thing."

"To be honest, I'd like to see the transition myself. Believe it or not, I've never seen a person change into a wolf."

"It's not pretty. Bones break, sometimes there's blood... it's not something a father would want to see his daughter suffer through. Not that you're in the running for any father of the year awards or anything, I still think I'll just save you the nightmares."

"Suit yourself." He stretched out a foot and nudged the bowl. "That's some ground beef with a little gravy poured over it. Num-num."

"Yeah? And how much wolfsbane did you put in there?"

Keighley shook his head. "Not a bit. Trust me, when we want you to lose your head, we'll let you know." He stood up. "Eat, don't eat, doesn't really matter to me. Eventually you're going to want to get out of here. You won't get far, but you'll get farther if you're fed and rested. So come on, Ariadne. Eat. Take a nap. We've got time before you put on your big show."

Ari said, "Have you ever actually seen a *canidae* dosed with wolfsbane?"

"Yes, as a matter of fact, I have. There were tests to determine the proper strength. I witnessed some of the trials."

"Then you know there are moments of lucidity before we go crazy. I was exposed. I know what it feels like to slip. So trust me when I say that if you try to use me against Dale, or my mother, or anyone, I'll have the presence of mind just long enough to kill myself before I harm either of them."

"Big words from the dog in a cage." He walked to the door. "We'll see just how much presence of mind you have when the time comes. And we'll see how easily you lose that mind when you wake up with your girlfriend's blood in your mouth. Have a nice day, sweetheart. Daddy's got some business he needs to take care of. Wolf manoth is just getting started."

Chapter Twelve

7:55am

DALE USED her own car to drive over the bridge to the island, figuring that Keighley already knew who she was and how she was involved in the *canidae* world anyway. It was still pre-dawn when she parked down the street from Keighley's house and used her phone to access the map of the area again. She held the phone so Mia, Milo, and Owen could see the screen. "Mia, Owen. You're going to come in from the north, through these trees. If you run into any obstacles..."

"We run into obstacles all the time," Owen said. "We end up on a lot of private estates back home. Fences, walls, we can get around it."

Mia said, "And if there's automated security systems we can usually tell. There's a hum, or an electrical stink. We'll only trigger the ones we want to trigger."

"Okay. Just remember to be safe." She checked her watch and looked at the sky. "We only have about five minutes before the sun is completely up. The clouds will give us some shadow, but we're going to be doing a lot of this out in the open. Everyone still on board?"

Milo said, "Ariadne would do it for us."

Dale nodded. "Okay. Mia and Owen, you get onto the property and raise the alarm. While they're chasing you, Milo and I will rush the front gates." She pointed to the guest house on the screen. "Ari is probably being held there away from the main house. We'll need the guards as far away from that place as possible. So when you come in..."

Owen leaned over the seat and pointed. "We'll come onto the property there. We'll cut across the lawn to make sure we're seen, then cut back across to the south. You cut across the drive, east to west, right up to the house, Bob's your uncle. Then we get the hell out of Dodge as quick as we can, leave them kicking the bushes for us while you make a quick getaway with Ariadne. We meet up on the south side of the bridge and head back to Milo's place for tea and strumpets."

"Knock on wood," Dale said. "Okay. We have the plan. Mia, Owen, you're up. We'll wait until we hear your signal before we make our move. Make sure it's noticeable."

Owen grinned as he settled into the backseat. "Don't worry. You won't be able to miss it." They began undressing in the backseat of the car so they could transform.

Milo chuckled and bowed her head, scratching her eyebrow with her index finger. She glanced at Dale, looked into the backseat, and laughed louder. "I was just thinking that your reputation will be forever ruined if someone comes by on their way to church and sees these two stripping down in the backseat of your car."

"You don't know me," Dale said. "This could be my Sunday ritual."

Owen coughed out a laugh, but the sound transformed into a choked growl before it was finished. Dale closed her eyes and gripped the steering wheel tightly as Mia followed with a drawn-out groan. Dale flinched at every snap and crack, turning to look at the shrubbery through the window until the sounds faded and she knew there were two wolves in the backseat. She twisted and reached back to open the door for them, and the two wolves piled out. They were both gorgeous wolves, Owen's fur slightly darker than Mia's, and they had the same golden eyes when they turned to look back at the car.

"Have fun and be safe."

Owen chuffed, nudged the door shut with his head, and then turned to follow Mia down the street at a fast trot. Dale settled back in her seat and took off her cap to run her fingers through her hair.

"You really don't like it, do you?" Dale glanced at her. "The transformation."

"I don't... hate it. I just know how much it hurts Ari. I know there's nothing I can do about it, so hearing those sounds really grates on me. But I can cope. It's just nails on a blackboard."

Milo hissed and hunched her shoulders. "Ah, why'd you have to go and say that? Damn it, made me imagine it." She shuddered and checked the dashboard clock. "Almost sunrise."

"Yep." Dale drummed her fingers on the steering wheel and sucked her bottom lip into her mouth. "Do you think it's disgusting? Me and Ari?"

Milo started to answer, stopped, and then sighed. "Last summer when my granddad told me this plan, when he said it involved me marrying a human?"

Dale cringed at the memory but she nodded.

"I was utterly disgusted at the thought. I've been with normal people before, don't get me wrong, but the idea of any kind of relationship, even one just for show, I couldn't bear the idea. It would be like getting married to a man."

"Ew, do women still do that?"

"In some parts of the world, I hear," Milo said with a smile. "But then I met you and thought, well. All right. She's hot. I guess I can make do with that for a little while at least. But then I met Ari, and I saw you together, and I... I realized it could work. A wolf and a normal person could work. So I put my nose to the grindstone because I thought it was what my people needed to survive. But I got to know you and I realized it's not as easy as it looks." She rubbed her lips together. "I don't know if I'm totally in favor of mixed relationships. But I do know that you and Ariadne belong together no matter what you happen to be on a DNA level."

Dale smiled. "Thank you."

Milo reached over and rubbed Dale's shoulder. "We'll get her back, Dale."

"Your lips to God's ears," Dale whispered.

It was then that they heard a loud bark echo from down the street. They both turned toward the sound as it was followed by a chorus of other barks that rose in number and volume until it sounded like a pet shop was being raided.

"I think that's our cue," Milo said.

Dale started the car.

8:01am

Ari had spent the past hour theorizing her escape. She wasn't a big physics fan, but she assumed she could put her feet against the front of the cage, push while holding onto the sides, and tilt the cage so that it was standing on its door. Then she could crouch on the door and lift the sides while standing. Her full weight combined with the upward momentum wouldn't break the padlock, but there was a chance it could snap the weak metal hinges that held the cage in place. She was about to put her plan into action when the door opened and Lorne walked in, followed by Keighley. During the brief moment the door was open she could hear barking outside.

"Hey, sounds like the gang's all here."

"Don't worry about them. They'll be put down as humanely as possible. Unfortunately, one of my security cameras picked up your girlfriend outside in a car. Detective Lorne convinced me that we don't kill humans, even when they're working with wolves the way your little lady seems to be. There are some lines we don't cross. But we can find loopholes." He held up two objects that Ari hadn't noticed when he came in. "Not your run of the mill smoke grenades," he said. "We've been working on these for a while. What better way to thwart a rescue attempt than by having the damsel in distress kill her saviors?"

"You son of a bitch..."

Ari tried to retreat as Keighley pulled the pin on the grenades and lobbed them toward the cage. One landed on top and Ari pushed her fingers through the bars to knock it onto the ground. It bounced on the concrete as it began to spew a thick cloud of sickly-sweet white smoke. Ari pulled her shirt up over her nose and sucked in as much clean air as she could before the smoke enveloped her. She heard the latch on the cage being unlocked and threw herself forward through the now-open door. Keighley was anticipating the escape attempt and grabbed the collar of her shirt, hauling her up and out before dumping her on the floor. She could hear Lorne coughing as the smoke filled the room.

"This is a very concentrated dose, Ariadne. I know you threatened to kill yourself if we tried this, but I think that was just a bluff. Wolves don't kill themselves. A wolf will chew off their own leg to get out of a trap. And despite my genetic contribution, you are a wolf, darling. You'll do whatever it takes to survive, up to and including killing those foolish girls who are on their way to save you."

Ari got to her feet but Keighley struck her with something heavy that sent her sprawling. She smelled the blood before she felt it trickling down her face, angry that he had hit her. Furious, even, that he had drawn blood. The smell overwhelmed the smoke and she began taking deep breaths, her back arching as she dragged her fingernails across the concrete. Her nostrils flared with each exhale and with a suddenness that surprised her even in her current state, the bone beneath her face cracked down the center.

"Detective Lorne, I believe that sound means you're about to get the show you asked for."

His voice was nothing to her now that the transformation was underway. Bones popped and her spine pulled up into an arch, her face stretching as the skin hardened into a pelt so it wouldn't tear. She heard Lorne say something but the words were lost as she pulled her knees up close to her side. She thrashed her head as fur erupted along the full length of her body, her clothes ripping as became something else. She threw her head back and howled through the pain before spinning to face her captors.

She felt rage. She saw the men who had hurt her, one who had hurt her mother, and she smelled her own blood as it continued to drip from her fur. Now it was matting the fur on the side of her face, running down to the side of her mouth where she could almost taste it. She wanted more blood, but not her own. She bared her fangs and lowered her head as she stalked forward.

Lorne was pale, his beard standing out against his ashen skin like soot, and he fled almost immediately. He left the door open so that the wolfsbane smoke could start clearing out, and she saw Keighley smile.

"Give my regards to Miss Frye, if you would. It was so nice to finally meet you, Ariadne." He turned and followed Lorne out of the room. Ari let out a growl as her claws scratched the pavement to gain purchase. She ran out of her prison and into a narrow hallway, following the cloud of Lorne and Keighley's mingled scents toward the exit. They had left the door open and Ari ran into the clear fresh air. She could only see red, could only think of biting and tearing and killing and tasting fresh blood on her tongue. She lifted her head and gave a low howl.

A familiar car sped across the grass, bouncing over the edge of the driveway. It fishtailed slightly when it hit the grass but the driver kept it under control. Ari was distracted by the vehicle's appearance, for the moment forgetting her pursuit of Keighley and Lorne. She paused with the car looming a few feet away, and both doors flew open. The girl who got out from behind the wheel was familiar to her, strawberry pink skin and red hair and a green hat. The girl in the passenger seat was familiar as well, but Ari could only think of attacking.

"Ari!"

"Dale, don't!" the other familiar woman shouted.

The pink girl ran at Ari, and Ari bared her fangs before deciding on the convenient target rather than one she would have to chase. She dropped her shoulders and pounced with teeth flashing at the pink girl running toward her.

8:05am

Dale had never been frightened of Ari's wolf. She understood that when the wolf brain kicked in, the thing that made Ari human went to sleep and all that remained was the wild animal. She knew that wolves rarely attacked humans without provocation and she had extrapolated that knowledge to Ari's wolf. It was the reason she never panicked when Ari transformed during the night. Waking up with the wolf was no different than waking up with a large dog. She'd never had the misfortune of seeing the wolf without Ari's controlling influence, had never experienced what the beast was like when all humanity was stripped away.

She cursed her own stupidity as she realized her emotions had gotten the better of her. By then it was too late, and the wolf had chosen her as its prey. She dug her heels into the grass to stop her forward momentum and brought her arms up in an X in front of her face as Ari hit her and knocked her to the ground. Milo's sneakers skidded on the dew-wet grass and she used the car to keep from falling over as she raced to Dale's aid.

Dale pressed the juncture of her crossed arms against Ari's throat and pushed up, but the wolf was unbelievably strong. It bared its teeth, snapping and growling as it tried to close its jaws around her face. Dale, eyes wide and panicking, pulled her arms together to make a tighter X that would cut off Ari's windpipe. Milo grabbed Ari from behind and pulled her up and off, falling on her back in the grass with both arms wrapped tightly around Ari's waist in a full nelson.

Ari scrambled and kicked free, twisting her head back and forth in an attempt to bite the attacker underneath her. Dale rolled onto her hands and knees as Ari bucked out of Milo's grip, spun, and dug her teeth into Milo's right arm. Milo howled in pain, blood splattering on her chest as Ari let her go and turned on her main prey. She lowered her head when she saw Dale on all fours, taking it as a challenge. Dale met Ari's eye and held her gaze.

"I know you're hurting right now, Ariadne. I know you're in pain, and you're confused, and you're angry. But you also know where you can go when you feel that way." She felt a tear on her cheek but didn't dare wipe it away. "You come to me. You come to me, and I don't know if I always make it feel completely better, but I always help. When you feel pain, I make it go away. When you feel alone, I'm there. I'm not your girlfriend or your secretary or your fucking therapist. I'm your pack. I'm your pack, Ariadne, and I'm here to save you."

8:08am

I'm your pack.

The words touched something deep in Ari's mind. She took a breath and caught Dale's scent, and it triggered her memory. Dale, whom she hadn't seen in two days. The woman she loved more than life, the woman she had defiantly claimed she would kill herself to protect. The tension went out of her body, her legs relaxing so much that she swayed to one side as she lowered her head and looked at the ground. She wanted to rip, to tear, to kill, but she couldn't kill Dale. She flattened her ears against her skull and dropped so that her belly was touching the ground. She crawled forward until her face was pressed against Dale's stomach, and Dale wrapped her arms around Ari's head.

"I'm here," Dale whispered.

Ari shivered violently and began to whimper, confused and disjointed, unsure of anything except the fact she didn't know what was happening. She heard voices, Dale and Milo speaking, and remembered the taste of Milo's blood in her mouth. It had tasted sweet, thick and delicious on her tongue, and she wanted more. She wanted to tear Milo open and spill all the blood she could, but she pressed tighter against Dale and breathed her scent.

"Can you help me get her in the car?"

"Yeah... Christ, she's got a vice of a jaw!"

She let herself be guided into the backseat where she promptly crawled into the floorboards and tried to make herself as small as possible. Milo climbed in behind her, and Dale got into the front seat. Ari barely felt herself starting to change as it was more of a release, the grip of the wolf fading as she was allowed to retake her human form. Milo scooted forward and took a jacket off the front seat, draping it over her body before the fur receded enough to make nudity an issue. Ari remained in the floor but lifted up to rest her head on the seat. She was covered with sweat and felt as if she'd stood in front of a pitching machine for a few hours.

"Sorry about your arm, Milo."

Milo grunted. She had torn off the sleeve and had it wrapped around the wound. "You're just lucky you can't infect me with your disgusting American wolfism."

Ari threw a weak punch at Milo's leg. She looked between the seats and her breath caught in her throat when she saw Dale's profile. "Dale..."

Dale glanced back and smiled before she went back to watching the road. "Yeah, Ari?"

She grimaced as another paroxysm of pain caused her to fold in on herself. When she was able to speak again, she smiled and said, "Nice to see you again."

"You too." Dale's voice was tremulous, full of tears she was refusing to shed. "Oh, by the way, I'm billing this whole weekend as work hours. Plus time and a half."

Ari rested her cheek on the seat. "I guess that's fair. Send me the bill..." She felt herself slipping into unconsciousness, sleeping even through the brief stop where Mia and Owen got back into the car. She didn't wake again until they were halfway back to Milo's house. She looked up and saw a stranger looming over her, legs bent to one side to accommodate the woman crouching on the floorboards. The woman had a strong, square jaw and dark eyes that seemed to examine every aspect of Ari's character without moving.

"You must be Ariadne."

"I guess so."

"I'm Mia Cohen. The man in the front seat there is Owen Kiernan. We're friends of Milo's."

Ari nodded and slurred, "Good to meet you."

"I hope you're worth all this trouble."

Ari chuckled and let her head sink back down, fading quickly back into safe unconsciousness. "You and me both, sister..."

CHAPTER THIRTEEN

January 5

WHEN THEY arrived at Milo's house, Dale climbed into the backseat to help Ari into a T-shirt and jeans. Ari was able to get out of the car under her own power but she sagged against Dale halfway up the drive. Someone slipped under her left arm and she found herself being carried up onto the porch. Only once she was inside did she look to see that the person helping Dale was her mother.

"Mom."

"Hello, Ariadne. You've looked better."

"Well, you know. Weekends with Dad aren't exactly how I pictured them when I was little."

She faded in and out of consciousness, fighting the twists in her memory and thoughts as she was guided into a bedroom and put down in a bed. She was aware of time passing quickly, and of a woman seated in a bed across from her. Sometimes the woman was watching her, other times she was looking out the window or dozing. She looked Asian, her hair loose around her face. She was dressed in a tank top and shorts that showed off her tattoos.

"Nice ink," Ari said at one point.

"Thank you. It's nice to finally meet you." The woman said her name at that point, but Ari was already unconscious again.

She had dreams of violence, of blood and viscera. During the worst dream she woke in a cold sweat, choking on a scream, but she was pushed back down onto the mattress and held there by strong arms. She fought Dale, kicked and scratched at her, but she had enough control to never bite her. She woke on the first night with Dale in her arms and she spooned her from behind, sniffing the back of Dale's neck as she stroked her stomach through the thin shirt she slept in.

"I'm sorry."

Dale shushed her and Ari turned her head so that Dale's hair brushed against her cheek.

In the morning she woke nauseated and spent a half hour kneeling in front of the toilet trying to purge the wolfsbane out of her system, then spent another fifteen minutes in the shower. She was hanging her head under the spray when the curtain was pushed aside and Dale joined her. Ari turned and embraced her, holding her for a long moment as the water washed over them.

"I'm sorry," she said again, kissing Dale's ear. "The phone call, the last time we spoke, I said some truly horrible things and it's been killing me that I couldn't apologize."

"You didn't have to. I know you were just trying to protect me. I know you didn't mean it." She kissed Ari's jaw. "I have been worrying about the fact I didn't say I loved you the last time we saw each other. So... Ariadne, I love you."

"I love you, too. You've made me so proud these past few days. I heard you cursing on the phone. He tried to make it sound like you were angry at me, but I'm too smart for that." She grinned. "So what were you really telling him?"

Dale thought for a second. "I'm not sure. What part did he play?"

"Something like 'go to hell' and 'fuck you.'"

"Oh, that. He wanted to trade the wolfsbane for you. I knew you wouldn't want us to do that, so I told him to take a flying leap."

"You were right. How did Mom take that?"

"She took it well. I don't think she necessarily agreed with it, but once I made the play she backed me up. She said you had run away from her and ended up with me, so I got to make the choice." She hesitated before going on. "I know you've been working with her."

"I figured that would slip out."

"I understand why you did it. I would have tried to help, and that's not what you wanted. Going to her was a means to an end, and you didn't need me complicating it with feelings and trying to rebuild bridges."

Ari leaned back and brushed the water out of Dale's face. "I guess. I didn't really think it out that far, but I'm glad you understand. And I'm sorry I left you here to deal with my mother all by yourself."

Dale shrugged. "She's not so bad. She accepts us as a couple, so that's something." She rested her arms around Ari's waist, stroking the small of her back. "How do you feel? Any lingering effects from the wolfsbane?"

"I don't feel homicidal anymore. Just woozy and hungover. I feel like I could sleep for about a week." She kissed Dale between the eyebrows. "God, it's good to see you again. I can't believe it's been two days."

"Technically three. You slept through all of Sunday, pretty much."

Ari grunted. "How is Milo's arm?"

"Patched up. And to answer your next question, we have no idea where Keighley and Lorne went. His men chased Mia and Owen for a while, but they managed to get away without too much trouble. I thought it was more important to get you the hell out of there than try anything too risky. Owen went back while you were out yesterday and he said the house was quiet. No signs of anyone, not even security. Looks like they cleared out quick. I can't help but kick myself for losing them but~"

"Don't. You made the right choice." The shower had pushed Dale's hair into a wide curl across her forehead and Ari pushed it back behind her ear. "You were very badass, swooping in there to fight a ravenous wolf to save your lady love. I wish I could remember it more clearly."

Dale smiled, but it was a short-lived expression. "Ariadne, is this our life now? Hunters and kidnappings and rescuing you from bastards who drug you to attack me?"

"No. One way or another, we're going to find a way to stop this. Even if we have to move somewhere the hunters won't think to look for us."

Dale said, "I hear Vegas is nice this time of year."

Ari grinned and tilted Dale's head back to kiss her lips. "Does Mom still have the wolfsbane?"

"Yeah. She said it's in a secure place, but we still don't know what we're going to do with it."

"Okay. I think I might have an idea." She shut off the water and they toweled each other off. Once they were out of the tub,

Dale picked up the collar she'd been wearing since she found it on the office door. Ari smiled. "I was wondering where that went. How'd you end up with it?"

"Keighley used it to let us know he had you. Want me to put it on you?"

"More than anything." Ari moved her hair out of the way, and Dale slipped the collar around her neck. She bit her bottom lip as she fastened the clasp. Once it was on she reached up and stroked the leather. "That's more like it."

Dale smiled and stepped away from her to take her clothes off the hook. Ari had some clean clothes she'd borrowed from Milo, and she grimaced as she put them on.

"I feel like a little kid playing dress-up. The clothes are nice and all, but if we're going to stay here for a while, I'm going to need some clothes. Maybe later we can find time to run by the apartment and pack a bag."

Dale paused as she pulled her underwear on. "About that. Uh. After you were captured, Keighley and Lorne searched your apartment. We don't know what they found because, ah, they... they set fire to it when they were done."

Ari leaned against the counter. "They burned down my apartment? How bad was it? How much did I lose?"

"I don't know. We haven't had a chance to go check it out because they might be watching for us." She put her hands on top of Ari's. "Are you okay?"

Ari shook her head, but then she shrugged. "I don't know. Sure. Maybe. I mean, everything I can't live without is over at your apartment anyway. So I guess when this is all over, I'm going to officially be moving in with you. If that's all right."

Dale thought for a second and then slowly shook her head. "No."

"Oh. I understand. That's fine. I'll find a place..."

Dale chuckled and put a finger over Ari's lips. "Hey. I just meant that when I moved into that apartment, I got it for me. For a college student who didn't have any idea what she was going to grow up to be. I'm not that person anymore. I think we should find a place for us. We should find a place we can make our own rather than just plunking you down in my apartment."

Ari smiled. "Are you sure? If we stay in your place you can always just kick me out when you get sick of me."

"Yeah, I'm sure."

They moved in for another kiss but they were interrupted by a knock on the door. Milo said, "Oi. This is a big house, but you got eight other people here who would like the chance to pee sometime before lunch. Stop being romantic shits and free up the room."

Ari said, "We'll be out in a second." Dale chuckled as she finished dressing. She opened the door to find Milo leaning against the wall with her arms crossed. "Sorry about that. And sorry about that." She gestured at the bandage on Milo's arm.

Milo lifted her shoulder and affected nonchalance. "It was either my arm or Dale's face. I'll make that trade any day."

"So would I, by the way," Dale said. "Sorry about hogging the bathroom."

"S'awright," Milo said. "You guys have had a time of it this weekend. You deserve a little time. But seriously, out of my way."

Ari stepped aside and Milo ducked into the bathroom.

Downstairs, Gwen was in the kitchen with Paige. The other members of Milo's pack were seated at the kitchen counter or around the dining room table. Dale quickly introduced them to Ari, and ended by saying, "Everyone, this is Ariadne Willow."

"Ah, finally a face to put on the myth," Tarun said.

"And quite a face it is," Owen said, earning him a kick from his wife.

Ari looked at Hannah, who was the woman she'd shared a makeshift hospital room with. "I assume you were the one who got shot during the attack."

"I was. Hannah Milsap." They shook hands. "I owe my life to your girl."

"So do I." Ari looked at her mother, still amazed to be in the same room with her after all these years. "Dale said you were trying to figure out what to do with the wolfsbane."

Gwen nodded. "It's far too much to just bury and hope no one finds it. In addition, if we put it in containers that leak, and it gets into the water..."

Ari said, "Right. What about concrete?"

Owen straightened slightly and said, "Concrete. Huh. Would that work?"

"I think so. I had some time to think while Keighley had me in that cage. The hunters are putting it in food, in water, so we know it can be mixed with something else. We put it in concrete, let it cure, and that renders the wolfsbane inert. If it ever gets broken by construction or an earthquake, the dust would be harmless because the drug will have lost its potency. There's a construction site near my apartment... my old apartment, I guess I should say. Someone could get in there and mix the drug in with their concrete. Then it would be safely buried underneath a building from now until... well, until who cares."

Owen said, "It's worth looking into. We'd have to know a lot more about what the drug is made of."

"We can find that out. Orarian Group."

Gwen said, "Their security will be heightened after the stunt we pulled."

Ari shook her head. "Heightened, maybe. Impossible to break, I don't think so. The hunters are just piggy-backing on Orarian's labs. The people producing it probably don't even know about wolves or hunters, they're just being used for their facilities. I think I can get in and snoop around a little without drawing too much attention to us."

"You?" Mia said. "After everything that's happened I think you might be a little too conspicuous for any kind of undercover operation."

Dale said, "Yeah, and I don't like the idea of you wandering around somewhere with wolfsbane being produced all around you."

"So, what, we're just supposed to let you do everything because you're not affected by the drug? We have to take risks."

Gwen said, "I think you've taken enough risks this month, Ariadne. You need to take some time to rest and recuperate."

"I'm fine."

"You were dosed with God knows how much wolfsbane, you've been held hostage..."

Ari said, "I know what I've been through, thanks."

Dale put her hand on Ari's wrist. "Someone else can go undercover in the lab, Ari. With all the stress you've put yourself through because there was no one else, now you can share the responsibilities with everyone here."

Tarun cleared his throat. "I, um, I have a degree in biochemistry. It could get me in the door, at least. Be nice if it came in handy for once in my life. As for the wolfsbane itself, I doubt there will be much risk of exposure in the lab itself. It's probably created under the strictest of safety regulations, just like everything else that gets made in labs."

Owen said, "I've worked in construction. I can check out a few sites around town to see which ones are the best candidates for disposal of our little time bomb."

Gwen said, "I know you're used to doing things on your own, Ariadne, or only relying on Miss Frye. But for the time being, you're dealing with something much bigger than you. You have a temporary pack to help take some of the burden from you. Let them."

Ari nodded. "You're right. But I'm not going to just sit on my ass and let you guys have all the fun. Keighley is still out there, and Lorne has a bite that's not getting any better. If I have to step back from the front lines, I'm going to focus my energy on making those bastards pay for sticking me in a cage and making me a danger to my partner." She picked up a piece of bacon off her mother's plate, her appetite returning with a vengeance. "You guys focus on the war. I'll focus on taking down their leader."

Gwen knocked on the bathroom door and Ari opened it from the other side before cupping her palms under the sink faucet. She let her hands fill and then splashed the water onto her face. Gwen took a towel off the rack and handed it to her. "Are you certain you're okay?"

"Yeah. I just wanted to get that queasy feeling out of the way before we hit the road."

"You're still suffering the effects of the wolfsbane. You should be in bed right now, not going off on some vengeance quest."

Ari shook her head. "Is that your professional opinion? I mean, it's a little poetic that the only people who have ever dosed me with wolfsbane are my parents."

Gwen looked down at the floor. "I regret that, Ariadne, but I had to make you see how dire the situation was. I didn't think you would be willing to sit down and have a conversation with me, so..."

"So you decided the best course was just to drug me. No, I get it. It makes complete sense."

"I apologize, for what it's worth."

Ari sighed. "Small potatoes. But thanks. As for resting, the best thing I can do right now is stop Lorne and Keighley from getting away with their shit. I'll let you and the Brits handle the big-picture stuff, but these guys are mine."

"Understood. Let me know if you need any help. Especially with Keighley."

Ari looked at her mother in the mirror rather than meeting her eye. "It's bizarre to meet him after all this time. Especially like that."

"I can't even imagine. I'm sorry you had to go through that. I never wanted you to know him."

"Did you know him?"

Gwen was silent for so long that Ari almost let her off the hook by withdrawing the question, but she finally said, "Yes. We weren't friends, but I had seen him around. He and his friends spent a fair amount of time confirming they were right about what I was before they acted. And I suppose to work up the courage to actually do it. I thought they were interested in me. I found their attention flattering, not that I ever would have acted on it."

Ari turned to face her. "Did you act on it with anyone?"

Gwen blinked. "I beg your pardon?"

"No, it's not an angry question. It's just that I've never seen you date. I've never heard you talk about a past boyfriend or girlfriend or anything. I guess at some point I just decided you were asexual, but... I don't know. I guess now that we're being forced to spend time together, I want to know more about you. Was there ever someone special?"

"Before..." She looked at the sink. "Before what happened, there was someone I had feelings for. He was *canidae* like me, and we used to go for runs. We went to Canada once on spring break, talked of getting married once we graduated. After the... afterward, when I told him what happened, he tried to be supportive. But he could smell them on me. Deciding to keep the baby was the final straw for him. After that I didn't feel like dating."

"Thirty years," Ari said. "That's a long time."

"Well, it's not like I was celibate."

Ari held up her hand. "Whoa, stop, don't need to know *that*."

Gwen smiled. "That's one reason I was so suspicious of Dale when I met her. But she's proven me wrong at least a dozen times in the past few days. You're very lucky to have her in your life."

"Believe me, I know."

She pushed away from the wall. "I'll go tell her you're almost ready to go."

"Mom." Gwen stopped and came back into the room. "I don't forgive you for what you did to me when I was a baby. If you want absolution for that, it'll be a long time coming. But with everything that's happened the past few days, and knowing the whole story, it changes things. I don't know what I would have done in your shoes so I can't keep punishing you for making a choice. You were doing what you thought was best for me. And having seen the alternative,

I don't know if I could live with myself if you'd let the hunter side take over."

Gwen steadied her shoulders and kept very still, as if afraid of frightening away Ari's statement if she made any sudden movements. Finally she just nodded. "Thank you."

"It's been long enough."

Gwen stepped into the bathroom and hugged her daughter. Ari tensed at first out of sheer instinct, unaccustomed to displays of affection with her mother, but eventually she brought her hands up and rested them on Gwen's shoulders. She closed her eyes and breathed in the scent of the first wolf she'd ever run with, the first pack she'd ever had, and felt an unexpected swell of emotion.

"I've missed you, Ariadne. You've made me so proud, sweetheart."

Ari opened her eyes to blink away the tears. "Dale is waiting..."

"Yes." She stepped back and wiped at her own tears as she smiled. "We have a war to focus on. Be safe. Protect that girl of yours at all costs. She's extremely good for you."

Ari laughed. "So she tells me. I'll check in later."

Gwen nodded and took a step back so Ari could leave the bathroom. Dale was sitting at the kitchen island with Tarun discussing ways she could finesse an ID for him so he could get a job at Orarian without citizenship. She arrived in time to hear Dale say, "...not legal in the law-abiding sense, but close enough for us to get away with it for a few days."

"Don't let her corrupt you, Tarun," Ari said. "Once you're down her rabbit hole, you're in for life."

Dale smiled and slipped off her stool. "Feeling better?"

"Better, yeah. Ready?"

"Yeah. I'm going to figure some things out and get Tarun credentials so he doesn't raise any red flags when he joins up with the Orarian Group, but we can do that at the office." She turned to him. "I'll call you when the stuff is ready."

"Much appreciated. Thank you."

"My pleasure. I do it for Ari all the time."

"Are you sure your office is safe?" Tarun said. "That is where they left the message."

Ari said, "They burned down my home. I won't let them run me away from my office. If they're lying in wait, I'll smell them."

They said their farewells and left the house. Ari waited until they were on the street before she revealed her news. "Mom and I had a talk. I said I still don't forgive her for what she did, but I understood it a little more."

"Wow. How'd she take that?"

"She hugged me."

Dale smiled. "How'd you take that?"

"I'm not sure yet. But I guess if you and she are going to be all buddy-buddy, I might as well make the effort."

Dale took Ari's hand. "It was a big step."

Ari linked her fingers with Dale's. "Thank you. For everything. This past week, you've been phenomenal, Dale. If there was some kind of *canidae* Medal of Honor, I'd award it to you."

"How about you just stay with me, love me, and help me find an apartment for us to move into?"

"Is that all? Hell, I could do that with my eyes closed."

Dale retrieved her hand so she could drive. She offered to take Ari by her apartment, but she rightfully said that they couldn't risk being seen by any hunters who were staking it out. She was curious about her things, what had survived and what she'd have to live without, but the risk was too great. Dale parked outside the office and remembered the graffiti on the glass just before Ari spotted it.

"That's ironic."

"What? How so?"

Ari said, "The door already said 'bitches,' so the graffiti says 'wolf.' Usually it would be the other way around."

Dale chuckled. "I didn't think of it that way." She pushed open the door and Ari held up a hand to stop her from going inside. She sniffed the air, scanned the room slowly, and then moved to the door of her private office. Once she had declared everything was clean, she finally nodded. Dale shut the door and shuddered on her way to the thermostat so she could turn on the heat. Ari took off her jacket and went into her office, hung it on the hook, and came out as Dale sat behind her desk and booted up the computer.

"Get Tarun's stuff situated first. I want him in that lab as soon as possible. They probably put the wolfsbane production on the fast track as soon as Mom got her hands on their stash. I don't want them building up another cache of it. Once it's all set, I want everything you can find on Keighley. I mean everything you can find on him. I'm going to look over the stuff you found me on Detective Lorne." Dale grinned. "What?"

"Nothing. It's just..." She waved her hand between them. "This? You and me? After the past few weeks, it feels normal again. It's really nice, despite the situation."

Ari smiled. "I know what you mean. Now back to work."

"Aye-aye, captain." Dale turned back to her computer screen and got to work.

At noon, Ari volunteered to go back to Dale's apartment to retrieve some food for lunch and some fresh clothes. When she returned to the office she also had a small white grocery bag. Dale nodded at it as she took the food. "What did you buy?"

"I wanted to get rid of that graffiti as soon as possible. It kind of turns my stomach thinking of it on there." Dale nodded and Ari went back to the door. She took out one bottle of water and another of dish soap. She mixed the two in a spray bottle and then spread a newspaper out on the floor underneath where she would be working. Dale ate her sandwich as she watched Ari work, fascinated by the way Ari's muscles worked under her shirt as she scraped.

"Where did you learn to do that?"

"I did my fair share of graffiti when I was on the streets. It was something to do. I got caught a couple of times and had to clean it off."

Dale hissed through her teeth. "That must have been scary. All those shop owners screaming at you for defacing their property."

"Oh, no, I hoped for angry screaming. Angry I could deal with. I hated the ones who were... disappointed. The last shop I ever painted up, the woman asked me if I knew how much the business meant to her. She asked if I understood what it meant for her to walk down the street and see my stupid little drawing covering up the name of the work she'd been doing for years. I was ashamed then, but I understand now how she felt. It hurts."

"Yeah," Dale said. She looked at the remaining LF of the message. "Ariadne... I... when I suggested the name of the agency, I didn't think." Ari looked at her without understanding. "Bitches. I didn't think about what it might mean to you. The whole pejorative thing... calling your people wolves and dogs..."

Ari smiled. "Dale, we went over this back when Milo showed up. I'm fine with you calling me a wolf, and I absolutely love it when you call me your puppy. Hell, you could call me a mutt if you did it lovingly. That one is true, actually." She tapped the glass scraper against the paint. "This was hateful. This was a slur. So yeah, I hate looking at it. There's a difference. Meaning is everything, and I never have to worry about what you mean."

Dale nodded slowly. "I guess..."

"No guessing, Dale." She put down her tools and went to rest her hands on Dale's desk. She leaned down until they were eye-to-eye. "I've never met anyone who accepted what I am the way you have. You're the girl I dreamt of finding one day. I dreamed of finding someone who wouldn't just go with the fact I was a wolf but took it as part of the whole package. Someone who would make me a better person. I set up these goals and I was willing to settle for a seven out of ten. I would have settled for a C-minus, Dale. But you came along and aced the test without even knowing you were taking it."

Dale hooked her index finger under Ari's collar and pulled her forward. "You pass my test, too." She kissed her. "I needed someone like you. Someone I could take care of, but who could turn around and take care of me if I was the one who needed it. You're my strong, independent basket case."

Ari laughed and pecked Dale's nose and eyebrows. "Let me go. I have to finish with the door." Dale let go of the collar and Ari went back to work. She washed the glass when she was done, and Dale had to admit the finished product looked even better than it had before. Ari wiped her hands on a paper towel, folded the newspaper she'd used as a drop cloth, and shut the door with her foot. "Where are you on Tarun's stuff?"

"Oh. He came by and picked up what he needed while you were out getting lunch. I've been digging up dirt on Jacob Keighley."

"Daddy dearest. Anything interesting?"

"Depends on your definition. He started working at his father's company just out of college, climbed the ladder through hard work and nepotism. He seems to be good at his job, though. They have stores in Oregon, Idaho. They're planning to branch out into Canada later this year."

"All places with heavy wolf populations. He's basically a supplier for the war against wolves."

"Looks like. What about Lorne? Find anything?"

Ari shook her head. "Nothing we didn't already know, but I did remember one thing. There's at least one cop who doesn't like him. Remember Diana Rios?"

"Your ex-girlfriend?"

"Jealous?"

"Nope. I won, she lost, and I can be a gracious winner. What about her?"

Ari smiled. "She's a detective now. And married, by the way. She took her wife's name so she's Diana Macallan. When she found out I was working with Lorne she warned me to watch my back. I thought I'd give her a call."

"Is that a good idea? Lorne's probably got half the cops in the city looking for you right now."

"I can get around that."

Dale raised an eyebrow but let the matter drop. Ari knocked her knuckles on the edge of the desk. "Are you at a place where you can stop for an hour or so?"

"Probably. Why?"

"There was another shop I wanted to visit, but I didn't want to go there alone."

"You want me to protect you?"

Ari shrugged. "Sort of."

"Is it in a bad neighborhood? Should I pack my brass knuckles or my nunchucks?"

"It's not that kind of dangerous."

"So you consider this dangerous?"

"When I'm alone, yeah. It's incredibly dangerous."

Ari held the door open to let Dale lead her into the store. The front windows were covered so casual passersby couldn't see inside, and for good reason. The brightly-lit store looked like a typical strip mall shop, with bright fluorescent lighting and shelves of products ready to be bought. The difference was that everything in the shop was designed to inspire or enhance sexual intercourse. Ari eyed a display of rubber erections and stuffed her hands into her pockets, quickly moving past the front counter. Dale hooked her arm around Ari's elbow and chuckled.

"Do you need me to hold your hand?"

"No, I need you to keep me from feeling like a pervert."

Dale picked up a package. "Why in the world are we here now? I mean, I'm all for stocking up the bedroom and everything. But don't we have higher priorities than... oh, wow, this has seven speeds."

Ari took the box away and placed it back on the shelf. "We're not here for that. We're here for something that actually is necessary. It's back here."

She led Dale to a section filled with black leather accessories, whips and a wide assortment of padded eye masks. Dale glanced at a shelf of furry handcuffs and looked at Ari.

"I didn't know you had this kink."

"I don't." She stopped in front of the wall display and searched until she found what she wanted. "Here. This... it attaches under the mattress, and you can secure my hands and legs. I was also thinking some sort of gag. Not a ball gag, because I think my jaw would be killing me in the morning, but maybe a bit? Something that slips easily into my mouth, something I could bite down on..."

"Ari." The amusement had left Dale's voice. "What's going on, puppy?"

"The last time we slept together, I transformed into the wolf without realizing it. It's far from the first time that's ever happened. I still have the wolfsbane in my system. I'm fighting it, and I've been purging as much as I can, but there's still a chance, however remote, that I'll... lose control."

Dale stroked Ari's cheek. Ari leaned in and rested her forehead against Dale's, her eyes closed as she tried to push away the mental image she'd just conjured. Dale slid her hand to the base of Ari's skull and massaged gently with three fingers until the tension in Ari's face relaxed.

"So a bit? Something tubular, maybe? Something you can just bite down on without having your jaw stretched out all night?"

Ari sniffled. "Yeah. That's basically what I was thinking."

Dale stepped back and took Ari's hand. "Okay. Let's see what we can find."

CHAPTER FOURTEEN

January 6

THE ROAR of traffic echoed off the concrete passageways of Freeway Park. Ari paused in one of the dark corners and watched as Diana Macallan arrived at the spot where Ari had instructed her to wait. Diana paced around one of the blocks, eyed the entrances to the clear space with both hands in her pockets, and checked her watch before she finally took a seat and crossed her legs. She took out her phone and began tapping the screen and Ari stepped out of her hiding place and approached her from behind. She eyed the screen as she came around the block and confirmed that she was typing an email.

"You're not texting your pals to hold off until I show myself, are you?"

Diana jumped and rolled her eyes as Ari held out a cup of coffee. She took it as Ari sat down next to her. "Could you have chosen a more crime-ridden part of town to meet up?"

"Probably," Ari said. "I have to be careful. I don't know what Lorne is telling people about me."

Diana sipped and touched her top lip with her tongue. "Nothing good. Out of the blue, you're public enemy number one as far as he's concerned. I thought you two were tight."

"We were. I remembered you warned me about him so I thought maybe you'd be willing to help me out a little."

"A little. Maybe."

Ari sipped her own coffee. It had grown cold while she was waiting for Diana, but it was still warm enough to ease the wind chill. "I'm not asking you to break any laws. I just want to know what the temperature is like. Lorne and I had a falling out and I'd like to know what I have to expect when I pop my head back out."

"He's telling people he tracked down the van used in the hit-and-run. He connected it to your mother, Gwyneth Willow, and told everyone you were involved. You helped set it up and coordinated the attack with people in the other van. The video techs were able to identify your partner Dale Frye on one of the videotapes. Is it true?"

Ari bounced the heel of her foot on the ground. "Sort of. Technically."

"Ari..."

"Look, Diana, it's complicated. Technically, yes, I was involved. Dale was in the van, as was my mother." She wasn't concerned about the confession since she'd chosen the park not only for its maze-like construction but because the I-5 roaring by underneath would have rendered any recording device useless. "This thing that's going on right now is a lot more complicated than cops and robbers or good guys versus bad guys."

"Then explain it to me."

Ari looked at the small opening on her coffee cup lid. "Is there an inventory of what was stolen from Orarian?"

"No. They only said it was a proprietary formula. Since Lorne was in charge of the transport, they're talking about a lawsuit against him and the city of Seattle for losing it. If your mother stole it..."

"She's not going to give it back. It's dangerous."

"Help me out, Ariadne."

Ari sighed and straightened, trying to think of the best non-answer she could give. "It's a method of waging biological warfare against a certain group of people. The drug is being manufactured in secret so no one knows they're working on a weapon."

Diana said, "What do you mean it targets a certain group of people? A certain race, or...?"

"It's something to do with their DNA. It responds to this drug and it makes them go berserk. It's a... it's a werewolf drug. It sends them into a rage where they think they're werewolves, and it makes them kill. That's what happened on the first of January, it's what's been happening more and more often throughout Seattle. People being torn apart by their friends and relatives, killings with their bare hands. This drug is causing that, and Kyle Lorne is a member of the group that's spreading it."

"And you know this how?"

"Because I'm a member of the group that's affected by the drug. I've been dosed twice. I'm still feeling the effects of the second exposure."

Diana looked at her for a moment and reached out, brushing the hair away from Ari's temple. "You were exposed to a chemical agent?"

"Yes."

"Against your will?"

Ari looked at her and frowned. "Of course against my will."

Diana said, "Ari, come on. We've known each other way too long to do this dance. I know you used to be an addict. If you've fallen off the wagon, you don't need to concoct this whole conspiracy just to explain it to be. I understand. I can help you get~"

"Whoa. I've never been addicted to anything stronger than caffeine. I've had a joint from time to time, but nothing harder. Where'd you get the..." She closed her eyes and chuffed softly. "Well, I guess it's not really surprising you'd think I'm a drug addict. Homeless when I was a teenager, then all those nights you found me wandering around in a daze. It's the logical conclusion. Diana, I swear, I'm not an addict. This is really happening."

"I wish I could believe that."

Ari stood up and walked a few steps away. She'd known Diana longer than she'd known Dale. She sighed and said, "Diana, I'm going to have to ask you not to freak out when you see what I'm about to do. But it's going to take less time to do this and then deal with your reaction than it'll take to convince you I'm not insane." She took a deep breath and remembered Milo's lesson about changing just one part of her body. "Remember when I said that the drug affects the DNA of certain people and makes them react like they're werewolves? That's because they are."

She held out her left hand curled into a fist. The bones elongated and compressed, her fingers retracting as dark brown fur spread out across her knuckles. By the time Diana dropped her coffee and backpedaled away, a wolf's paw extended out from Ari's shirt sleeve. She cursed quietly and the transformation reversed itself, her hand snapping back into place with enough pain that she had to flex her fingers to make sure they weren't broken.

"Son of a bitch."

"What the hell was that?"

"We're called *canidae*. All those times you caught me half-naked and out of my mind? It's because usually I'd been a wolf five minutes earlier. Lorne is a hunter. His people are trying to make wolves into killers so they'll be justified killing us. That's what happened with Logan Ahearn. He was exposed to a drug called wolfsbane, it made him kill his friend, and Lorne shot him right in front of me. The accident my mother was involved in, they were transporting the entire supply of wolfsbane to a secure location. But we got it, and it's not going to be used to kill anyone else."

Diana had gone pale. "This is nonsense, Ariadne. This... this is..."

Ari held up her right hand. "Want me to demonstrate again?"

"No. Please don't do that again." She put her hands over her stomach and leaned forward. "This can't be real."

"It's real," Ari said softly. "Lorne held me hostage for two days this weekend. When Dale and some friends of ours came to break me out on Sunday morning, he helped expose me to wolfsbane so I would attack them. This is what's happening in this town, it's why Lorne is suddenly treating me like a terrorist. In his mind, I am."

"He didn't know you... that you were..."

"No. Until this weekend he thought I was a hunter, like him."

Diana straightened and sat down on the block again. She took a deep breath and after Ari had mentally counted to five, let it out again. She closed her eyes and furrowed her brow. "What was that word you said? Not werewolf, you said you were something else."

"*Canidae*."

"Lorne used that word the other day. Monday. He said that he'd connected the theft to the Canidae Coalition. This can't... mm." She stopped herself from denying it again and looked at Ari. She laughed incredulously and shook her head. "You're a werewolf. The strangest thing is that it explains so much about you."

Ari smiled. "Sorry to eradicate the mystery, but I really do need your help."

Diana put her hands on her hips. "If Lorne is really guilty of everything you've said, we need to get him off the streets. But we can't hold him accountable for a drug that for all intents and purposes can't exist. If we say he's trying to recover a werewolf-targeting drug, no one is going to take us seriously."

"That's why we can't do anything official."

"We damn well can. We can charge him for unlawful

imprisonment. You said he held you hostage for two days. The crazy falls on him in that case, if he claims you're a werewolf that stole his werewolf-go-crazy pills..."

"It's actually a powder."

"That doesn't... I don't care about the logistics of it. The point is, the man was holding you against your will. He's the one who has to come up with a plausible reason for that, and if he can't, he's going to jail. At the very least he's going to lose his badge. All you have to do is press charges and he'll never work as a cop again. So? Is that what you want to do?"

Ari rubbed her hands together. "We'll see."

"Ari, the only other option is trying to sell your crazy version of events."

"No, there's another option. It just makes me feel a little sleazier than I'm used to feeling. Is Lorne on duty now?"

"He came in for a little while but the lieutenant sent him home. He looked rough."

"Yeah, he would. Okay. Thanks for the help, Diana. I'll be in touch."

Diana grabbed her arm. "Hey. No, you don't get to do that. You don't get to come here and drop something like this on me, then just walk away. We're going to discuss this."

"We are. But not right now. We're on a really strict time table, and my people are at risk every minute we sit around talking. I think I can force Lorne to help us, but I have to go now. We'll talk, we will definitely talk. Maybe at that dinner you mentioned, with you and your wife. I really want to meet her. And come on... is this really a conversation you want to have in Freeway Park?"

A host of different emotions passed across Diana's face before she finally released Ari. "I can't believe I was actually starting to miss you. I forgot what a menace you could be."

Ari held her hands out. "It's not my fault I'm an interesting person."

Diana rolled her eyes and walked away. Ari gave her a head start before following her into the park's maze.

Lorne sniffled as he let himself into his apartment. He felt weak all over, each part of his body having seceded from the whole in order to air their grievances separately. He'd exhausted every pain reliever in his apartment and finally found the strength to trudge down to the corner store to refresh his supplies. The trip had taken its toll on him and he was practically sleepwalking by the time he finally stepped into his living room and found Ariadne Willow lounging on his couch. His gun was on his hip but he lacked the strength to even reach for it.

"Ariadne Willow, I'm placing you under arrest~"

"Save it, Detective." She took her feet off his coffee table and leaned forward. "How are you feeling? Achy and tired all the time? Can't get comfortable?"

He grunted and, though he meant to deny her accusations, he was attacked by a sudden bout of lightheadedness and swooned. Ari stood up and caught him before he could correct himself. She guided him to the couch and, as he sank into the cushions, he realized she had taken his gun. He watched with detached interest as she put it on the dining room table and then sat on the coffee table in front of him.

"You don't have a month left, Kyle. The full moon is a week away. Most of the mythology is bullshit. I don't care about moon cycles, but for newborn wolves? People who have been bitten? They feel the urge stronger during the full moon. Even if they've been able to fight it up to that point, when the moon is full they just completely give in to the urge. After that, it's pretzel time. If you're lucky the physical trauma will kill you. If not... well. The deformities aren't pretty."

Lorne said, "If you came here to torture me..."

"I didn't. Despite what you did to me, I'm not here for payback. This is bigger than me."

He glared at her. "What do you want?"

"I want you to help me stop this war."

He laughed. "That's not going to happen. Not on my say-so or yours. I'm just a foot soldier."

Ari said, "Keighley isn't. Huxley from the cab company seemed to be a pretty big player, too. If they give the order to stand down, I bet the hunters will listen."

"We've waited years for wolves to be open season again. Now that they are, we're not giving it up lightly."

"Yeah. That's big with you guys... waiting years for the chance to kill all us dirty wolves. But you're not taking advantage of it. You're making us kill ourselves. You manufacture that wolfsbane shit so we'll turn into slobbering self-destructive maniacs. How many wolves have you personally killed this week? How many wolves has Keighley straight-up murdered? I think you guys are too civilized.

Just like we are. Wolves have become productive members of society. Those who prefer the wild are out there, living in the woods, minding their own business. You hunters are the same way. Some of you armed up on the first day of January looking for wolves to murder. But the rest of you? The rest of you took the time to design a drug to make us dangerous. People like Jacqueline Ramsey put themselves in the line of fire rather than just killing in cold blood. Wolfsbane was an excuse you hunters needed, and that's all gone now."

"We'll just make more."

Ari smiled. "Yeah. How long do you figure that will take? You can make a little bit, spread it around, but you'll never get your whole supply back. You guys have been wasting the shit left and right. Spreading it all over the Bull and Terrier, infecting salad bars with it... I'm willing to bet the supply you have on-hand is slim to none. This war is a non-starter."

Lorne shifted on the couch and looked away, stifling a cough with a trembling fist. Ari leaned closer and took some of the edge out of her voice.

"You're going to die, Kyle. It's not going to be a good death, but you can make your last days count. You chose to become a cop. You chose to make a difference. Do you really want to spend what little time you have left trying to kill my people, or do you want to help me find a way out of this mess?"

He leaned forward and met her gaze. Ari saw that his eyes were bloodshot, his face under siege by a series of micro-tremors. "Let's say you're right and the majority of hunters don't want this to happen. They don't care about wolf manoth because the tradition fell apart or they weren't trained by their father. That doesn't change the fact that there are other hunters like Keighley and Huxley who have been waiting for this since they were children. They were raised in a cult mentality and taught that wolves are lesser creatures. Midnight of New Years was like a starter pistol to them. They aren't just going to lay down their weapons."

"That's why I need your help. I need you to help me convince them that this is pointless."

Lorne shook his head. "They won't go for it."

Ari said, "Then we'll take them out. We won't fight an all-out war, but we'll go after the people who are threatening our lives. Do you know how I'm living these days, Lorne? I'm buying my food from another state. I can't eat anything from delis or restaurants because I can't trust anything I didn't make myself. Last night, I had my girlfriend tie me to the bed with a gag in my mouth so I couldn't attack her if the wolfsbane you dosed me with took over in the night."

He took a deep breath and, as he released it, his entire body trembled. When he had control again he stared at her for a moment before speaking. "And why would I agree to help you?"

"Because you've been keeping secrets. Hunters and wolves are verboten, so you can't just flat out use wolf manoth as an excuse for your actions this past week without looking insane. All I have to do is tell them what happened this weekend. You kidnapped me, put me in a cage..."

"You're a wanted criminal."

"A criminal who wasn't officially wanted until after I escaped Keighley's garage. That's going to make your whole spiel look a little odd, won't it? Kind of like a personal vendetta rather than the result of any actual police work. You had me in a cage, I got away, and out of nowhere I'm your prime suspect in an ongoing case?" She pursed her lips and shook her head. "Hard to slide out of that one. Especially if I give them word that a few days earlier I'd rebuffed your romantic advances. You're going to look like a stalker, Kyle."

She could tell from his expression that she'd hit a nerve. "You wouldn't do that."

"Hell yes, I would. Even wild wolves don't attack humans on a whim. But we'll fight if we're forced, and we will attack if we get cornered. You're cornering us. We're giving you one last chance to back off before we turn on you. If you're smart, you'll heed the warning."

She stood up and looked down at Lorne. He looked as if he was going to stand up as well, but his arms wouldn't produce the strength to push him up off the cushions.

"That's going to get worse. You're going to start to feel like the only relief is to just give in to what your body is trying to do. At that point you might as well just surrender to the inevitable. I'm telling you right now there's no coming back from that decision. Make a decision you can live with before it happens."

"Live with," Lorne said.

"So to speak."

He nodded slowly and looked away from her. "Get the hell out of my apartment, Willow."

She picked up his gun off the table and brought it back to him.

"Don't shoot me in the back as I'm leaving."

"Don't tempt me." She handed the gun back and he slipped it back into the holster. She started for the door, but he stopped her by saying her name again. "If you weren't gay... and, you know. A wolf. You think I would've had a chance?"

Ari said, "I don't know, Kyle. You try so hard to be a good guy. I like to think that would have counted for something."

He nodded and leaned back, closing his eyes as his body shook with another round of small seizures. Ari left the apartment without looking back, tempering her pity for him with the memory of Logan Ahearn's body after Lorne shot him. She stuck her hands in her pockets and jogged across the street, walking to the corner where she'd parked her car. Dale was in the passenger seat fussing with the small GPS tracker they had bought but hadn't yet used. She got behind the wheel and looked at the screen. The tracker she'd placed on his gun would most likely be discovered the next time he cleaned it, but she was confident it would be live long enough for what they needed.

"Anything?"

"Well, we're getting a signal, but he's not moving much."

Ari said, "He's in bad shape. I haven't seen many bite victims, but he's the worst by far. I honestly don't know if he'll make it to the full moon next week. Even if he doesn't agree to help us end the war early, hopefully he'll still lead us to wherever Keighley is hiding before he surrenders to the inevitable."

Dale nodded. She wore a scarf pulled up over her chin and kept the brim of her cap pulled low over her eyes, ready to cover her face if Lorne happened to leave the apartment again. She was hunched down in her seat knees up in front of the steering wheel. Ari kept watch on the front of Kyle's building but her mind kept wandering.

"I've been thinking about our arrangement. I think you should take the PI test so you can become a full partner in the agency."

"What?" Dale looked up from the screen. "That's not... I mean, thank you. I'm not really angling to be a private investigator, though. I've been thinking about it since you brought it up as a joke. I know I have the hours to qualify, and all I'd have to do is pass the test~"

"Which you'd ace, by the way."

"Thank you, puppy. But every time I think about it, I think it would be a bad idea. We work well like this. If I took a step up, it would be six weeks, two months at the most, before I got bored and begged you to demote me. Or an alternative... if it works, we'd have to hire someone else to answer the phones. And you have a habit of falling in love with your assistants."

"Just the smartass redhead ones who are named after singing cowgirls."

Dale chuckled. "Seriously, I'm honored you think I'm worthy of being a Bitches Investigations detective. But I'm happy to do the paperwork, the nerd stuff as you once so lovingly called it." Ari chuckled. "This, hanging around in cars and waiting for something to happen, or taking pictures of people cheating? I don't need that. What I need is to be safe and sound by a phone in case you need me to swoop in and save you."

"I like that, too."

"What brought this up again? Is it about that phone call?"

"I called you a secretary, Dale. You have to know I see you as more than that."

Dale rolled her eyes. "God, Ari, of course I know that." She reached over and took Ari's hand. "Tensions were really high that morning. We were both trying to look out for each other, and we lost our heads. If you're really feeling anxious about what we said, we can keep that contraption on the bed and I can give you a proper spanking when this is all over."

Ari smiled. "Okay. I'll let it drop. But I want you to be a partner in the agency regardless of your status as a private investigator. The agency would be impossible without you at the wheel and I want that reflected in the arcane, strange web of ownership. I don't want the agency to be mine anymore. It's ours. It always has been."

Dale raised an eyebrow. "Moving into a new apartment together, now you're putting the agency in my name. You sure you want to go all-in like this with me?"

Ari sighed and brought Dale's hand to her mouth to kiss the knuckles. "I'm not tying you into everything. I'm making everything tied to you so you can't get away from me. The alternative is losing the agency, going back out on the street, working at Zeeks Pizza just to have a little cash in my pocket. That's if I don't freeze to death one of the nights the wolf decides to take me halfway to Oregon when I let it off the leash. You made my life while you were saving it, Dale, and if I thought it was the right choice for us, I'd ask you to marry me."

Dale stared at her for a long time. "If I thought it was the right choice, I'd say yes."

Ari smiled and raised an eyebrow as she brushed her cheek against Dale's hand. "That's good information to have. You know, for future reference."

"Give me back my hand."

"No." Ari put Dale's hand on her thigh and covered it with her own so it couldn't be quickly extricated. Dale chuckled and squeezed Ari's thigh through her jeans and accepted the theft as she used the GPS tracker with her other hand. Ari watched her for a while before she focused on the street in case Lorne came out but left his gun at home. It seemed unlikely but possible and she didn't want to miss him if he did. The plan was for Dale to be ready to follow in the car while Ari could follow on foot if vehicular pursuit wasn't possible.

She had worked with a partner while earning her work experience to get her license. It was a necessary evil but, when she moved on to her own agency, she had made a vow she would work alone like her boss and mentor Glory had. She hadn't anticipated how necessary it would be to share the load, how impossible it would be to do everything without help. She'd managed for a few weeks before Dale came along but there was no doubt in her mind it was a downhill slope toward failure. The only difference between crashing and soaring was the arrival of Dale in her life.

"He's moving," Dale said.

Ari looked at the screen and saw the little blue bauble had moved slightly closer to the bottom of the screen. Dale said, "It keeps going from side to side. Judging from the scale and the position in the building, I think he's going downstairs."

Ari climbed between the seats and quickly shed her clothes. Dale glanced back as Ari stripped out of her bra, taking the handful of clothes she was passed and looked to make sure no one was paying attention as Ari began to transform. Ari rolled through the transformation and dropped onto all fours as the change completed. She shook herself to ruffle her fur, bared her teeth, then waited as Dale reached back to open the door for her.

"Give 'em hell, puppy."

Ari chuffed, bounced her head, and trotted down the street. They had parked next to a stone retaining wall and Ari leapt to the grassy slope in a single bound. She moved through the trees, keeping the street in view as she moved into position. She crouched down and watched the front door of Lorne's building. As Dale predicted, he wasn't carrying his keys; he was smart enough to not risk driving in his current condition. He looked up and down the street before he lurched to the south. Ari gave him a good head start before she began loping after him.

CHAPTER FIFTEEN

WHEN SHE was certain she wouldn't be needed to follow Lorne across town, Dale took out her phone and got online. Ari was so focused on Keighley and Lorne, the men who had personally betrayed her, that she'd forgotten about the man Lorne took her to meet immediately following the robbery. Fortunately she had a secretary who was willing to pick up the slack. Dale smiled at the thought as she accessed the file she'd been working on the past few days.

Patrick Huxley was Lorne's superior in some way, shape, or form. He was the one who received the report of the accident so Dale figured it would be handy to know more about him. So far she'd discovered he was a bigwig in the Seattle elite. He owned the Alki Emerald Cab Company, a fleet of sixty cars that served the greater Seattle area. She recalled having seen the cars lined up outside the airport on a few occasions, and the blue-and-green cars were a common sight around town. He frequently made the news for donations to schools and education, and she found a photo of him smiling as he handed over a check to a teachers' association.

"Beware the smiling snakes," she muttered to herself. She dug a little deeper and checked anything connecting Huxley with Keighley. They were both well-off, so it stood to reason there might be some kind of affiliation between the two. Five minutes later she found what she was looking for. Both men were part of a business association that also supported the Police Athletic League. A quick scan of the PAL website revealed Kyle Lorne was a member.

Dale went back to the association's roster. "Huxley, Keighley... Beck, Vance, Levitt, Wakefield, Warwick." She chewed her bottom lip and chose a name at random off the list. The man whose name was in the middle of the list she found, a Mr. Colin Vance Esquire, who worked at Microsoft in some capacity. She read his title and job description and still wasn't entirely sure what his job entailed, but that wasn't important. What she needed was personal information about the man, his hobbies and affiliations, and she found a bio for him on a site for business professionals that listed his hobbies.

"Enjoys the great outdoors... I bet he does." She scrolled through his photo album and found a picture of him standing in a snowy field with a rifle resting on his right shoulder. He was decked out in the finest hunting gear, and clearly visible on the lapel of his reflective jacket was the logo for K1 Sport Gear. She checked the names of the other men and discovered they were also high-level, also loved the outdoors, and according to their online portfolios, they all seemed to shop at Keighley's sporting goods store. They all had ties to the police department. Dale tracked the information in a file and, when she was finished, she looked at the seven men she'd identified.

Two restaurateurs, a politician, a mass transit leader, a police officer, and the CEO of the Orarian Group. Dale could almost see the web between them, and she understood how they had used their influence to manufacture and spread the wolfsbane across the city. They had all the power and the reach, but the war had just shrunk from every hunter in the Pacific Northwest to seven men who were pulling the strings.

Dale sent the information she'd gathered to Gwyneth and backed up the file in her own email. She had gotten the addresses of the seven men and decided she would check them out while Ari was tracking Lorne. Her first stop would be Huxley to see if she could tell how he was dealing with the lack of wolfsbane. She would do reconnaissance on the other men she'd just discovered and, when Ari was ready to be picked up, the information would be available for her to do with as she wished. The wolfsbane was already out of play. Keighley was on the run, Lorne wasn't long for the world, and she had a feeling the other hunters were going to quickly lose their will to fight once it became clear the wolves wouldn't just lie down and accept their fate as victims.

The hunters had gotten almost a full week of their wolf

manoth. She would be damned if she let them have an entire month. The wolves had spent the past six days running, but it was time to turn and take the fight to their enemy instead of waiting for the enemy to come to them.

The building rose up from the surrounding greenery like a medieval fortress, an Art Deco tower that peeked above the treetops to look out over Puget Sound. Lorne's walk had been brief, but it was marked by frequent stops for him to catch his breath that allowed Ari to keep up with him. Now she could tell he had finally arrived at his destination by his suddenly cautious body language. He stopped to make sure he wasn't being observed, overlooking the wolf crouched in the park half a block away before he crossed the parking lot to the main entrance.

Ari waited until he was inside before she closed the distance. The property was surrounded by a waist-high wall topped by a wrought-iron fence. The two stone columns that flanked the driveway had plaques, one which presented the building's street address and the other gave the name of the building as The Venatorial Club, est. 950. Most people probably assumed it was a mistake on the engraver's part, but she knew the plaque referred to the first historic hunt that created hunters in the first place.

She slipped around the gate, hyper-alert for sounds she had been spotted as she crossed the open grass to the landscaped trees that would serve as cover so she could get closer to the building. The small private woods concealed a parking lot from view, and she saw two cars parked close to the building, along with an Orarian Group van that was parked at the far end of the lot. She ran along the side of the building, aware of each window she passed. She sniffed near both cars and identified that one belonged to her father before she continued on.

When she reached the door she closed her eyes and focused. She had done the trick that morning to convince Diana her story was true, but doing it again required effort. The bones of her left forepaw stretched and cracked until it was a woman's hand, the thick fur closing in around her wrist. Her fingernails were still smudged gray and black as if they were still claws. Her hand ached as she stretched the fingers and lifted her hand like a dog offering to shake. She gripped the knob with effort, twisted, and pushed the door open.

The room in which she found herself reeked of spices and the ghost of long-served meals but currently stood empty. She let her hand transform back into a paw, a slightly less painful alternative to leaving herself half-changed as she crossed the floor. As a wolf it was easier to remain unseen behind the kitchen islands in case someone came in looking for a snack. She crossed to the kitchen's entrance and listened to the sounds of the house. Her father's voice boomed through the wood-paneled corridors and she paused to determine the difference between source and echo before she turned to track it. There corridor from the kitchen led through an empty dining room and out into a wide receiving area that included the foyer. Lorne and Keighley were on the other side of the foyer in the den, and Ari stayed low as she crept past the foot of the stairs and slipped into the shadows behind the credenza.

"Tell me you understand that," Keighley said.

After a long pause, Lorne said, "If she was, then consider it mission accomplished. She wants us scared, we're scared. It was great while we were sitting around here smoking cigars and talking about how we were going to confirm our position at the top of the food chain. But this is reality. People are dying, people we care about are dying. You can't tell me you're still excited about how this is all going down."

Keighley said, "People we care about? You mean Ariadne?"

"Your daughter, apparently? I mean, holy shit, Jake. You didn't think to mention that?"

"I didn't know until I saw her. She does look very much like her mother."

Lorne was quiet for another long beat. "You know, maybe you were the wrong person to bring this to."

"What is that supposed to mean?"

"I mean, Christ. You raped a woman because she was a wolf. Surely you have to see that was crossing a goddamn line."

Ari heard the clink of glasses. "A woman, sure. I would be horrified at the idea of someone violating a woman in that matter. Gwyneth Willow is a wolf."

"And that means less than human."

"Yes. You've heard them howling about how they are *canidae*. They consider themselves a different species. Left unchecked, these animals will overrun cities, they will become powerful, and then we will be the ones running because we lack the ability to transform. We cannot allow them to advance beyond us."

Lorne said, "So this is just an extermination."

"That's what this has always been, Kyle. Wolves overrun England, the king decides that wolves need to go. We were knighted in order to restore England for its people. People... not beasts. The *canidae* we ran off the island were remnants of a darker age, a bygone era of monsters and magic. They should never have survived to the second millennium."

Ari crawled closer to the door, now able to see that the room was a study. Judging by the vague shadow moving across the wall, Keighley was the only one standing. She assumed Lorne's worsening condition left him seated while Keighley paced.

"I'm a cop, Jake. This sort of thing goes against everything I believe in."

Keighley's voice became angry again. "This isn't coming out of the blue, Kyle. We've discussed this for over a year. We've planned, we've prepared... and now you're losing your nerve. Because of her. We should have killed her when we had the chance."

"She's your daughter, Jake, for~"

"She's a side effect I should have made sure to take care of at the time. Believe me, if I'd known the consequences of our little game, I would have finished the job with Gwen before that little abomination could see the light of day."

Ari bristled, but she didn't feel any personal betrayal. She wasn't his daughter, and he certainly wasn't her father.

"We're going to get the wolfsbane back, and we're going to get this wolf manoth back on track. This region, hell... this entire city has been overrun by those beasts. It's about time someone did a little extermination. The wolves we don't get need to receive the message that they're not welcome here. This is our town." A bell chimed, and Ari retreated into the shadows as Keighley put down his drink. "That will be the others. Clean yourself up before you join us. You look like shit."

Keighley came out of the study at such a brisk pace that he didn't have time to spot her hiding behind the furniture. He opened the front door and a tall, gaunt man she recognized from the news came into the house. His hair was an odd mixture of brown and gray, swept back off his forehead. Only when he craned his neck to look into the study and then extended his hand to Keighley did she recognize him as Scott Levitt, the mayor's chief of staff.

"Everything okay?"

Keighley nodded. "We're brainstorming ways to track down the 'bane."

They continued talking as they passed the stairs, coming within inches of spotting Ari. She tensed until they went through a swinging door and their voices faded. A few seconds later Lorne came out of the study to follow them. He had his head bowed, hands up to massage his temples. The pained position left his eyes angled downward so he was looking directly at Ari when he entered the foyer. He straightened slightly and he dropped his hands to return her stare.

Agonizing seconds ticked by. Ari was poised to move if he went for his gun or raised the alarm, but he surprised her by turning on the ball of his foot. He moved like a marionette tangled in its own strings, each step punctuated by a quiet burst of air pushed out through his lips. He opened the door, turned around, and followed the path Keighley and Levitt had taken.

"Willow?" His voice was soft enough that she knew he wouldn't alert anyone that she was there.

She chuffed and nodded her head up and down.

Lorne sighed and shook his head, dismissing her with a wave of his hand. "Go. Get the hell out of here."

Ari waited until he was out of the room before she got up and ran for the door. She paused before going outside to make sure there weren't any other guests on their way. The drive was clear so she darted across the porch, onto the grass, and ducked into the trees. She stopped and hid again as a truck pulled up. It followed the drive past the front of the house to park near the back, and Ari took the opportunity to leave the property before anyone else arrived.

When she crossed the street she was so focused on the safety of the woods that she almost ignored the sound of a car door being opened nearby. The shrill whistle that followed made her turn her head, and she skidded to a stop when she saw Dale leaning across the front seat of her car to push open the passenger door. Ari changed direction and charged with her head down, nails clicking on the pavement, and Dale retreated just as Ari scrambled into the car.

She climbed into the backseat and dropped onto the floor. Half a minute later she reached between the seats and Dale handed her the clothes she'd left behind earlier. She dressed as quickly as she could and slid up into the backseat. She was panting, sweating, too inflexible at the moment to even squirm between the front seats to sit next to Dale. She pulled her lank hair out of her face and tied it into a sloppy ponytail just to get it out of her eyes.

When she'd caught her breath she said, "What are you doing here? Did you follow us after all?"

"No, actually... I was following a lead."

"I thought you literally just told me you didn't want to be a detective."

Dale shrugged. "This case is different. I'm not going to tell you to lay off Keighley and Lorne to focus on something else. I knew if your father~"

"Could we stop calling him that? He's not my father, he's just someone who..." She grimaced and shook her head. "Let's just stick with calling him by his name."

"Okay. I knew if Keighley wasn't involved, you would have followed up on Huxley. He seems to be more important than Keighley in the grand scheme of things. So I headed to the headquarters of Alki Emerald. I had just pulled up when Huxley came out."

Ari stretched her back. "How did you know what he looked like?"

"He's got pictures all over the internet."

"See, this? This is why I think you'd make an excellent private eye."

Dale grinned over her shoulder. "I don't want to be a PI. I want to be your, uh.... your housekeeper. I clean up the messes you don't have time to take care of yourself. I was thinking I would tell you everything I'd discovered over dinner. I didn't think we'd both end up in the same place. I guess I'm busted."

"I'll be sure it's reflected in your pay."

Dale looked at her again. "Are you okay? You look hurt."

"I'll be fine."

"What's with your hand?"

Ari looked at her left hand which was curled into a tight fist. Now that she was aware of it, the fingers throbbed with pain. She tried to relax her hand, but the ache radiated up her forearm as if she was trying to walk off a leg cramp. After a few seconds she managed to move the fingers, and soon the resistance faded enough for her to open and close her hand without pain. She knew it had to be a result from her partial-changes, but she didn't want to worry Dale.

"That was weird."

"Like the cramps you used to get after a run? Those seem to

have become really infrequent lately. It's almost like once we started dating, you stopped complaining about how much you hurt."

Ari winced. "I have a good workout partner these days."

"Ari, if you're hurting, you have to tell me. Okay? I worry about you regardless. At least if I know you're in pain I can try doing something about it. No more secrets, no more grinning and bearing it. If that thing with your hand happens again, I want to know. Understood?"

"Yes, ma'am," Ari said.

"Good girl." She rested her hands on the steering wheel. "So what did you see in there?"

"It's some kind of club. Venatorial?"

Dale narrowed her eyes. "Latin, I think. It means hunting."

"Thanks, college girl. Keighley was in there with Lorne, who was sharing our offer of peace. The mayor's chief of staff showed up."

"Scott Levitt?" Dale said. "He's on my list."

"What list?"

Dale took out her phone and handed it over. "I played connect the dots and found a group of people I think are possibly the... council or whatever. Lorne said there was sort of a committee who was overseeing things in the Pacific Northwest? I think this is them, or at least the Seattle branch of them."

Ari nodded. "These people make sense. I'm not sure where Mr. Microsoft fits in, though. Is he sticking wolfsbane in people's computers?"

"I don't know. Maybe he's just the numbers guy. But whatever... these other people are in good positions to spread the drug around. Cabs, restaurants, the mayor's staff. We're lucky there's not an epidemic."

"That's what I was telling Lorne earlier. The hunters talk a big game, but when it comes down to an actual war they're all gun shy. Even with the so-called justification of wolfsbane they're just not pulling the trigger. I think we can calm everyone down. Lorne saw me in there. He saw me and opened the door so I could get out."

Dale turned in her seat. "Really? That's huge."

"I think he's just got nothing left to lose. The hunters are pissed at him, he's got that bite getting worse and worse. I guess he figured there was no upside to sounding the alarm."

"Still, I think it's a breakthrough."

Ari shrugged. "Even so, Keighley won't be easily convinced.

This guy has walked the walk since thirty years ago when he attacked my mother. He's been waiting all this time for the rest of the hunters to start up wolf manoth again." Another car passed them, and Dale looked at the driver while Ari slid down so she would be less visible. "Could you tell who it was?"

"I saved pictures of the group... this guy was blonde with a big chin." She scrolled with her thumb and then held the phone up for Ari to see. "Adam Beck. He had that cooking show for a while, and now he has the restaurant downtown."

"Glad I never took you there."

"Me too. I think it's a dating-don't for your girlfriend to attack your waiter."

"Only at the real hoity-toity places, and even there people turn a blind eye if he screwed up your drink order."

Dale laughed and reached into the backseat. Ari took her hand, curling her fingers around Dale's to prove she could.

"I love being with you, Ariadne."

"Where did that come from?"

"I don't know. Just the two days we were apart, and just now... we're sitting here talking about something that could kill you or get you killed, and you still manage to make me laugh. I want to say, about the fight we had the other day? You can say whatever you want to me. I know how you feel in your heart, and I know that sometimes you speak before you think. You love me. I'll never doubt that."

Ari bent down and kissed the back of Dale's hand. "When this is all over, I want to take you somewhere. I don't care where, as long as it's just the two of us without cases or clients."

"Granddad's cabin? We could buy a week's worth of groceries, hide out on the island... you could go for runs on the beach, through the woods..."

"That sounds fantastic."

Dale rubbed her thumb in a circle on Ari's palm. "I'll pencil it in. And you know, in all honesty, when it comes to meeting the parents, things could be going a whole lot worse."

Ari laughed. "Is that so?"

Dale said, "Yeah. I could have ripped the seat of my pants right before dinner, or introduced myself as Fale Drye because I'm too nervous to remember my real name."

Ari grinned. "Both of those things really happened to you, didn't they?"

"A good girlfriend wouldn't ask me that."

Another car passed while Ari was chuckling, and Dale took her hand back to look at the phone. "Vaughn Wakefield. He owns the Orarian Group."

Ari frowned. "Levitt, Lorne, Huxley, Keighley, Beck. Now him? They're war rooming."

"What does that mean?"

"It means within the next few minutes, anyone on that list who isn't already in the house is going to show up. It means whoever is calling the shots is anxious about losing the wolfsbane."

"This is good, right? They're scrambling to find a plan B."

Ari nodded. "Yeah, but that also means everyone who could end wolf manoth is going to be in that castle in the next hour."

Dale glared at her. "Ariadne, no. Don't even think about going in there alone."

Ari said, "Who said anything about going in alone? I have to make a few phone calls."

She wasn't sure how long it would take to set up the plan she had in mind, but she doubted the hunters were planning a short meeting. She had time to get all her ducks in a row and put her plan in motion without worrying they would finish up and scatter before she was ready.

CHAPTER SIXTEEN

TYSON WARWICK was the final member of the Venatorial Club to make an appearance. Ari and Dale observed him park well away from the other vehicles in the parking lot and then angrily stalk across the parking lot to the front entrance. Ari checked her phone to make sure everything was in place, then squeezed Dale's shoulder before she stood up and jogged to catch up with him. She approached from an oblique angle so that he didn't see her until she was right beside him. He flinched and she pretended not to notice, mirroring his angry demeanor as she fell into step beside him.

"You have any idea what this bullshit is about?" she asked.

"No. I'm about ready to tell them to shove my membership. I don't have time for this."

Ari laughed humorlessly, thrilled by his attitude. Hopefully his fellow hunters would be equally put-out. "You and me both, buddy. I haven't seen you around. I'm Adrian Wall."

He shook her hand. "Tyson. Ty."

He held the door open for her and she nodded her thanks as she stepped inside. She let him get ahead of her so he could lead the way, pushing open the door through which Keighley and his first guest had vanished. Ari closed the door behind her and scanned the room. All eight members of the club were present, with Lorne stretched out on the divan while Keighley and Huxley huddled near the window. Everyone else looked like frustrated passengers who had just been told their flight was delayed.

Vance frowned at Ari. "Since when do we allow huntresses in this club?"

Keighley's eyes flashed. "Ariadne."

Tyson looked at her. "I thought you said your name was Adrian."

"I lied about that. Go sit down with your pals." He moved away from her with some confusion and took a seat next to Adam Beck. Lorne had sat up at the sound of her voice and glared at her from the couch. Keighley started toward her but Ari held up a finger. "Hold on, Papa." She narrowed her eyes and looked toward the ceiling. "Right about..."

A car alarm began wailing from the parking lot, and half the men turned toward the window. When a second alarm joined it, Scott Levitt rose and looked out the window.

Ari smiled. "Nothing too criminal. No vandalism, just a little nudge to set off the sound effects. Some of you in this room know me. Some of you don't. So let me get us all on the same page. My name is Ariadne Willow, and I'm a private investigator. I'm Jacob Keighley's daughter, on a technicality. I was born when he assaulted and raped my mother thirty years ago at college. Now, I know what you're all thinking. 'Jake is no rapist.' He would agree with you. He doesn't consider it rape since she is *canidae*. I get that from her. Well, that and my eyes. People say we have the same eyes. Mostly it's the wolf thing, though."

Huxley looked at Keighley. "What's she talking about, Jake?"

"He's been looking forward to this day for most of his life. He's a true believer, someone who really carries the banner of hunting like nobody's business. I bet there hasn't been a hunter as dedicated as him since... God, probably since the Napoleonic Wars." She walked across the room to the wet bar and picked up one of the bottles. "Wow. This is the really good stuff. I was in here earlier and I smelled cigar smoke, brandy, all kinds of stuff. It's ingrained into the texture of the carpet. The walls and the ceiling, this place just reeks of dude.

"That's when I realized. That's what this is. You guys are the top of your respected fields. Mr. Levitt, you work for the Mayor. Adam Beck, celebrity chef. It's really hard not to ask for your autograph right now. My girlfriend used to watch your show religiously. So it makes sense you needed a place like this to unwind. Get away from the cloying public and their cameras. This is your haven. And then one day Jake Keighley came along and reminded you why this place was built. He reminded you of those trips with your papa, those stories he told. Werewolves are real! Werewolves are a menace! And it's up to you to stop them from spreading."

Huxley said, "He reminded us of our heritage. Our responsibility to the people of this world. We were entrusted with the safety of humanity against this scourge~"

"Hogwash," Ari said. "Maybe in the year eleven-hundred, when we were just a bunch of tribes hitting each other with swords because we had a tiny little island to fight over, maybe then I could believe this whole extermination bullshit. We've spread out a bit since then. Wolves take the forests and humans have the cities. To be honest, if anyone needs to be exterminated to protect land, it's you guys and your urban sprawl. But I'm not here to hurt anyone. I'm just here to talk."

The door behind her open and Milhous stepped into the room. Ari hooked a thumb at him.

"If anyone needs to be hurt, I'll let him do it for me."

"Gentlemen," Milhous said. A few of the hunters shrunk away from the giant.

Ari laced her fingers in front of her. "We have the wolfsbane. The vast majority of it, anyway. Mr. Wakefield, I know your Orarian Group is in the process of making more, but they have to do it quietly without raising any eyebrows. So it's going to take a while for you to have enough to make a difference, and by then wolf manoth will be over. And I think that's the only thing justifying what you guys are doing. When this month ends you're going to shake hands, pat each other on the backs, and go back to your real lives."

Levitt said, "What is your point, young lady?"

"I'm here to say... stop. Stop this war right now. It's archaic, it's pointless, and none of us want this." She looked at Keighley. "Well. Almost none of us. You were all born hunters, but it wasn't a tradition for you. It wasn't engrained the way it was with Mr. Keighley. He truly hates wolves. I bet he was the one who brought up reinstituting wolf manoth. I bet he convinced all of you to throw in your specific contribution. The restaurants, the cabs, the mayor, the police. He took this place you men had turned into your refuge and he turned it into a war room. He convinced you that the wolfsbane would justify whatever damage you caused."

Huxley said, "What makes you think the wolfsbane was his idea?"

"Oh, it was him. The rest of you built lives, empires. You found something with purpose and you followed it through. Captains of industry, leaders in your fields. Not Keighley, though. He had a sporting goods store. A place where hunters could equip themselves for battle against the true enemy."

Footsteps thudded on the floor overhead. When the men looked up, Ari snapped her fingers.

"Pay attention now, because this is where it gets important. You followed him because he said your hands would be clean. You weren't slaughtering people in cold blood, you were killing monsters. That's some heroic shit. But without the wolfsbane, we're going to go back to being normal, everyday citizens. You won't be able to shrug and point to the havoc we've wreaked to rationalize violence. You'll have to make a conscious effort to kill another human being.

"But that's not the only thing you need to think about. For the past week, we've been defending ourselves. We've spread the word about wolfsbane, and we've taken measures to make sure we and our loved ones aren't exposed. That's the only reason there hasn't been a slew of vicious attacks throughout the city. As of right now, that changes."

Lorne said, "You're threatening us?"

"No. You threatened us. Wolves generally don't like to fight unless they're provoked or their territory is invaded. You invaded our territory. You poisoned our food. This war has been one-sided up to this point. If you continue to come after us, we're going to go on the defensive."

Something crashed in the hallway. Adam Beck stood, but his posture was more fearful than threatening.

"There are wolves in your house, Keighley. One of them is the partner of a wolf Detective Lorne shot the other night. One of them is a woman whose home was turned into a bunker in anticipation of an attack. We're done running. We're not going to hide anymore. We took the wolfsbane so this will be a fair fight. A fair fight you will all lose."

Keighley said, "You're asking us to stop. Just... asking."

Ari met his eye. "Jacqueline Ramsey. Who in this room was getting updates from her?"

After a moment Huxley raised his hand. "She's in Ireland."

"She's dead in a garage out on Yarrow Point. She was killed by the wolf she was assigned to watch over. And..." She looked at Lorne. "Sorry about this, Kyle. But your friend here isn't just sick.

He was bitten during the robbery. Look at his arm."

Lorne stood up. "That's bullshit. We're..."

"Kyle... shut up." Huxley crossed the room and pushed up Lorne's sleeve. The bandage was evidence enough that she was telling the truth. Huxley looked angry, but his expression quickly faded into grief. "You could have told us."

Lorne pulled his arm away and tugged the sleeve down.

"How many friends are you prepared to lose in this fight?" Ari said softly. "End this war right now. Today, in this room. Call off the hunters you have hiding all over the city. Have them get rid of whatever wolfsbane they have left in a safe manner. We go back to our lives, you go back to yours, and neither one of us has to worry about being hunted."

Huxley said, "And if we refuse?"

The door behind Ari opened and Milhous stepped aside. Gwen entered, followed by Milo, Paige, Owen, and Mia. They formed a wall behind Ari, blocking the exit.

"If you refuse, then we bring the war to you."

Milo said, "The hunters become prey."

Owen said, "We'll track down your families and make sure the hunter line ends."

"And we'll make sure this is the final wolf manoth ever," Mia added.

"No wolfsbane," Gwen said. "No excuses. Just wolves versus hunters." She lifted her chin, eyes locked on Keighley. "Are you confident you would come out victorious?"

Tyson Warwick stood up and fished his phone out of his pocket. Huxley watched him as he dialed. "What are you doing, Ty?"

"I'm calling my restaurant and telling them to get rid of that wolfsbane shit. I wasn't exactly keen on putting it in my food in the first place. This?" He shook his head. "This is too far. We're ending this, just like they said."

Keighley said, "Put down the phone, Ty."

Tyson ignored him and turned his back to place the call. Once he began speaking, Adam Beck took out his phone as well. Ari looked at Colin Vance, the Microsoft employee.

"What exactly did you bring to the table?"

Vance looked at her, looked at Huxley, and then sighed. "I accessed profiles and private information of people who we believed were genetically hunters. I brought them into the fold. But I'm done. This? This is madness, Keighley. Even you have to see that."

Keighley said, "Even me? What is that supposed to mean?"

"It means you're delusional," Wakefield said. "This has gotten out of hand."

Huxley grabbed Wakefield's arm. "This is exactly what we signed up for."

"This is what you talked us into. There's a pretty big difference, Patrick."

"You cowards..." Keighley stalked forward into the center of the room and turned to face his men. "This is what we've been working for. What we've been waiting for all our lives."

Vance said, "It's what you've been waiting for, Jake. You just conned us into going along with it for a while. We're done."

Keighley didn't telegraph his punch when he swung at Ari, he simply spun on the ball of his foot and brought up his arm. The blow glanced across her chin and knocked her back, forcing Milhous to catch her before she hit the ground. Keighley sidestepped the bulky bouncer, but he was stopped by an outstretched arm across his chest. Gwen was on top of him before he hit the ground, her weight forcing him down even faster. She put her arm across his throat and leaned in until their faces were inches apart. When she spoke, her voice was barely more than a low growl.

"If you ever raise a hand to my daughter again, I will not hesitate to make you bleed."

He grimaced as Gwen grabbed his collar and hauled him onto his feet. She closed her hand around his arm just above his elbow, squeezing hard enough that Ari figured his hand would go numb in a matter of seconds.

"What exactly is the plan now?" Wakefield asked.

Gwen hauled Keighley back to his feet and shoved him toward the couch. "Now we do something that is reprehensible, but may be for the best. We let you go. Despite the deaths you've caused, despite the harm you've done and the wolves you've killed... we will let you walk free. Consider it a gift for laying down your weapons and leaving us alone. I think it's a fair deal. It's one way we can walk out of this room and we all get to keep our lives."

Levitt said, "We need to discuss this."

"Do you?" Milhous said. "Do you really?"

Tyson shook his head. "No. We're finished with this." He looked down at Keighley. "This has gone on far too long. People have died, and more people will die if we allow it to carry on. You called us all here to try talking sense into Mr. Lorne, but the truth is he was right. I would suggest a vote, but I doubt that will be necessary. Anyone disagree? I think we know how Mr. Keighley will vote..."

The men around the room began voicing their agreement with Tyson. Soon the only holdouts were Lorne, Keighley, and Huxley. Lorne stood up and stepped away from Huxley. "I think seeing as my outlook isn't exactly peachy, I should abstain from voting for any long-term plans. But I also think you know which way I was leaning, Mr. Keighley. It's over."

Huxley said, "It's lose-lose, Jacob. They have our names, they know our faces. I'm assuming we're not looking at the full force of the wolf army. If anything happens to them, I have to believe our names get sent to the authorities. Someone will pay attention, and we'll lose everything."

"Why did you even follow his lead in the first place?" Ari asked. "All it would take is one health inspector noticing granules of an unidentified substance in their food and your restaurants would be shut down."

"He had us convinced it was the moral thing to do," Tyson said glumly. "And we all remembered growing up, the family stories about wolves and the righteous hunters who cut them down. We thought we were playing the hero in a story about monsters."

"Reality is a little different than that. Enough lives have been lost. Last time this war ended in a peace treaty," Ari said. "A hunter and a wolf declared their love for each other. I think this time we should do something simpler." She stepped forward and held her hand out to Huxley. "Mr. Huxley, I suggest we declare a truce between our people."

He stared at her for a moment and then looked at her hand. "Hell." He reached out and clasped her hand. Ari squeezed and he returned the pressure without trying to crush her fingers. "For what it's worth, Miss Willow... I apologize for my part in this ill-conceived endeavor."

"I appreciate that."

Wakefield cleared his throat and rubbed his hands together. "The wolfsbane that's still out there... one reason we mass produced so much is because it has a very brief window of viability. The shelf-life is something like five or six weeks."

"That's good to know," Ari said. "Thank you."

"No, thank you." Vance seemed legitimately relieved. "This war has already gone on far too long. We were just too stubborn to admit it."

Keighley bent his knees and threw his weight back, pressing his shoulder into the center of Gwen's chest. She slammed into the wall with a sickening crack, crying out in pain as Keighley brought his elbow up into her chin. She rocked back against the wall and went limp, releasing her grip enough that he managed to get his arm free. Milo lunged for him but Keighley anticipated her. He grabbed her arm and pulled so that her own momentum sent her flailing onto the floor. He jumped over her, caromed off the wall, and ran out of the room.

The entire scuffle lasted barely thirty seconds. Ari overcame her shock and confusion to drop down next to Gwen.

"Just got the wind knocked out of me," she gasped. "Go! Get the bastard... go!"

Ari ran out of the room, no longer thinking about the monumental thing she had just achieved and focused only on catching up with Keighley. He'd left the front door open when he fled and she raced through it. She saw a flash of movement from the corner of her eye and realized she'd fallen into a trap. Keighley had been waiting next to the door and grabbed her as soon as she was through the door, spinning her by the arm and letting her go. She was pulled off her feet and landed hard on the driveway, tucking and rolling to minimize the damage. The pain was exquisitely sharp, and it took her brain a moment to process just how much it had hurt. She pushed herself up with her left arm, vision swimming as she watched Keighley flee toward his truck.

Someone came up behind her, hooked both hands under Ari's arms, and hauled her off onto the grass. She was unceremoniously dropped on the soft ground just as Keighley's truck sped past them, his tires veering off the pavement in an attempt to hit her as he fled the scene. Ari looked up at her savior and smiled.

"Hey. You saved me."

Dale said, "It's kind of a habit of mine."

"I've noticed."

"You okay?"

"I hurt." She sat up with Dale's help, hissing through her teeth. Her blouse was ripped from skidding across the pavement, but the skin underneath had been spared.

Dale stroked Ari's hair out of her face, then gently probed her shoulder to see if it was broken. "What happened in there?"

"I ended the war."

Dale's eyes widened. "Ari, that's amazing."

"Not yet. We've got a rogue general out there. I think he's going to do his best to end the war with a bang instead of a whimper."

CHAPTER SEVENTEEN

ARI HAD passed K1 Sport and Outdoors hundreds of times, on foot and in cars. She was fairly sure one of her stashes, maybe the one in St. Mark's, was buried in a bag that originally came from K1. In all that time it had just been a building to her, an innocuous part of the scenery. Now she knew that it was owned by the man who had attacked her mother in college, a man who had dedicated his life since then to a wolf manoth that would put past hunts to shame. Dale had helped her up and Ari limped to the car with her. Gwen came out of the house and Dale rolled to a stop long enough for her to get into the backseat before leaving the Venatorial Club behind them.

"His store," Ari said, unable to elaborate her entire idea.

Gwen nodded. "That makes sense. Are you okay?"

Ari grimaced and rolled her shoulder. "Yeah, I'm fine. I just took a tumble. I'm used to it."

Gwen gripped the headrest of Dale's seat as she took a sharp corner. "Detective Macallan called us when we were on our way to the club. They found Jacqueline Ramsey's body. She's handling the investigation and she'll do everything in her power to make sure Serena Ahearn doesn't go to prison for defending her family."

"Good. Thank you."

"You did all the work," Gwen said. "I'm just reporting. Do any of your friends on the police force happen to be working traffic?"

Ari shook her head. "No. Dale, you might want to slow down."

Dale eased off the gas. "Sorry... I don't want to give him too much of a head start."

Gwen said, "We know where he's going. We can get there before him."

Dale said, "Where is K1?"

"It's off Olive, near I-5." She rubbed her eyes and tried to visualize the address. "You know that little gray building that says BEST RIBS IN TOWN, and you thought it was a barbeque place? It's like two blocks away from there. Big, ugly glass building with an oval sign over the door..."

"It's got a fish on it," Dale remembered. She scanned the cross streets, envisioning the late night trips through abandoned streets to pick Ari up from wherever the wolf had taken her. She had gotten good at finding the quickest route between two points, and even with the traffic of early afternoon getting in her way, she could clearly see a path. "Okay. Hold on. I can get there before he can." She slowed to take the next turn and pressed her foot down on the gas. Ari and Gwen both held on tight as they were thrown around the car by Dale's driving.

Gwen said, "What was it?"

Ari said, "What was what?"

"The little building. If ribs isn't barbeque, what was it?"

"Oh." Ari smiled. "Comedy club."

"And that's the joke they advertise with?"

Ari chuckled as Dale took another turn and pressed her against the side of the car. "Geez, Dale!"

"Sorry..."

"Don't apologize, just a little warning next time."

"Consider this your warning." She pulled the wheel again and Ari flattened her palm against the window as she looked over her shoulder to see if there were any cops speeding up behind them. When she looked forward again she saw that Dale had swerved to avoid a sawhorse attached to a tall orange bucket by a string of yellow tape. "Uh, Dale, this is a construction site. Dale, this is a construction site."

Dale nodded. "I know. But they finished the road first so they can get their vehicles up to the building."

"Is that a fact?" Gwen said.

"It's close enough to a fact," Dale said as she pulled up onto the sidewalk to avoid a gap in the asphalt. The car was jostled by its passage over broken rock and turned-up dirt. Dale didn't bother driving around the next obstacle, choosing instead to snap through the caution tape like a marathon runner reaching the finish line. She turned the wheel almost violently and the car fishtailed right, tires squealing as they passed Best Ribs in Town.

Gwen pointed. "There!" Ari saw the glass building that housed Keighley's company, but her mother was pointing at the truck that had just run up onto its front curb. Dale slammed on the brakes at the corner and squealed the tires again as she came to a stop. Keighley turned at the sound, shouted something they couldn't hear, and ran for the building. Gwen threw open the back door while Ari looked at Dale.

"Don't take this the wrong way..."

"Stay here?" Dale said. "My part of the danger was getting you here. Go!"

Ari took a second to kiss her before she got out of the car and followed her mother into the building. Keighley had close to a full minute lead on them, but the front of his store was so crowded by customers that he had to slow down to get through them. Gwen was blocked by a family buying their gear in bulk and she took half a second to search for a way around them before she pointed at Keighley and shouted, "That man stole my purse!"

The nearest man instantly reached out and grabbed Keighley's jacket. Keighley spun and threw his weight against the Good Samaritan, knocking him backward against a glass display case. Ari cut across the front of the store, past the checkout aisles until she found one that wasn't open and therefore wasn't blocked by a row of shoppers and gear-laden carts. She ran through the shortcut and grabbed for Keighley's jacket but he sidestepped away from her.

He cut through an archery display on his path to the back of the store. Ari passed a golf display and grabbed a sleeve of balls, tearing it open and throwing it. She doubted it would work, but it hadn't cost her any time and there was always a chance. Keighley heard the clatter and looked back to see the three golf balls bouncing uselessly in three different directions. Ari cursed the idea as idiotic at the same moment someone pushed their cart out of an aisle and Keighley slammed into it at full speed.

"Oh, my gracious!" said a woman far too young to be using such quaint colloquialisms. "I am so sorry! I had no idea..."

Ari caught up and stooped down to grab Keighley. He grabbed her arm and pulled her down, lashing out with his foot to catch her knee. Her shoulder was already injured from her earlier fall so she twisted so she wouldn't land on it. She crashed down onto the tile and felt a spike of pain through her hip as she lay dazed. Keighley rolled onto his knees and slammed his arm across Ari's back.

As she sprawled, the woman whose cart had impeded his escape yelped in horror. "What on earth are you doing to that poor girl?"

"She's not a girl. She's a monster." He got back to his feet and took off again.

The woman crouched and helped Ari up. "Goodness. Are you all right? That brute..."

"I'm fine." She saw Gwen coming and pointed to where Keighley had gone. Gwen nodded and changed direction. The woman watched Gwen go, then looked at Ari.

"Is this some sort of hidden camera thing?"

Ari nodded. "Sure. Yeah. You might want to do your shopping elsewhere." She looked into the lady's cart and saw she was buying baseball bats. She grabbed one and said, "I'm going to take this, though, if that's all right."

"After the way he treated you?" The woman held up another bat. "Take the aluminum one."

Ari grinned, made the swap, and chased after her mother.

The doors to the back of the building were still swinging when Ari reached them. She pushed through and nearly tripped over a tangled pile of clothes. She used her toe to move the blouse, confirming it was her mother's before she moved on. The storeroom was heavily packed with rows upon rows of merchandise waiting to take its place on the shelves at the front of the store. She heard running footsteps but they echoed off the tall ceilings until it was impossible to tell which direction they were coming from. Ari knew her mother had changed to utilize the wolf's heightened senses and prowled forward with the bat resting against one shoulder.

She heard someone coming up behind her and spun around to see not Keighley, but a man in a grey polo shirt with the K1 logo. He was short but walked with his shoulders back and his chest out like a tin-pot dictator. He glared at her and raised a hand as he approached. His nametag identified him as Brandon.

"Miss? Miss, do we have a problem?"

"How many people are back here?"

He put a hand on her elbow and leaned to one side, half-ushering and half-guiding her away. "Miss, I'm going to have to ask you to come with me. We've gotten several complaints of you disturbing customers in the store, and..."

Gwen barked loudly, a sharp and piercing sound that didn't echo as much as footsteps, and Ari pulled her arm away from the manager.

"If there's anyone back here, get them out. I'll leave the second I stop the man who raped my mother from killing her. Is that okay with you, Bradley?"

She didn't wait to hear his answer as she ran toward the bark. She heard Keighley's voice as she approached.

"Should have just finished you when I had the chance."

Ari came around the corner to see Keighley standing his ground in front of Gwen. Her mother was a beautiful wolf, tall at the shoulder but long and lean, her coat bearing more silver than Ari remembered from their runs. Her teeth were exposed and her ears flattened against her skull as she and Keighley faced off. Ari started forward but slowed when she realized her mother was facing the man who had changed her life so completely. He took away her plans, put her in the center of a war she wasn't prepared for, and had given her a child she didn't want. Ari lowered the bat and watched as the two silently dared each other to make the first move.

"Keighley!"

He flinched and looked toward her. Gwen took advantage and pounced on him. Keighley realized his mistake at the last second and brought his arms up to protect his throat as Gwen hit him. They both fell and Keighley pulled something from his belt and thrust it toward her belly. Gwen yelped in pain before closing her teeth on his forearm. He shouted a curse and twisted to get away as blood spattered the ground around them. Gwen twisted her head and pulled away from him, muzzle darkened by blood as she fell to one side.

Keighley looked at the horrific wound on his arm with the numbness of shock. His fingers trembled as he turned his arm to see the extent of the damage.

"What have you done," he gasped, shock quickly replaced by horror.

"She's infected you," Ari said. "Turnabout is fair play, huh?"

Keighley glared at Ari and lunged for her, but she swung the bat before he got close enough to grab her. She hit across the side of his head, just above the temple where she would have caved in his skull and killed him. He was unconscious before he hit the ground, and Ari moved to where her mother was transforming back into her human form. Ari unbuttoned her own blouse, leaving her in a T-shirt as she moved to cover Gwen's nudity. She stopped when she saw the slashes across Gwen's side and the slick of blood running over her hip.

"Mom," she whispered, dropping hard onto her knees to press her hand against the cuts.

Gwen's eyes were open, but only barely. Her face was ashen and beaded with sweat. She focused on Ari and smiled.

"You ended my war."

Ari pressed harder against the wound. "No. No, you're fine. You're going to be fine..."

Gwen closed her eyes and grunted. "No, I don't... oh." She exhaled sharply and shook her head. "Ariadne... I love you. You were never a burden to me. I never..." She swallowed hard and whimpered, the pain changing her features ever so slightly before she put her stiff upper lip back in place. "I never once regretted the decision to have you. My baby girl. You were my only accomplishment."

"I love you, too," Ari said. She twisted and shouted for help, hearing her voice echo. She wondered if Bradley or Brandon or whatever his name was had stuck around. She heard footsteps and looked down at Gwen. "Someone's coming. They're going to get you help."

Gwen closed her eyes. "Tell Dale..." She wet her lips. "Tell Dale to take care of you."

Ari sniffled and shook her head, tears finally falling from her eyes. "She doesn't have to be told. She's good at that."

Gwen swallowed and tensed. "It hurts, baby."

"I know, Mommy. Just hang in there."

She turned and called for help again. The footsteps were coming at a run now, but they still seemed impossibly far away as Ari struggled to keep her mother from bleeding to death.

There was no transition from sunlight to darkness that day. Ari happened to look out the window of Dr. Frost's kitchen and realized it was full dark without a second of warning. To be fair, she had been distracted since arriving at the house. She was sitting in an armchair meant for one that Dale had managed to squirm her way into. They were pressed together almost painfully but Ari would have protested if Dale tried to move. She'd fallen asleep sometime after their tiny dinner, her cheek on Ari's shoulder and her lips slightly parted as she murmured through a dream. Ari held her and looked at the woman across the room, her peaceful features and dark hair combed back off her face.

She was in agony, both emotionally and physically. She'd donated as much blood as she could to replenish what Gwen had lost on the floor of K1, and her altercations with Keighley had left her bruised all up and down her side. She was exhausted, but she refused to sleep so long as her mother was still unconscious. Gwen's spleen had been damaged enough to require removal, and three hours later he had stitched her up and told Ari that all they could do was wait.

Jacob Keighley had been taken into custody by his own security, who decided to err on the side of caution in regards to the naked, bleeding woman lying near him when they arrived. Ari's story was that he was to blame for a drug causing people to spontaneously attack each other and they'd been trying to stop him. She also revealed that Keighley was her father, and she was born as the result of a rape thirty years ago. The DNA tests were pending, but she knew it was just a formality. Detective Macallan called to tell her that the statute of limitations on rape was one year from the positive identification of the suspect. Once he was identified as her father, they were going to try him for what he'd done to Gwen.

Ari turned her head and brushed her lips against Dale's forehead. Dale murmured, and the sound was echoed from across the room. Ari watched Gwen until her eyelids fluttered open. She eased away from Dale, who woke long enough to understand what was happening. She scooted to one side of the chair so Ari could get up and kneel next to her mother's bed.

"Hey. Are you awake?"

Gwen stared at her. "I don't know. Everything's..." Her eyes rolled back. "I think I'm high."

Ari smiled. "Well, Dr. Frost pumped you up with a lot of stuff before the operation."

"I operated?"

"No..."

"I'm not a doctor. Don't let me operate on anyone."

"I'll do my best."

Gwen focused on Ari again. "Hum. This is awkward. I death-bedded you. Said a lot of things."

Ari nodded. "Yes, you did. It was very nice to hear them, but I won't hold them against you." She took her mother's hand.

"Keighley is in prison, Mom."

"Mm. Good, sweetheart." She smiled and squeezed Ari's hand. "Oh, boy. I think I'm going back to sleep now."

"Okay. I'll be here when you wake up."

"No, no, no." Gwen shook her head. "Go home. Don't watch me sleep. Take Dale home."

Ari considered arguing, but she knew it wouldn't do any good. She leaned in and kissed Gwen's cheek. "I'll see you tomorrow, Mom. I love you."

"Ah... so I didn't dream that."

"No. I'll say it again when you're not dying or drugged."

Gwen smiled, and the expression slipped as she passed out again. She kissed her mother's cheek again, letting her lips linger as she remembered all the years she'd hated the woman she was currently crying over, all the hurt feelings and rage that had fallen away like a veil. Now she could only remember the woman who had taught her what it was to be a wolf, how to survive in the streets when all she had was her wits. The strong woman who had taken it upon herself to fight a war to protect her daughter. She sat up and freed her hand from Gwen's, smoothed down her hair, and then went to where Dale had fallen back to sleep. She kissed Dale's lips to wake her.

"Mm. What? What's wrong?"

"Nothing's wrong." She held out her hands and Dale took them. "Come on. We're going home."

CHAPTER EIGHTEEN

January 17

THE NOTE said that he didn't have any family, and that he found a certain irony in hiring her for the job. He paid her usual rates, hiring her for two days in order to follow his instructions properly. Ari told Dale to donate the check to a charity for the families of fallen police officers and picked up the package from the mortuary. She drove north to a cabin in the foothills of the Cascades where Kyle Lorne and his father had bonded over hunting techniques. She hiked into the wilderness behind the cabin until she came to a clearing and looked out over the Salish Sea.

"Well, Kyle, you were right. Breathtaking." She looked at the box of ashes. "I can see why you'd want it to be here."

He'd gotten progressively worse during the days after the war's end. He decided he was done waiting and finished the job Gwen's bite had started. Ari tapped her thumbs on the side of the box and looked over the water again. It sucked that there was no one to give him a proper funeral, but the note he left behind said that the hunters were his only family, and "recent events" had soured him on the entire group. So there was only her, and she was at a loss.

"You were a good man, Kyle. You did some shitty things, but in the end you overcame your upbringing and did what was right. I just wish it could have ended differently. I'm going to miss you, Detective."

She let the ashes loose and watched until the wind spread the cloud too fine to see. She tucked the box under her arm and took in the scenery for a long time before she finally walked back to her car. She drove back to Seattle thinking about the wolfsbane outbreak. Tarun had used his position in Orarian Group, combined with the newfound support of Vaughn Wakefield, to destroy the components being used to create the drug. Every hunter in town was ordered to surrender whatever supplies they had on-hand or face the consequences. No one elaborated about what the consequences would be; no one needed it to be clarified.

Diana Macallan and Dale oversaw the destruction of the wolfsbane Gwen had stolen. Owen managed to get them into a construction site afterhours and they spent a good portion of the night mixing the wolfsbane in with unmixed concrete that was due to be turned into a basement floor within the next few days. They made sure there were no wolves on the crew just to be safe, and Milo watched from across the street as the blended concoction was poured and left to set. In a few weeks the poison would be harmless even to wolves, but until then it was buried so deep no one would be at risk.

Ari got home in time for the farewell party being held at the Bull and Terrier. Hannah and Gwen were both back on their feet, albeit shakily, and the Brits were preparing for a triumphant return to England. Their pack leader had flown out as soon as he heard about Hannah's injury, and Milo introduced Ari to Anton Clarke. He was older and amicably gruff, with thick blonde curls and a shaggy beard. He shook Ari's hand, then eyed Dale.

"This is the human?"

Dale resisted the urge to gulp. "Yes, sir."

He narrowed his eyes, looked her up and down, and then huffed. "Could've fooled me. You act like a wolf, from what I hear."

Dale smiled with relief. "Thank you for the compliment, sir."

He raised an eyebrow and then smacked her on the arm. "Thanks for saving Hannah. Shame to think she wasted all that ink on her tattoos just to lose them all now."

Dale laughed. "Yes, sir, that was my main concern, too."

They drank, they laughed, and they celebrated the early end of wolf manoth with free bottomless pitchers provided by the owner of the bar. Milhous made certain that everyone through the door knew that Ari and the Brits had single-handedly saved every wolf in Seattle, and they were inundated by offers to buy appetizers and drinks were stacked on top of drinks. Dale's presence was accepted by all; she had more than earned her spot in the back booth, but she tried to be unobtrusive.

Ari went to the bar for a refill and Milo joined her. "Hey."

"Big night."

Milo nodded. "It's not every night a war ends. Looks like this time it might actually keep. Well done, wolfy." She bumped Ari's arm with hers. "We were thinking of going for a run after we leave here. The others haven't had a chance to really roam in America. It smells different here. It's a good smell."

"Good enough to stay this time?"

Milo shook her head. "My family is in England."

"I understand. I'll miss you."

"I'll miss you, too. You and Dale." She looked over her shoulder at Dale, who was matching Owen shot-for-shot. "There's a good pack. Two-woman pack... who needs more?"

"Not me," Ari said.

Milo's eye was caught by movement near the dartboard. "Looks like someone told Ant that your mother took over as Alpha in his absence."

Ari looked and saw Gwen and Anton standing together against the wall. They were talking animatedly, but it didn't look angry to her. She was about to say so when Gwen laughed, and Anton reached up to brush his hand over hers on the pretense of taking her glass. Ari's eyes widened just as Milo reached the same conclusion and said, "Oh, bloody hell!"

"Your Alpha is hitting on my Mommy."

"Doesn't exactly look one-sided there, pup!"

Ari laughed and covered her eyes. "Oh, God."

"Good on 'em, though."

"Yeah," Ari said. She took the glass that had just been left in front of her and toasted in the general direction of her mother without looking. "Cheers."

They both drank and Milo chuckled at the thought. "You want to come on the run with us, you're more'n welcome to. Be happy to have you."

Ari shook her head. "If I'm going to get naked and work up a sweat..."

"Dale's gonna be there."

"Damn skippy," Ari said. Milo held up her glass and Ari tapped hers against the side of it. "I've stopped getting nauseated every half-hour, so I think the wolfsbane Keighley infected me with is completely out of my system."

Milo said, "So you're not gonna have her tie you up tonight?"

"I didn't say that." She winked at Milo and then smiled. "When do you head home?"

"Tomorrow morning."

Ari held out her hand. "In case I don't see you before that, thanks for showing up. You saved the day as much as I did."

"To us," Milo said. "We may have been a temporary pack, but we were damn good."

"Hell yeah, we were."

Milo finished her drink with that toast, then tapped her knuckles on the bar. "We're out. Go. Take that girl of yours home. Try not to think about what your Mama is doing with Ant."

Ari groaned and threw a handful of pretzels at Milo's head as she retreated. Ari retrieved Dale, who had to extricate herself from the booth amid the groans of everyone she'd been entertaining. She kissed the top of Owen's head, gave both Hannah and Mia kisses on the cheek, and then finally allowed herself to be dragged out into the cool night air. Dale sighed and sagged against Ari as if she'd left her energy behind and the tether was snapped when the door closed.

"I like your family."

"Our family," she corrected, kissing Dale's hair. "Come on. You're drunk."

"I am. Very very."

They leaned against each other as they walked up the street. Dale glanced at an alley and said, "That's where I kissed Milo."

"More info."

"She was naked."

Ari said, "More information?"

Dale chuckled. "I thought she was you. I mean, a wolf swoops in and saves the day? It was an honest mistake. Besides, you kissed her, too."

"That was different. And she kissed me. This is the second time you've kissed her. It's starting to become a habit."

Dale sighed. "Good thing she's going back to England tomorrow."

"I'll just have to find a way to make you forget her."

"Tall order."

Ari slipped her hand into the back pocket of Dale's jeans and squeezed, holding on tight as Dale squealed and tried to twist away from her.

"I think I'm up to it."

Dale nuzzled Ari's neck. "Everyone thought I was a hood. We could play that tonight."

"You want me to change while we're~"

"No! But I have a scarf I could put on over my hair... and I could come into the bedroom." She added a breathy note to her voice. "Gran'ma! What a big, lovely mouth you have..."

Ari refused to play along with the tease, but she smiled and pulled Dale close as they let the cold night air take the edge off their drunkenness enough so they could drive home. She didn't know how drunk Dale was or how long it would take before one of them was confident enough to get behind the wheel of a car, but she didn't care. At the moment, despite the weather and the lingering ache in her left side from where she'd been thrown around by Keighley, she felt as if she could walk until dawn as long as Dale was by her side.

EPILOGUE

January 20

THE CELEBRATIONS had ended and Dale declared it was way past time to get back to business as usual. She went through the backlog of calls, contacting clients and arranging meetings for those who hadn't moved on to other agencies. She sorted the cases by order of importance based on their time-sensitivity and made the appointments for the following day. When she left for lunch, she took a check Ari had signed the night before and drove to Dr. Frost's office. He had just sat down for his own break, but he agreed to see her. His politeness turned into genuine happiness when he saw she'd brought him money.

"This is unnecessary, Miss Frye. We were at war. I considered myself a medic, like... Hawkeye. I loved that show."

"Yes, but even those doctors got paid. It's the least we can do. Hannah and Gwen were both... well. Let's not dwell on that." She smiled. "You saved my girlfriend's mother. We want to make sure you're compensated for that."

Dr. Frost nodded. "Thank you. It's very much appreciated."

"You're very welcome."

She stood, but Frost stopped her with an upraised hand. "You could have mailed this. Avoided the whole attempt where I try to give it back. Was there a particular reason you wanted to drop it off in person?"

Dale shook her head. "No... not really. I mean." She twisted her lips, fought her desire to just smile and walk out, and took her seat again. "Have you heard of *canidae* half-shifting? They turn a paw into a hand, for instance, just for a few seconds?"

"I've heard of it. Most don't attempt it because it takes a lot of energy for not a lot of reward. Has Ariadne been doing that?"

"Milo... you remember her? She taught Ari how to do it a few weeks ago. She hasn't done it much, to my knowledge, but during this whole wolf manoth thing she did it twice. The second time she couldn't unclench her hand for a few minutes afterward. It was like a full-arm cramp. Is that normal?"

Frost considered the question as he chewed a bite of his sandwich. "Well. You have to understand, of course, that very little is 'normal' when it comes to Ariadne. She was turned into a *canidae* through a very unique procedure. All *canidae* feel pain when they change, but none feel it to the extent she experiences. I've been monitoring her since she started coming to see me, and her pain is only going to worsen as she gets older. By the time she's forty, if not before, she may be walking with a cane. But if..." He wiped a crumb from his lip and shook his head as he stared at a spot on the table. "If she experienced even mild paralysis after a change, it could be a worrying indication of how her condition is progressing."

Dale swallowed the lump in her throat so she could speak. "You mean Ari could be paralyzed."

"Not any time soon. Changing only one limb causes extreme reactions, but yes. It could be indicative that sometime down the road, Ariadne could find herself permanently paralyzed in one form or the other."

Dale was certain she was polite, that she thanked Frost for his time and left without simply walking out of the room, but she couldn't remember details later on. She stopped at a trail and walked until the heat left her face, until she could breathe normally. She wiped her hands over her face and went back to her car and continued composing herself on the drive to Ari's favorite deli. It would be Ari's first non-home-cooked meal in months, so Dale wanted to get her favorite sandwich. What was the point of breaking a fast if she didn't do it right?

She drove back to the office and presented Ari with the sandwich. "Oh, bless you. Oh, my God." She opened the wrapper and inhaled, leaning back in her chair with a near-orgasmic moan. "God, I've missed that smell. Thank you so much."

"My pleasure."

"Where were you?"

"I, uh, stopped by Dr. Frost's office to give him a check for helping Gwen and Hannah."

Ari nodded and took a bite of her sandwich. It ballooned out her cheek but she spoke around it. "What did he have to say?"

"Nothing much," Dale lied. "He tried to refuse it, but... you know. I insisted."

"Good girl."

Dale smiled. "Did you want me to do the background check on that nanny?"

"Would you mind?"

"Not at all." She stopped at the door and said Ari's name. Ari looked up and Dale smiled. "It's good to be back at work."

Ari smiled and wiped her little finger across her lip to clear it of sauce. "It's really good."

Dale winked and went to her desk. Frost had said the paralysis was only a potential problem, and even then it wasn't necessarily fated. She would keep an eye on Ari's condition, and she knew Dr. Frost would keep on top of it as well, and she would keep track of any tightness she felt during a massage in case any of them became chronic. Ari didn't need another thing to worry about, not so quickly after putting the lid on wolf manoth.

For the time being, Dale was happy to do the worrying so Ari could focus on living day to day. There would be time enough for worry down the road.

For now they had work to do.

Red in Tooth and Claw: An Underdogs Novel (4)

Canidae private investigator Ariadne Willow and her girlfriend Dale have had a hectic couple of years, dealing with murderous clients while attempting to stop an all-out war between hunters and wolves. After stopping the onset of wolf manoth, Ari decides it's well past time that she and Dale take a vacation. Two weeks of rest and relaxation at the cabin where their relationship went from business to romance sounds like exactly what the doctor ordered. Dale hopes the opportunity to slow down will ease some of the pain Ari has been suffering from her transformations.

Their plans are thrown for a loop when Ari goes for a run and stumbles over the body of a dead girl hidden deep in the woods near the cabin. When she returns with the police the body has vanished and the scene hastily cleaned up. The police don't see any evidence to confirm Ari's claims but her enhanced canidae senses confirm the body was there and has vanished. With the police refuse to investigate based only on her word, Ari and Dale begin digging for the truth and quickly learn that the and there are some secrets people will go to any lengths to keep buried.

Riley Parra: Season One

For years the forces of good and evil have waged war in the confines of No Man's Land, the wasteland on the edges of Detective Riley Parra's city. When what should have been a routine case opens Riley's eyes to the true fight going on behind the scenes, she finds herself drawn into the endless battle between angels and demons. Reluctantly taking up the mantle of good's champion, a mortal fighting on the side of the angels, Riley can only rely on the guidance of an angel in human form to help her survive the coming war. A war that will put her closest friends at risk and make Riley question her sanity before it's over. Becoming a champion wasn't Riley's idea, but she's not going to let her city fall without a fight.

Tilting at Windmills (Claire Lance, Book 1)

Claire Lance is on the run. For the past year, she has kept on the move, keeping her head down, keeping out of trouble. Until she reaches a tiny town in Texas and trouble finally corners her. Forced to take action to save another woman's life, she suddenly finds herself over her head. Blood on her hands, forced to go on the run with the woman she was protecting or end up in prison, Lance finds herself forced to revisit the life she thought she had left behind and reopen painful old wounds.

www.ingramcontent.com/pod-product-compliance
Lightning Source LLC
Chambersburg PA
CBHW061254210726
48293CB00003B/962